a cool, dark place

a cool, dark place

SUPRIYA DRAVID

PENGUIN BOOKS

An imprint of Penguin Random House

PENGUIN BOOKS

USA | Canada | UK | Ireland | Australia
New Zealand | India | South Africa | China | Singapore

Penguin Books is part of the Penguin Random House group of companies whose addresses can be found at global.penguinrandomhouse.com

Published by Penguin Random House India Pvt. Ltd
4th Floor, Capital Tower 1, MG Road,
Gurugram 122 002, Haryana, India

Penguin
Random House
India

First published in hardback by Random House India 2013
This paperback edition published by Random House India 2015
This edition published by Random House India in 2021

10 9 8 7 6 5 4 3 2

ISBN 9788184007220

For sale in the Indian Subcontinent only

Typeset in Adobe Garamond by R. Ajith Kumar

Printed at Repro India Limited

www.penguin.co.in

FSC
www.fsc.org
MIX
Paper from
responsible sources
FSC® C047271

For my father Shekhar Dravid
who keeps my heart in the safest place (inside his).
For my mothers
Sukanya Dravid and Shampa Dhar-Kamath
who taught me to always love more.
(Because really, how do you love less?)

Acknowledgements

Arjun Krishnan, my love, my life, my most compelling axis. For letting the light from your life reflect on to mine.

Binoo John for realizing that I had this book in me before I did.

Jiggy George for being a kind and patient reader who pulled me up if the plot was 'travelling without moving'.

Divya, Mahima, MayaG, Neha, Shhiv and Shimauli, protectors of my sanity, my everyday heroes.

David Godwin, agent provocateur. For your faith in helping me map my way under this unfamiliar sky.

Meru Gokhale and Faiza Sultan Khan for their Olympian strength in shaping this book into what it is. For being the best and most perceptive editors a writer can hope for.

Appu, Arjun, Beulah, Chika, Faye, Mandy, Madhusree, Manjul, Maurya, Mika, Renate, Rick, Riju, RohanM, Shaalu, Shailesh, Sruthi and Tara for feeding me your stories, deep-fried love and support through the years.

The Kichus for making me one of their own.

And finally, Madras Thatha. For your lines, and for your life.

Thank you.

Chapter 1

'Memory is a beautiful, generous thing. But it is also such a bastard. It is the contamination of the mind.'

I read that line, the only line, in my father's suicide note.

My father's death came two weeks before I was supposed to start university. One year, three months, twenty-seven days ago.

We were your average family, close-knit and a little cuckoo. But then two years ago, my father's twin sister (younger by 3.25 minutes) killed herself by jumping off a building, and the year before that my father's older brother returned from a wedding lunch, went to bed and never woke up. No one even realized that he had been dead for ten hours until the family pets surrounded him and started wailing. And just as our family grappled with that sadness, my father made it easy for himself by exiting this world. We weren't even a political dynasty. It had to be a family curse; there was no other logical explanation.

At his funeral I heard my grandmother whisper to my grandfather that she had cried so much in the past two years that there was no salt left in her tears. But a fresh batch of tears started all over again. Her universe had been hijacked. My grandfather didn't respond. He just stood there, his face hollow with helplessness, fighting gravity to stay standing. I was convinced that his purple, mute soul had left him in permanent disgust. All the emotion had drained off his face, and his soft, kindly features had hardened. The folds on his face had multiplied so quickly in the last three years. The book of life implies teaching children to fly from under the wings of their parents, to learn to survive without them, but how do you teach parents to survive without their children?

There were no speeches. A priest, organized by my grandmother, was conducting the token rituals that precede the departure of the dead by burning them on the ground to send them skywards. He was mumbling some prayers in Sanskrit without opening his mouth properly; enunciating the words in a metronomic drone that occasionally rose to a high pitch like a steam liner announcing its presence on rocky seas. He wore only a dhoti and a sacred thread around his untrimmed chest, which was so hairy that it looked like he was wearing a black sweater. The little knotted ponytail at the back of his head bobbed up and down. I remember staring at him wondering if he was okay, considering he was drenched in rain, or sweat. Or both.

At some point my mother interrupted the prayers by stepping forward to caress my father's face as he lay in front of us. I didn't stop her. No one did. She tried to open his eyes, which had been stitched shut haphazardly with a black thread. I wondered what had gone through the mind of the person who had sewn my father's eyes up, the same eyes that would never see me grow up. Perhaps my mother thought that if she stared hard at my father's face he would come back to life. She held him in her arms, and looked at me with a panic-stricken face and said, 'Zef, I can't remember his laugh . . . the sound. Do you know how it went?'

I said nothing.

My father wasn't just the love of my mother's life. He was her heartbeat, a beat that she would never replace.

My mother was trying to stalk her memory. She placed her jaw against his collarbone. She kissed him hungrily, hoping that he might wake up. But what use are kisses to the dead? She kept mumbling that my father, Gravy, a man with one-and-a-half eyebrows, ran away with her words, and her world. Eventually, my grandmother enveloped my mother with her frail, parched, crooked black hands, so that the rituals could be completed. Everything had to be done by noon. The priest continued chanting like a robot, from the same point at which my mother had interrupted him. He must have been used to the outbursts of madness that the dead bring among those who are left behind.

This would be the last time I would see my father. I stared at his still, preoccupied face and tried desperately and hurriedly to memorize everything about it—the stamp of startled confusion, the exact placement of the mole under his right eye, the bald patch of skin next to half of his left eyebrow, his dishevelled hair; how his earring clung to his right earlobe; how his thick cheeks hung low with anguish; his lips pursed in an upside-down smile. I tried to pray that time would never bend this image of his face in my mind. I placed his favourite book of Marathi short stories by P.L. Deshpande next to him, the one that he read repeatedly for several years while he ate his meals. But I think it was also the book he unconsciously stopped reading some time ago, because he decided that he didn't really want or need to laugh any more. Perhaps I hoped the book might make him smile a little in his other life. I also put his snuff box between his hands.

I played with the idea of reconstructing bits of my father like a life-sized doll with a heartbeat. It consumed me with its hypothetical optimism. But then there was the reality of what was happening in front of me. The rituals seemed to take forever. I didn't complain. I didn't want it to end, because then my father would be gone with no tangible trace. Soon my world would be ablaze, and there was no one who could salvage me. I was trying to see his form in the smoke that arose from his funeral pyre, but it kept changing, kept charring. What was the point of seeing his life downsized to ash in an urn? What was the point in anything any more? My father's death just burned my heart. I lost the only man in my life who had promised to love me more than any other man, and who loved me more than anyone could possibly love me. It was a love that could not be touched.

My mother and I left soon after the funeral, scurrying under the weak, scrawny sunlight like a couple of old bats, rushing as though to some pressing engagement. We hurried home with eager eyes, almost expecting him to be there. We were fooling ourselves into believing that the man we had just sent into the wild stretch of unruly fire—to be free?—was his doppelganger, a twin ghost, as though all of this was just another bad dream. Neither of us exchanged so much as a glance, but we both knew what we secretly wanted. It was so stupid but you couldn't argue with us then. It was only when the empty room slapped us in the face that we realized the truth of what we didn't want to confront. Now we were left with nothing but Hitchcockian memories of him—some happy, some silly, but mostly of his spiralling into the descent of doom.

For a long time before my father ended his life, he'd hidden himself in the darkness. So my mother had hidden there with him, in the forlorn shadow of his helium heart, in the never-ending nuclear light, under sunken iron beds and love-sewn quilts. I think she hoped her Olympic tolerance would help him map his way back to the living, and destroy the lonely world, the Prozac paradise he had cocooned himself in. But it didn't help. She became an exhausted lady with an unpleasant husband to tolerate.

My father had a mental problem which seemed to have burgled

his rational brain. First he dyed our beautiful brown dogs purple and pink. Then he said that the dogs were staring at him, and he didn't like it. Then he worried that they had turned into jackals in the night and were out for his blood. So one day when my mother and I were out, he took the dogs and disposed of them somewhere. I never did find out what the true story was. He said he had cremated them, and gave us a phony number where he took them to get cremated, and when that didn't add up, he said he drove them to a busy market area and tied them to a lamp post and returned home. He told me he would kill himself if I told my mother. This was not the normal behaviour of a sane human being.

On the face of it we seemed like a loving family. That was before the sinister undercurrents started sucking us all into some kind of sequence of synchronized drowning. It was a crazy way for things to have ended for a man younger than spring, who had Elvis hair and cocktail eyes, who never raised his voice, who brought me skyfuls of joy, hung dreamcatchers above my bed, read history books for fun, preferred the use of commas over full stops, taught me to write instead of ride a bike, believed in unicorns and tree houses and the power of love, a man who made water colours of all the things I couldn't see, and encouraged me to colour outside the lines of the things I could see.

He put all these pink dreams in my head, and kept my heart in the safest place possible—inside his. A dreamer at the windowsills. Maybe he wasn't so normal after all, maybe he was gazing out of the windows at bigger worlds. Who knew what had played in the mind of someone so fragile, so weak, so broken, so sad? You'd have liked him. Everybody did. It was impossible to not like him. He was like a cute beagle in human form. So I think it was actually a sneaky thing for him to just go off and kill himself. I felt a burst of rage and just so bummed out.

After my father's death, my mother lost herself in some hormonal snake pit. Maybe she was terrified of her own grief. Something had changed in her. To her, it was the end of love itself. She seemed to act like some sort of a thief, stealing from life. She didn't know how to behave with me. I think she didn't quite know how to love me; it was a case of upside-down love. She loved me as one might love a pet—a cat, or a pigeon or a peahen perhaps—because the pet loves its master and the master loves the pet for doing so.

My mother's hair greyed very early on ('that's because of all the bloody steroids I took when you came out of me,' she used to say), but she still looked regally indifferent on a good day. She was as much of a character as she appeared. She was born under a lunar sky with a tooth that hadn't *yet* fallen off. A slightly discoloured birthmark on the right side of her face slithers its way on to her right eye. Her nail-bitten fingers seem leperish, but that's not the first thing you'd notice about her. It would be her misty eyes and pale lips, her fiery red hair haphazardly bundled up inside oddly shaped, out-of-date hats. Once upon a time she used to look infinitely delicious, as though she had traipsed out of an interesting past, or maybe even an appealing future.

Growing up, she had had many lovers, my mother. She had this empathy and intelligence that came straight from the heart. Maybe it was her infectious laugh, her full-throttle passion, or the burning intensity inside her that made the men she loved yearn for her long after she had left their rooms and their lives. Well, that's the impression that she had given me.

During her space-out sessions, she'd start talking about my father and how they had met at a bus stop. It was a moment of fated collision, brimming with ease and reassurance. How he had dexterously spun their thick love out of thin air, like a paean of passion. It was this memory that she clung onto now. This relationship *was* her—she stood right in the centre of their love story—no, she stood a little off-centre, dreaming obsessively about its enchanted, fairytale-ish beginnings. She just wouldn't allow herself to let go of the cauterized ruins. Somehow it seemed that when the fire consumed my father's body, his soul consumed hers.

She kept popping pills to stand still. She dressed as though she had a permanent headache. She became someone who kept forgetting her trolley in supermarkets. She couldn't look me in the eye—she became a child, a Phoebe, a ditsy dolly, a crazy widow organizing dinner parties. Once, she went to a store to buy groceries but came back instead with a pet parrot and got so engrossed in the peripheral act that she forgot to invite the guests.

I had contemplated taking a gap year to look after my mother and, well, heal myself and us. That was my Oprah-fication. I was going to start university in a couple of weeks in New Zealand. My father had naturally assumed that if the world was going West, I was going to head East. So I went along with the idea. But one day between her tears, my mother confessed to me that he wasn't my father.

She slipped that bit of information in with such deliberate casualness I almost thought it was the Valium talking. The information hit me with the silent surprise of a cotton ball, but it kept playing in my ears over and over again, louder and louder, until it came at me like a hellfire rising inside of me. I stared at my mother, but her words seemed to play out in silent slow motion, muffled by the stampede of horses rushing inside my head. She didn't make eye contact while talking (did she ever?), choosing instead to stare at a framed black-and-white picture of my father holding a 5-year-old me over his shoulders, his enormous palms covering my buttocks. I took that picture from her hand and smashed it on the ground till the glass splintered. I felt an anger swelling up in my gut, taking control of me, as though someone had stuck a *Wüsthof* knife in my windpipe—I couldn't breathe and I couldn't come up for air. I didn't understand the need to tell me something right now when I didn't need to know. Why the secret revelation when the man was dead? I couldn't even hate him because he was dead.

Something snapped inside me. It wasn't so much dealing with my father's death, but facing the fact that he was not who I thought he was. I didn't want to hear any explanations, didn't want to indulge in any speculations. Frankly, it was all too much. People I loved were dropping around me like flies, and on top of it, this. *This?* I just didn't need to deal with this right now. I wanted to leave this shattered room, this toxic air my mother and I were breathing, these broken walls, harrowing nights, this broken, secret life. I decided against the gap year and just left.

Chapter 2

I barely managed a year away at university, which I spent in a tectonic blur. It was brain death. I don't know what I was doing besides ransacking my local pharmacy. I could barely keep my head above sea level. As much as I surrounded myself with new faces, places, too much noise, I couldn't get myself to tell anyone about what had happened. I was too embarrassed. I stole so many lives that I forgot which one was mine.

My so-called father's suicide and the angst preceding his decision was like a scar, a secret that a lover reveals to another, between the sheets. Not something to be discussed in public. I wanted to hear other stories and be a part of other people's lives—I tried really hard, but the truth was I couldn't even hear a joke. I built walls so high that I lost myself inside them.

For the time that I was away in New Zealand, I tried to fade into the mist, ignore the stain of my new reality. I didn't want to remember the thing my mother had told me, which left me sick to the pit of my stomach. I wanted to jump off the train of this journey of remembering.

This volcano of morbidity left me feeling abandoned. But in the process of not dealing with things, I had abandoned my mother too. We kept in touch, of course. Conversations with her were stilted on my part; never easy, always an act. 'Do you need money, have you found a house to stay, don't talk to boys with light eyes, go to school, sleep but don't oversleep, don't fail but even if you do, it's okay.'

But that was about it. I knew she wanted and tried to tell me everything, but between my vacant breaths and her hysterical sighs, she didn't really get a chance. She knew that.

Eventually, when I sobered up a year later, I began to miss her. I missed her smell, the smell of stale jasmine, the smell of her cigarette-stained smile, the smell of her funny anger, the smell of her impulsiveness and the smell of her filter coffee. The loneliness in the Land of the Long White Clouds got to me. I started to miss who I used to be. It seemed as though I took a walk so far away from the centre of my core that I needed to make the journey back to the mean. Mathematical, really, if you look at it.

I was tired of being upset. I missed being happy. I didn't want to run around overdosing on a three-course meal of complicity, caffeine and cocaine. I couldn't walk the line, all I could do was cut one. I couldn't make the bus, I couldn't sit still. Eventually, everything came at me like a ghost with a kind voice—because in the end despair, like all things, eventually exhausts itself. It sweats itself out of the body on bitter winter mornings. Ironic, isn't it. Our greed stains our new desires, our old longings. But we will be destroyed when we eventually receive what we have been craving, and then will always yearn for something more comforting from our past.

On one of those weekly calls with my mother, I broke down. She told me to come home and this time I didn't argue. She had moved from Delhi to Madras, where she had been born and raised, to be with her father, Don, a caballero with filthy, light grey-violet absinthe eyes hiding behind his thick, black square frames, a champagne socialist, a fantasist who could never really be trusted, who relished wearing capes, or sometimes a white linen suit and wingtip shoes with a gold coin taped on to the right sole (for luck). There was also a slutty tattoo of a naked woman on his forearm—each time he contorted his muscles, it seemed as though he was making her voluptuous breasts move up and down. It was his own perverse polysexual, erotic inventory, marked on his body as a souvenir, maybe as a remembrance of his boyhood days in the army. I was convinced that he had the blood of wild animals in his nerves. He was a daemon, a humanimal. I loved him. Now his life was hanging by the last drop of blood on a drip by his bedstand.

I took a year out of university (I was failing miserably anyway) and made my way to Madras to my mother's childhood home, a shambolic, Versaillic, moth-ridden empire of despair, where a tree rose to the ceiling right in the centre of the living room. My grandmother, Sancho, had insisted that it shouldn't be chopped off while the house was being built. So there it remained even now, brown and brittle, as though it were an old man, a bit like the man lying inside, slurring in his sleep. I knew I would have to struggle with every emotional muscle in my body to get through the next few months. I needed to get out of my own head for a while and sit still in the buzz of silence—the kind of cold, calculated silence you employ while cleaning a shotgun before engaging in a massacre.

It's true that everything comes to us when we are ready to make the space to receive it. Maybe now was my time to scribble down the love-worn story of my family. Maybe writing was my methadone. I suppose, as Byron poeticized, if I didn't write to empty my mind, I would have gone mad. I was writing to bring a part of me alive.

One year, three months, twenty-seven days after my own father's death, I was in the courtyard of my mother's childhood home, waiting for this old man with a magical life to die. Helping my mother come to terms with the fact that Don was dying—in the next minute, in a week, in ten days, but definitely by the end of the month. Hoping that in his death, we might both finally start living.

My mother bided her time in Madras until I arrived. When I opened the faded yellow gates, they creaked and then echoed with the chimes of the 417 tiny bronze bells that hung onto them. The house felt like a cadaverous warehouse whose vampire residents had just left in a state of disarray to suck someone's blood dry for dinner. Now it was a cemetery of memories, a preface to the truth that would unfurl.

An intense mould had climbed over the house's façade, shrouding it like a temple of desolation, a disturbing tableau of times past. The eighteen glorious Chettinad Burma-teak columns that lined the three-hundred-foot length of the house were now rotting elegantly as the sun's sharp rays chewed into their bones. Don had bought them from a poor, cataract-eyed cousin who had been breaking and selling different parts of his old village home in Tanjore, and had sent them to Madras on a bullock cart. Bits of the now ash-coral veneered walls had chipped away to reveal dusty brown bricks, and also a stash of cognac bottles hidden behind them. Deterioration never looked so enchanting, my mother said.

The house always managed to overpower when you enter. But it is like a zircon that fades away after too much bathwater. It was starved of a heart, crumbling away all alone in its decayed beauty, as though an army of white ants had decided to eat it away bit by bit, with slow, quiet, steadfast vengeance, until there was nothing but dandruff-like dust. Scrawny cats lazed around, looking frozen as they stared vacuously ahead at nothing. They looked like they had the weight of the sky inside them, the heavy soul of the house in their breathing. I waded my way through a herd of goats that had made the garden their new home (Garden was perhaps not quite the word; it was a sloth heaven, a jungle with lovesick flowers, broken leaves, sharp, dry blades of grass reaching nearly six-feet high and crisper than potato chips). All the sculptures in the garden were lying headless, as though wrecked by a demolition spree held in the last century. It was the kind of home where ghost stories were born and bred, where a child wandered to recover a stray ball never to return, it had haunted grounds forgotten by life.

My mother and I had not planned to be here. We really thought Don would live forever, long after we came back in another life as the fly he would swat or the cat he would indulge.

My mother grew up in a house that was dogged by Don's cranky wisdom of fascist ideologies. His years as an army stock keeper in Europe had made him into something of a pastiche of a 1920s Eurotrash man-baby—part Gatsby; part Hemingway. While he had led a colourful life, he suffocated my mother with unreasonable restrictions. Personally, I think his wiring went haywire when he was faced with the crisis of fatherhood. Some people should never marry, and never have children. Don was one of them.

He had a series of affairs. In hindsight, he was just greedy for the smell of skin, the smell of sex, the smell of skin after sex. He was a tyrant at home—his daughter's back must never face him; she couldn't be late for dinner and if she was late, then she had to face the wall for thirty minutes and/or go to bed hungry; she had to dress the way he wanted her to, often with him handpicking her clothes; he convinced her that the sun shone out of his bum; he was her Jesus Christ, her Sodom, her Gomorrah. He controlled everything. My mother said that she couldn't just go to a store and buy a pencil. If she needed a new pencil, she had to show her old one to Don who would then bring out his ruler to examine if the pencil was at the prescribed amount of shortness (1.5 cm), and if the remaining lead could be of absolutely no use at all before he would give her the money to buy a new one (rarely), or buy it himself (almost always).

For the fifteen years or so that she walked to school, my mother never steered away from the route her father had ordained her to follow. The timing of the school walk would not be more than thirteen-and-a-half minutes, which included a quick stop en route at the temple ('an absolute must for a God-fearing Hindu girl of noble lineage' according to Don), registering her arrival with the priest, drinking the holy water and doing the quick salutation lunge on her knees with legs crossed (the left over the right) as her forehead touched the ground.

'I had to take the same route every single day,' my mother said in a flat voice as her stubby index finger moved from point A to B to signal the distance travelled.

For most of her life, my mother was plagued by a consistent fear of uncertainty, because she had seen the whole rollercoaster of fortunes sway in and out. Don had amassed copious amounts of wealth too soon, and the excesses were experienced at a frantic pace. If you looked at photos of her as a young girl, she looked every bit the desi heiress, vacationing on her country estate, reflexively prim.

When Don had money, he was funny. It was all now or never, nothing was too little or too much. He employed two uniformed drivers, a rarity back in those days. Their lonesome cream-coloured Fiat and red Ambassador—both with lace curtains—would traipse on Madras's empty roads.

The home breathed heavily with wasted indulgences. Don played it like the symphony of an orchestra. No wall remained white. Extensions multiplied as the money grew, a parade of the owner's obsessive addiction for the absurd. Stone corbels of tigers glared at every turn. He had built a curvy sliding board that made its way into an emerald pool in the backyard; there was a separate home for their dogs, silk carpets were hand-woven for his pets—that sort of thing.

The porch had an incongruous life-size bronze statue of a cow with the head of a horse. While the face was shaped like a magnificent, equine Trojan beast made by the hand of God, the body looked like a clumsy doodle of a lazy, fat, gouty cow as sketched by a baby. A garland made of six faux fish (which looked ridiculously real) was strung around its neck. It was so grotesque that you had to love it.

The statue had been in the same spot since the day it was placed here, some sixty years ago, when Don had first got it home from Gokarna, a sleepy beach town, unheard of at the time. It was a fleeting glance, a passing look at this remarkably ugly statue that had made Don do a double-take. Restless (and a little possessed) that night, he traced his way back to where he thought he had seen it. When he eventually found the village schoolyard where it held pride of place, he waited like a stalker with unfailing determination until the next morning, so he could ask the caretaker about the statue's owners. Upon finding them, he was told that it was a family heirloom, a guardian angel that was passed on as dowry, and that they had one girl in the family left to be married, so no, they couldn't part with it.

And that's how Don married my grandmother. He was young enough to swim against the tide and had the potential to turn water into wine, the girl's father was led to believe. A 17-year-old Sancho was brought out to be introduced to her city-slick suitor who was Steve McQueen, Al Capone, Tom Wolfe and Vronksy all rolled into one king of cool. She fell madly in love with his flamboyant disposition. Everything was fixed, hands were shaken, ties were bound, the marriage was arranged. It all seemed as though it was meant to be.

The statue would be sent first with Don, followed by Sancho soon after.

Sancho's father gushed about how grateful he was to have met Don as a chance encounter—this date with destiny that only a benevolent God could have orchestrated—and that his daughter was lucky to have found a husband who had literally come knocking on their door. Don had got what he wanted and was already out of earshot, urging the driver to speed up as fast as he could. Just as the tyre tracks of the open truck containing the statue rumbled its way out of the gates, Don gave Sancho and her family his big barroom grin and waved at them in the way glazed-eyed sportsmen do during their victory spin. When Sancho's family had parted with this monstrosity, they had placed a garland of fish around the neck of the statue, as a souvenir of sorts of the beach town, as a reminder of the smell of the sea with all the excited, hungry sharks in it, with all its whirling dervishes trapped inside, with all the rage churning in its belly, with all the fears repressed inside, with all of the ruined sky inside, and at twilight the diamond stars doing their ballet against the wrinkled tide. A stuffed crow had been placed next to its feet. Having got what he wanted, Don, the sly beast, promptly forgot about the promise he had made, and about Sancho for many years after.

At the time the garden was beautifully manicured in various shades of green, according to Don's instructions. He wouldn't allow my mother outside into the garden at night. 'The plants are sleeping, don't disturb them,' he told her. Four zebra-striped chairs were placed in the centre of the garden, where sometimes they used to dine. He made sure that the blades of grass never exceeded 0.97 mm, and the flowers were organized by colour.

There was also a beautiful bronze bathtub that Don had won as a bet (by winning twenty-one games of bridge in a row, at least that's what he told everyone at home). He placed it on the porch, right outside his study. He was often seen taking a bath post-midnight, under a starry sky. It would have made for a beautiful photograph, a magic flash of an insane man bathing under a bawling moon.

Don was the king of this cavernous lair. He was living a nineteenth-century life in a twentieth-century setting, my mother always said. It was the most luminous atmospheric space. He treated it like a huge stage set piece, and he was the star of that musical.

A hoarder and gatherer by instinct, Don kept adding, never subtracting from the house, as though he was rooted by his possessions, as though they would signify someone who had led a Czar of a life. The main door of the house was an eighteenth-century carved Islamic beauty that was brought from the Swat Valley in Pakistan. Right next to the door, a set of realistic-looking forearms jutted out of the wall, which served as fitting stands for handbags, hats and an umbrella. The furniture was carved from rosewood trees of Don's choosing.

Pure greed papered every surface of the house. There were all kinds of sprinkled ephemera, collages made of paper roses, there were framed moustaches of people Don once knew but didn't remember, little amulets of Lord Vishnu's footprints in every room to ward off evil, giant swooping chandeliers. There was even a bust of his favourite poodle Gunther (named after his favourite author John Gunther).

My mother had traipsed off on a long romantic walk to her makeshift room, a room where she was still living out of a suitcase. She never slept in the room she had grown up in. She brought out a wooden-framed photograph of Don and Sancho against an ash-green backdrop. He hadn't put his arm around her, as most lovers might have instinctively done before a click. Instead, they stood like two schoolchildren at an annual class portrait.

'When was this picture taken?' I asked.

'It isn't a photograph,' she said.

'What do you mean?'

'Look at it closely.'

I did. Don had commissioned portraits, and if he couldn't sit still during the session, he'd get the artist to paint the portrait out of a photograph. The portrait of Don and Sancho was painted with such precision that it could really have been mistaken for a photograph. Don was wearing cat-eyed, lightly tinted glasses, which revealed only a slight bit of his eyes, and his thick toffee-brown mane was parted in the centre. He was wearing a white shirt with club collars and a paper-thin leather tie. He had a little safety pin between the collar and the tie, for a little bit of sartorial spunk, I presumed. His forehead was scarred by a slight curl of hair taken from the left side of his face. His cheekbones were sharp enough to hurt you.

Next to him, my grandmother was radiant. There was a fiery dot of vermillion on her porcelain forehead, her kohl-smudged eyes seemed to hide a smirk, and her face sparkled like crazy kryptonite. She wore traditional flower-patterned earrings with seven diamonds that were held tightly together with the help of a little button that peeked out between the screw. Her nose was pierced on both sides, with a triad of diamonds on the right, and just one stud on the left. Thick strands of two gold chains cascaded delicately as they grazed down the bump of her sharp clavicles. She also wore another smaller chain with a little bone as a pendant. (My mother told me that it was a part of an anaconda's vertebrae.)

My grandmother's hair was up in a low, loose bun, the sort that she must have put up in a hurry en route to the photo studio, and decorated with jasmine flowers worn at the insistence of Don at the studio, I was told. In spite of that, she looked like a coiffured beauty, with her skin sowed in the sultriness of Madras's summer sun, beautiful, like the cover of a soul album. She didn't wear her grey-with-dull-gold-border Kanjeevaram sari the way it was meant to be worn. God, no. She had scrunched up the sari, and wore it tightly across her taut bite-sized breasts, revealing a concave patch of her almond, tanned, shimmering navel. On her gold-painted lips hung a delicate slim cigarette, dripping ash and perched precariously on a holder. Together, the two of them seemed so regal, so indifferent, so lost in this postcard from a beautiful era.

'Are there other portraits?' I asked.

She went quiet for a while.

'There aren't others because Sancho . . . she wasn't there,' she said, slightly rheumy-eyed.

'What?' I asked.

'Exactly that,' she said, '. . . one minute she was there . . . and the next . . . she . . . one afternoon when I was about seven, no, eight I think, I don't remember how young I was, Sancho said she was going to a bookshop to order a special 1923 edition of *War and Peace*. But she never returned, Zef. The book was delivered to Don five days later to mark their anniversary. I remember going to the bookstore with him to look for clues to find her but . . . but it was no use. Don told me that some people are too old to die, too young to live, just right to disappear. And I . . . I believed him. We searched for her everywhere for days on end until one evening Don told me that Sancho had called to inform him that she had chosen to live another life with another family and had also asked in passing—"just for the sake of it but hadn't really insisted"—if he would send me to live with her. But Don wouldn't hear of it. He said that he had "tried but couldn't persuade Sancho" to come back home, here. Who knows? As a child, you'll believe anyone who buys you everything. He had me convinced that Sancho treated motherhood as some vapid vaginal accident. The two of us, Don and I, just continued our life without her. So this portrait . . . it is the last real memory I have of my mother. There are other memories—tucked somewhere inside me but they all seem to blur out with what happened later.'

'What happened later?' I asked.

She didn't answer. I had lost my mother. Perhaps, she was trying to navigate her way through the secret hurricane in her head.

Life seemed to go on—a little lopsided when this third wheel in their auto went missing. But it went on slightly intoxicated, nevertheless. Everyone was merrily riding the wave of hedonism that went with

Don, who continued to live as he always did, as though Sancho was just a temporary aberration. The dining table was always set, and groaning with food, just in case someone dropped in. People often came at odd hours, and ended up extending their stay for days on end. Don wouldn't let them leave. Everyone came dressed up because it was just *that* kind of a house. Time was spent smoking the days into the evening or playing bridge with debauched royalty, and dinners often started just before breakfast under the fading moon, hazy stars and when the reluctant sun hadn't yet bled like egg yolk.

But all that went for a toss when he became a rum-gurgling rapscallion and spent the rest of his life sucking the lid off his hip flask. Not just that, he squandered away his money by making overconfident allowances on his leather business, which just couldn't sustain his whisky habit. He once gave away his Rolex to a musician because he was completely enchanted and mesmerized by his talent. But Don was like that.

Over the years, Don had become rather uncertain about his financial situation. It became about living the champagne lifestyle on a beer budget.

'You know, Zef, it is better to grow up knowing that you are either living hand to mouth, or have some wealth . . . and are comfortable with it. But, I was growing up in an atmosphere where we were meant to be wealthy but it was all a façade. Don spent all the money. And when you are not told, it can confuse your general role as a human being,' she said.

The truth is, all parents scar their children in some way.

So when the money became scarce, they carried on with past savings, horse-racing gambles, and by pawning off jewellery, antiques, art, land.

In the end, all they could really hold onto was the house—because my grandmother (while she still lived with them) would let the dogs out each time the auctioneers came visiting—she saved the rosewood furniture, two mattresses where the three of them would sleep, and a grand old piano that my mother played when the lights went out. (Ah, the piano, I would have forgotten all about its existence had I not been witness to Don's lunatic outburst at a houseguest who innocently tried to play it one day.) My mother never did like that piano—her father forced her to learn it. She'd often cover her fingers in black ink to stain the piano keys. I didn't really talk about it much with my mother, even though I was frantically curious. I guess when you have a terrible childhood, you are pretty much ready for life. That way you are ready to take on any form of disappointment.

A real skinny bunny, her friends often teased my mother for being so fragile she'd trip on blades of grass. She said that when she got pregnant with me and when she finally had me, she didn't have a clue about what it took to raise a nine-pound baby. The day she had me, she had actually just boarded a taxi to go to the cinema. 'It was a new MGR film, I just had to see it,' she told me. 'I figured that if you hadn't come out of me for ten months, then I may as well go see a film,' she explained.

Yes, she was like that. But her water broke, and I was born in that taxi.

'There was no better music than the sound of your first cry when you came into this world,' she smiled at the memory. 'Eventually, Don was summoned and he took her to the hospital for us to be cleaned up. I wonder how we survived it all. She said that when the nurse got me into the room bundled up in a light-blue wrap and a cream-coloured nappy (which she has preserved till this day, sometimes even ironing it) to be given to my mother for the first time, I had a frown on my forehead, and a curious sense of authority.

'You were trying to gauge me before you gave your seal of approval,' my mother told me. 'When your beady eyes darted towards me, it felt like you were giving a lazy shrug that meant fine then, it may as well be you,' she said. 'I felt as though you were selecting me to be your mother. Somehow, it's true. Children do that.'

Is that what makes us responsible for each other? I wondered. She read my mind.

'I think that when some children are born, they are already 10-years old,' she explained. 'They come with that in-built maturity. Because when children are being conceived as a thought of desire or in body or in spirit, their naked, innocent souls intuitively know how they want to be filled up, which womb they want to reside in, which accrued history they want in their blood, which history to build upon, become victims of, which home they want to grow up in, just as you did. It's like a lottery of life in a way. Children decide and select their parents. It is some sort of karma connection from the past life. Maybe it is a story written by the hands of a patient god?'

'So did I choose this other man to be my father?' I asked her.

'Yes,' was all she managed.

Silence.

After a while, she managed to say with a sly giggle. 'Your nose was so flat, Zef, you were just really black like a telephone, my goodness, what an ugly baby you were.'

Don't get me wrong. There was no malice in her voice; it was all just a matter of fact.

The memories of this house stung her. She went from room to room where everything was maintained with brothelish housekeeping tactics. She was searching for something, missing something, but didn't know quite what.

Eventually, my mother went through every square inch of Don's closets. Surprisingly, they were maintained very meticulously. Remember that line from Flaubert? 'Be regular and orderly in your life like a bourgeois, so that you may be violent and original in your work.' That was Don in a boring sentence.

'It was unnerving and eerie,' she said, 'to see the bookshelves stacked alphabetically and the closets organized via colour.'

All of it echoing so silently, sullenly. He maintained everything so skilfully, perhaps applying the same set of skills that a poet applies to prosody. There were all these dusty props of hits and misses of this plot called life. Don suffered from an obsessive desire to preserve everything. There were diaries, pins, bowties, shoes, socks, taxidermied housemates (one cat with a string of pearls around its collar, three dogs, one duck, one pelican, one raccoon, two hamsters, one tiger cub, one peacock, one framed box of exotic butterflies), a clay mould of Don's face when he was a young man preserved in a glass cookie jar, magazines from thirty-six years ago, worn down toys from some past life, bras that didn't belong to my grandmother, underwear that bore the initials of unknown people. Knowing him, he was probably anal enough to organize it systematically for a day like this. A day when he would be lying half dead while we scavenged through his life in boxes, in disarray, in ruins, while his organs prepared their mutiny.

Chapter 3

Before I had taken off for varsity in the desperation to live another life in another self, my mother lived rudderlessly. This was before she moved to Madras. She was consumed in her journey of remembrance. The days bled into weeks and months. Her love for my father, Gravy, was out of control—a trait I realized, much later, that I wished to hell I had never inherited. But blood is blood, and desire is desire, and I was half of her soul, and we can't edit our soul now.

She loved him a little too much, because it was hard to give less, or love less, she said.

Her wasted eyes processed every piece of memory she had with Gravy in super-slow motion, scene by scene, line by line, breath by breath, moment by moment, bottling it all under her skin, in her head, till she felt suffocated with its moth-filled smell. She reluctantly tried to get used to not being in the company of her husband any more. Oftentimes, she lived inside a television, as her eyes vacuously stared into mind-numbing *Desperate Housewives*, she instinctively turned to ask her husband and said, 'Did you just hear what happened?' only to find herself talking to an empty seat, in a lonely room.

She became one of those restless women who was only at ease while conversing with ghosts (my father's, who else's?). She imagined how her body would be found when she eventually died. *Eventually* was too far away. She stared into space for days on end; her face was always curled up in anguish and anger at having been left alone with me. The fridge brimmed with containers of foul-smelling, rotten food, with packets of milk that probably hadn't been opened for a month, or the stale old yoghurt that would have abominable forms of rainbow-coloured fungus floating all over it. The floor was lined with big bunches of dead hair taken out of a comb in a huff, quickly knotted up over the index finger, and then allowed to drift away until it accumulated with the rest of the webbed dust, becoming one big, lousy ball of dirt. I didn't think she could get herself to do anything. My father was her most compelling axis, and in his absence, she was paralysed.

It was not right, on my part, to think that her looking at me was a sign of her need for conversation. It just meant that she was lost in this passing of time. She abhorred company, barely tolerating mine. She was all over the place, running on Japanese time, I think. She refused to meet people, and when people stopped by, she sensed their arrival like a hawk, as though they were carriers of the bubonic plague, so she could quickly switch off all the lights, unplug the telephone, draw the curtains, fuse the doorbells, tape the windows shut (this time the storm was inside her veins) and disappear into the darkness as though we were bandits in our own home. She'd keep creating new ways to escape contact with human forms. And after they left, she'd heave out a sigh of relief and say with misplaced glee, 'Phew! That was a close call, wasn't it, Zef?'

'I wanted to meet them,' I told her once, meekly protesting her insanity.

But she broke down saying that she wasn't ready to face the world just yet and that I had to understand that. I wanted to tell her that I was tired of being understanding, I just wanted to be understood. But I stayed quiet. I was worried for my mother, but then she was grieving in her own way, in a way that I didn't even want to attempt to make sense of.

The only thing she would consume were nine pegs of scotch and a bowl of curd rice, morning, noon and midnight. The scotch because the liquid gold could seep into her veins and knock her out to slumber, numb the pain; the curd rice because it was my father's favourite comfort food, his staple diet of simple happiness.

'I didn't air out his room because . . . I just wanted to bottle his smell,' she said. (It was a chilly mix of citrus and Davidoff's Cool Water perfume.) She didn't throw out my father's last tea bag, preferring to keep it in a silver box with a lock. She triple bagged his ashes in a Ziploc, and fastened it with a rubber band, kept it amidst his clothes inside his cupboard, locked it and threw away the key. She'd taken out some of his shirts which she sometimes wore because apparently she could 'feel him inside the layers and folds'. She kept hunting for bits of his hair around the house, and once she spotted them, she'd twirl them with her fingers and play with them till the strands would break.

My father's side of the bed was left unmade. It was kept in the same position that he had left it when he had woken up on the day that he had decided to die. Who knew that he was already planning his trip to another galaxy that afternoon? If by chance my mother's hand tugged on his pillow during her hazy medicated catnap, she'd instantly wake up with a miserable jolt, realizing that he wasn't there any more and she would have to adjust the sheets and pillows back to their state of crumpled orderliness with military precision. She kept a cube of chocolate on his pillow, as she used to every day when he was alive, like those trained chambermaids who come to turn down your bed at a hotel. The last night that he lived, he didn't eat that chocolate. It had fallen underneath the bed.

She also made it clear that she wasn't particularly keen to hang around, even for my sake. She just wanted a way out. She daydreamed about death. She daydreamed about not waking up. She wrapped herself on the bed in a plastic sheet, hoping that it swallowed, no, suffocated her in its grip, until one day, boom, she would never open her eyes again. Can you even imagine someone doing this? Wrapping themselves up in cellophane on the bed? Who does that sort of thing? I told you her love for him was unconditionally, explosively, other-worldly.

I wonder if I can ever understand just how much of her belonged to him.

But even as she wanted to play dead, she still woke up every morning in disgust, as though her bed was ridden with scorpions. As much as I was selfish in running away, she was selfish, too, in not wanting to live, not wanting to deal with me or anything, or anyone. Our childish escapist strategies only proved that I was her daughter after all. We both just wanted a way out, but then you can't really escape what's planned for you until your time is up, really. We still have to live till we eventually finish our quota of breaths, I suppose.

My father had been kept under observation since he had attempted to kill himself before. He had started the process of dying. He was no longer in love with love. He was no longer in love with life. Convincing the Pope to drink a double shot of Patron from a stripper's pan-flat abs would have been easier than selling Gravy on the idea of living. He became a king among mumblers. Death, the idea of it, consumed the latter part of his life. But he didn't die. He used to joke that he was an unsuccessful suicidist. My mother and I used to stare while he would let out brief, nervous laughter.

'Do you think it was our fault that Gravy died?' my mother asked me randomly.

That felt as though someone hit me with a hot pressing iron on my face. Why would he kill himself because of us? We never treated him badly, I thought.

'No,' I muttered, appalled by the question.

'Are you sure?' she pressed on. She was smothered in the cynical stench of personal regret, and of what might have been.

'Yes,' I gritted through my teeth.

'Okay, fine.'

'There's nothing more you can do now. You looked after him,' I tried to be convincing. Why was there a need to be convincing when there was nothing anyone needed to be convinced of, I thought.

'Really? I think he is still somewhere here. His good side is angry that I didn't save him,' my mother said.

'You couldn't have saved him. He was beyond redemption,' I said.

'I guess no point allowing a man who doesn't want to live to live.' She seemed to justify to herself. 'Yes. Probably not a good idea,' she sighed.

I felt heat rising to every part of my face.

'It's . . . it's . . .' She was formulating what she wanted to say. 'It's like when you are trying to save a man from jumping off a bridge into a deep sea, even as he screams let me go, let me go, and you keep on holding on and say no, no, no and then he keeps asking you to let go, and then finally you let go. He falls down. Drops dead, drowns. Whatever, but then his last thought in the millisecond before he falls into the jaws of sharks is wow, she actually threw me in, what a cunt! But then do you become a murderer? If he was trying to kill himself anyway? What happens to the conscience then? Do we die of guilt or do we go about buying our daily bread saying he's at peace because he wanted to die? But then the last thought of that dying man is that I killed him.' Her voice seemed strained with the tears and cigarettes.

She had wondered if he'd died when he thought she could manage alone.

Manage? What was this woman saying? She was a mess, I was a mess. We had feared that he'd be dead soon. And now that he was dead, I wondered what was yet to rattle us more. He had left with every piece of us. We were doing everything but managing. Death wasn't like a heartbreak or severance from a lover where you cry for half the amount of time you were together and one morning wake up thinking that oh, great, I did good because I didn't think of him, I didn't feel as though someone punched me in my stomach.

'It's funny isn't it?' she said.

'What?'

'He must have thought that his death would be some sort of a closure, an end . . .'

'To what?' I asked, but she ignored my question. I may as well have asked her if cats liked butter.

'But it's just . . . it's just . . . just even more of a colossal mess . . . of complications . . . of our lives . . . everything is so tanglewood . . .'

I didn't ask her anything more.

In my secret life, deep in the filthy recesses of my twisted brain, I was ready to explode. Heartache is never part of the original master plan of the universe. I was ready to strangle myself, my mother and anyone getting in the way of my inching closer to the truth. But I maintained that façade of calm curiosity, like some class of Patrick Bateman's twin, juggling an alter ego in the same way I guess a million people do on Facebook; in the same way someone might write 'hahahah' for something that is not even remotely funny. I had no choice, had to keep calm, carry on, tiptoe with the delicacy of a ballerina ninja but with a hundred-ton emotional battle on my shoulder, as night after night went on by beating its weary load. You get what I mean? Because I wanted to know, I wanted to search for pieces that were conveniently hidden under the rug of disguise, because this is a story that is as much my mother's as it is mine, as much the man I thought was my father's as it is mine, as much my family's as it is mine.

But to get there from the broken social scene that I had inherited, I couldn't possess the capacity to fuck off. I needed a whole lot of patience before my mother started to erase herself from living. To live, I was what she needed to be reminded of. On one of those days, when I was sleeping in my room, she came in and gave me a magazine with a post-it marker on page ten. She had written an email to Ozzy Osbourne in the *Sunday Times* magazine, asking him how to deal with grief.

'Ozzy Osbourne, really?' I started to laugh but she seemed very serious.

'Yes', she replied curtly.

'Did they really accept your probl . . .?'

'Just read it.'

'I keep getting horrific panic attacks. It started when the love of my life killed himself. I've been to psychologists . . .'

'You didn't tell me you were having panic attacks.'

No response.

'Do you still get them?' I asked.

Silence. Did she have a cotton ball stuffed inside her mouth, I wondered.

'You went to shrinks? Why didn't you . . .'

'Just read it, Zephyr,' was all she said to me.

'Fine!' I wanted to hiss but stayed quiet.

'. . . But they all say that if I realize that I'm not going to die, the panic attacks go away. That's BS, because I know I won't die, but I still feel like I'm about to explode. Please help. —S, India'

The man had actually answered:

> Answer: It sounds to me like extreme grief, S. People don't take grief seriously enough: the loss of someone or even something, can be very hard to get over. When I was in rehab . . .

'What is this nonsense? Are you seriously taking advice from a debauched, has-been, drug-addled, rock star?' I asked, amused and angry—but more angry than amused—at the same time. She seemed to have become a little insane in the membrane.

'Are you fucking demented, Mummy? I just want to take your hair and tie you with it to the ceiling fan,' I screamed.

'My hair will fall off from my head,' she replied calmly. Then after a while, she added, 'so will I . . . I only have ten strands of hair left on my head.'

She looked at me, rolled her Rizla and patted it like it was some diamond tobacco. She placed it in her mouth but did not light up.

'Look, he and his wife, had this . . . this bond,' she murmured.

'Oh.'

'It was this insane connection, this strong unbreakable bond, as much as either of them likes to ignore it or pretend. She got him,' she explained.

'So?' I asked.

'So, what so? I wrote to him . . . why don't you just finish reading it?'

It was the stupidest thing I had ever heard but I am not one to argue with a confirmed crackpot.

So I finished reading Osbourne's reply:

> . . . I had to attend grief groups for the loss of drugs and alcohol in my life. I thought it was stupid at first—especially when I met a guy in there who was sobbing about his cat going missing. But I soon discovered that grief can really mess you up. I wouldn't be at all surprised if that's what's causing your panic attacks. Your body is overloaded with emotion, basically. So I'd say get on Google and find your own grief group. It's healthier than going to your doctor and getting some Valium: that'll just fix one problem and start five others.

'Really?' I looked at her. 'So then, did you?' I asked.

'Did I what?' she said.

'Join a Google grief group?' I tried to keep calm.

'It was just . . . I don't know. I was trying to work it out. I couldn't keep busy as much as I tried. I couldn't handle the silence, I couldn't handle anything, I couldn't handle you . . . I just couldn't,' she cried.

She was holding on to something that used to be there in this house, hoping it will come back, knowing it won't. The gravity of this grief made us feel like some sort of a fruit, like an orange or a plum, that was once lovely, ripe and beautiful but now had become rotten and stank.

I suppose that's why she decided to move to Madras soon after . . . maybe to deal with the absence of my father's hectic, broken soul. But then, going back to Madras for her . . . how can I best describe it to you? Imagine what getting back with one's high school flame would be like—remembering all the highs, but ultimately finding that all the reasons that broke you up back then are still valid now. Perhaps more so.

My mother, the queen of a thousand sighs, was a strange woman, and she became progressively kookier. She had a deeply ingrained sense of fatalism inherited from her devastating life experiences. When my mother was six years old, she was completely paralysed in an accident. It happened while playing with her mother's shawl; the damn thing fastened around her neck and strangled her.

The doctor said that she was afflicted with quadriplegia, where the patient loses sensation and control. In medical terms or maybe in everyday speak, my mother said, 'It's called a choking game where the player gets a pleasant sensation while being choked.'

'You are saying this as though you are savouring some vintage Bordeaux,' I told her.

'Hahahaha, you are funny. But it was random like that. I was admitted to the local hospital in Madras, St. Isabel's, and put on a ventilator. The doctors said that improved my breathing but I was comatose for five months. Bare naked bones. Everyone tried whatever they could do—from keeping my favourite food—rasam and rice—and flowers—gardenias—underneath my nose for the smell to seep into my brains, to talking to me non-stop, to pumping me with drips—all of this to bring me back to life, but there was no improvement. So finally, the doctor played old records of music, everything from the Beatles to Carnatic, via headphones, for three days continuously.

'I was in a dream where everything was illuminated by the light of a fire. That's all I can remember,' my mother told me. 'And I remember running, I just kept running. And then when I stopped running, I just woke up. The first words I said to Don were, "I'm fine." Then, after a few hours, I slipped back into a coma!' my mother continued.

'Just like that?' I asked her.

'Yes. It makes for a good black comedy, right?' my mother laughed.

The doctors said that my mother had some sort of stroke which put her back into a coma for another five months.

'All I remember was that the second I slipped back into coma,' my mother went on, 'I was starting out in a race. Don let out a whistle and then, as I kept running, you know, like that stallion, that show on the horse you used to watch . . . what was it?'

'*The Adventures of the Black Stallion*?'

'Yes.'

'You ran like that horse?' I asked.

'Something like that. I felt I was the horse in a race.' She looked at the expression on my face and said, 'Stop mocking me.'

'I'm no . . .'

'Anyway,' she interrupted, 'I kept running, and eventually I tried to slow down as my legs started to give way but I couldn't stop. It was like that . . . like that . . . running on a treadmill programmed to run you down for six years without stopping. All through it, I kept wondering if it was real or a dream because I was losing control. When I tried desperately to slow down, I saw that I was the only one running—there was no one next to me . . . I think that was when I started responding to music. I was told that they started playing music via headphones again. It got me all worked up. I could hear a faint tune and I was trying to hear it better. It was like trying to remember the lyrics to your favourite song. You know when you are juggling your iPod to tune your favourite song while running but then you end up tripping over because you aren't concentrating on running. So I tripped. You know when you fall in your dream, and you're jolted awake to reality. That's the only way to describe it.

'I thought I fell over a boulder and rolled down a rocky hill. I woke up with a shudder. I had no sensation in my legs. I had forgotten how to walk. But the funny thing was that when I woke up no one cared that I couldn't walk for three months—they were just thrilled that I had responded to their quack method of pounding my dead ears with music. There are some morons who are happy when you are alive as a vegetable even if you are so long gone that you can no longer take part in real life. So they keep you in the next room and are just so incredibly overjoyed that they are around in the same airspace and that's all that really matters. Well this was like that.'

My mother went on as if she were talking about something as trite as tiramisu. Poor thing, she used to be an electric and funny storyteller. But now she looked dazed and so fucking tragic like the filthy, ugly beauty of a Lucian Freud painting—filled with despair in all its naked, untamed, destroyed beauty. Clearly, her weirdness started very early in life.

Chapter 4

Funny how memories form us, and as we form we reshape our memories—we create and destroy them to fit in with our lives. We all carry rooms of each other inside our separate skins. We choose to remember only certain things, certain smells, certain feelings, and those memories become symbolic of entire relationships.

In all certainty, it probably would have continued like that had my mother not taken stock of her subconscious and opened her big, compelling marble mouth and resorted to honesty. What was the point of speaking the truth when it brings no joy? I don't understand why she had to confess that he wasn't actually my father when I was pretty sure I had erased or blocked it from my own brain. She sensed my irritation and apprehensions.

'I need to restore some sanity,' she frowned almost indiscernibly, as if she'd just remembered something she'd left in the rain.

Maybe it was like clouds piling up on her window and she needed to see the future ahead with a clean, unvarnished eye. Maybe there was a sense of agitation creeping into her bones, much like the chill silently creeping in between the blankets, and she chose to put the phantoms to rest. Sure, death makes one undergo an emotional earthquake, but honestly, she didn't really need to come clean and speak the truth. Because I had remembered to forget the truth myself. That might make me an unreliable witness to my own life but sometimes lies provide that comfort that help you lead a better life, at least in your head. Don't they?

Sometimes it's best to not disturb the tangled piece of pearl necklace at the bottom of the drawer. And as long as my mother never brought up the topic of who my real father was, it didn't have to be true. It's not as if I wanted to go on a wild goose chase trying to figure out who sired me. As it is, it felt as though my heart was in a state of intergalactic jet lag. All I wanted to do was cocoon myself in a semi-comatose state, and treat Gravy's death as a passing spectacle. That way, it would have been a simple, incomplete, tragic story. Father killed himself. His death came in quick succession after his siblings. Family coming to terms with a bizarre curse. Limited sorrow. End of. As in, it is the end.

It's like a bitter break up, really, if you come to think of it. Sometimes even after a relationship ends, it takes a while for it to really, really end. You consciously tell yourself to not look at the old pictures, delete all the numbers, even though you can recite them in the deepest sleep, and even when you are falling into death. You remember to forget all the funny moments, and never listen to the same songs, you work very, very hard to get to that level of faux emotional stability. So once you delude yourself into believing that you have the fleeting stamina to start building a new life as a hobby, as the ravages of grief ease up slowly, you are over cautious, less strong (horribly fragile like a burn victim) you believe in the power of a terrifying love, the kind of love you don't require, the kind of love that smells of endings, and no ever-afters, the kind of love that gives you a fleeting, deluded illusion that no harm has been done, the kind of love where you have sex differently, maybe even quickly, furtively, impulsively, so that you can block out what your body wanted from your former lover. But then, sometimes just when you think the wounds are about to heal, and you feel that your heart has seared its way from another skin and tucked itself into protection, you wonder why he won't fall back in love with you. You see a new picture of your former love somewhere, with the grin of a good life on his face, and wonder how in Judas' name dare he smile when he has destroyed you to your bones, or your hands deliberately, accidentally, unsteadily dial his number only to hear his voice and hang up, and that is enough for you to crumble into little pieces.

It took a lot for my mother to talk. Now, her confessing to something like this would only make me want to eventually question everything, open up an emotional can of worms, and all the Pandora's boxes that my two-, three- or five-year-old brain must have sealed shut. Truth be told, my mother wasn't prepared. I mean, can you really be ready for a sordid story narration, especially when it involves telling your daughter that her father is someone else.

'I am determined to look at reality firmly,' she said, not particularly to me.

She spoke in breathless sighs, fervently, excitedly, hopefully, uncertainly, with eagerness and without patience, foolishly. Talking to my mother seemed like a conversation with someone who had returned from a drunken trip to Venus.

I felt as if I was falling from some tall building and she decided to fire information at me as I fell. Or think of it as though she was filling me up like a big black balloon, filling me filling me filling me filling me up till the time I explode, and then eventually disappear into small, powdered smithereens. There were multiple dialogues and emotions, thoughts, bubbles and colours and various black-and-white pigmented versions of life crises running through my head.

My mother, after all, was constructing a story from uncertain beginnings in some form of morbid amuse-bouches of disconnected confessions. Even if I tried to interrupt, she didn't register any of it. Sorrow does that to you, perhaps. You don't realize that when someone says, 'So what's going on?' you can't seem to find the brakes in your vocal chords. Maybe she was just waiting to be asked? So I took it all in. There was no point trying to avoid it.

After all, it was about where she ends and I begin.

Deep down, it was hard for me to understand that my mother was a full-blown woman with a miry past that was dominated mostly by crazy needs, and an affectation most commonly associated with repressed convent-educated nutters (I've been there), before she wrestled her weak emotional muscle and finally lost her mind (not just metaphorically), body (always a problem) and soul to the man she declared would bring me up. Lust was the thread, and she had sewn an entire wardrobe out of it.

In many ways, it was as though my mother was slicing her heart open to remove the bullet lodged in it, while calmly talking at the same time so she could breathe better. She wasn't just scarred on the surface, she was split up within. She constructed the story of her life—where the past had arrived into the present—from its hazy beginnings. She told me these stories in the same haphazard manner in which she chose to live her life. These were words of desperate and imagined love.

'I blame my first. It's always the first. Isn't it?' she threw the question in the air, to an invisible audience that may have been privy only to her eyes.

I wouldn't know, I thought to myself. The closest to love I had ever been was lusting after Liam Gallagher. But these were thoughts that were better left in my head.

'The balance just shifts internally if the first ends badly,' she continued. 'The first always ends. Always remember that, Zef. Okay? That's how I got here, that's how you got here, asking me all these questions, the answers for which I have tried very hard to forget.

That's what maybe led me to your father, and to the man who finally adopted you as his own. I loved your father much more than I could have loved anybody because he saved me from myself. And over the years,' she paused as though she were searching for the words hidden somewhere inside her body, '. . . especially in the past few years, he became the demon that he had saved me from becoming.'

My mother reminded me of that character from Dostoevsky's *The Double* where the doppelganger wakes up and his double is following him around, taking over his life. In her case, I didn't know which 'double' was real. Because she was in a war with herself. It seemed as though her right arm had been cut off when the other hand was feeding the mouth some sandwiches.

'If I have to retrace my steps here, it means that I have to remember the terrifying anguish of my first love,' she said. Before I had asked her who it was, she added, 'It was . . . my piano teacher.'

So it was that simple. She'd fallen in love with her teacher. I was expecting something a bit more spectacular, a little more soap operatic, a little more Federico Fellini. Of course, the story was just beginning.

'I met him for the first time on my thirteenth birthday. No, wait, I was fourteen. Yes, I remember this because Don had gone to Spencer's in Madras . . . it was the only shop at the time that stocked dresses from England,' my mother said.

Apparently Don wanted her to wear a baby-blue dress because he had bought baby-blue lace socks during his last trip to England. He had got her small pearl earrings and patent black Mary-Jane shoes with half-inch heels. This was Don while he was still doing very well with his leather business. He never tired—no tired isn't the word, he had a ball—satiating all his whims—no matter how ludicrous they were. (My mother told me that once for her tenth birthday party, Don had organized an army of dwarfs to serve the food so that there were only little people at the party.) Anyway, there at the store, he had seen this man, all of twenty-eight, sporting a large nose, barely-there eyebrows, playing a jazz trumpet for an audience that didn't care for music really. So apparently Don went home with a goddess dress for my mother and also invited this gent over.

'I had heard noises coming from the hall,' my mother remembered. But she recalled dismissing it as one of Don's melancholic outbursts with vague friends when he was inebriated, which he was most of the time. 'A serene tune started filtering through the walls. I went downstairs and saw this man playing this old trumpet, engrossed in his own rhapsody. It was the loneliest sound an instrument can make. His head was arched back, his eyes closed, his body in a hobgoblin posture, moving like a rocking chair, his white pants torn, his light blue shirt crumpled and worn with a badly knotted tie, his hair dishevelled like it had never been combed. He looked like Jesus Christ on a Goan holiday. I thought my heart lost some five hundred beats, Zef. I didn't even know I could feel this way, as though someone sucked the oxygen out of the room. At first, I fell in love with his long, sinuous fingers, the sound of the slight guttural twang in his accent when he said hello, the origin of which I didn't care about. When I noticed the rest of him, his scraggy face, his ill-matched socks, his unkempt look, he looked like some class of a pirate cartoon hero. I was giddy with lust. Don declared that he'd be my piano tutor,' my mother told me.

Don had announced to my mother with a tone of finality that the real test of a musician was how smartly one could pick up sound by ear and that if she knew how to read music, then playing it shouldn't be a worry. So the deal was struck.

'I knew it would be a bit of a struggle learning like this,' my mother said, 'but I didn't want to show my incompetence in front of my new tutor,' she told me. 'You know, Zef, even though I hated the piano, I instantly fell in love with the idea of being around him. My heart was beating like a jungle drum. If music were what feelings sound like, then my nerves must be blaring like an unleashed goat that had just seven minutes—no actually, that's five minutes too long—to live before the axe goes down.'

My mother's tutor came over to the house—the very same house we were in now—to teach her lessons three days a week. He'd play a tune, and she'd try to recreate that on the piano.

'Were you good?' I asked her. It seemed ridiculous to worry about her musical ability at this point but for a moment there it almost felt like a normal conversation.

'I was miserable,' she said. 'I struggled because I wasn't naturally gifted to pick up on sound. I succeeded partially also because with each passing day, I fell hopelessly in love with him, his unaffected beauty, his squarely-cut nails. He was . . . he was unlike anyone I had ever met. He was so removed from the crazy set of hedonists that revolved around Don's debauched world . . . he came from a less sophisticated world . . . so genuine . . . how shall I put it to you . . . he was real . . . yes that was the word . . . real . . . so . . . normal, so poor, so sincere and he was at that age in his life when he didn't know quite what to do with his untamed beauty . . . he was . . . how can I put it . . . he was different from my world. But in hindsight now, I think, I must have confused lust for love.'

I suppose when you are fourteen, there is no caution in love, I thought. And a lot about love is also innocence and ignorance at its core, isn't it?

Anyway, my mother's lust for her tutor was festering like a boil. 'I just dreamt of having him. In my dream, I was almost there. That sense of ownership. It consumed me,' she told me.

Over the course of those days, my mother said that her tutor became extremely friendly with Don—the two of them were inseparable. He had told them about his nomadic upbringing as a child, and how he was brought up by only his mother, and how he valued all the anchors he built over the years, many of whom he had met so serendipitously. Don, too, believed in the trigonometry of fortuitous encounters—that's how he had met Sancho, hadn't he? The tutor had found himself in Madras after travelling around the country; it was near the sea, it smelt kindly, it wasn't rushed, this city. He had spent time as a full-time teacher in schools here but those opportunities depended on the moods of little children. He had looked for a job as a musician everywhere until he found one here in this store, three times a week in the evening. Being a trumpeter at a store didn't pay much—in fact it hardly paid anything—but it was better than nothing. During the day he composed tunes—in his head—while his hands transcribed old Bavarian texts (he knew the language) into English for the languages department in Madras University.

The two of them—Don and the tutor—seemed like old friends who had merely lost touch. After an hour of lessons, the two of them would play endless games of bridge, share a similar interest in reading intensely vague books because it served as a 'cloak over all human thought', a love for jazz, a fancy for long walks and banter. Don introduced him to all his friends and acquaintances by organizing musical nights so that he could showcase his talent. He really began to treat the tutor like one of his own. He even gave him some sort of an administerial job in his office—for a few days a week—so he could have some extra money, find a better place to live, look sharp, live smart, get some half-decent clothes to wear, move up slowly in the world, that sort of thing. Having him around the house worked well for my mother because all she really wanted was to breathe the same air around her tutor.

'But,' she said, 'for all the incessant camaraderie between the two of them, my tutor was terrifyingly chaste with me. He hardly even made eye contact. He was a strict tutor, almost detached in a way, and I tried hard to . . .'

'Impress him?' I interrupted.

She nodded her head.

'I practised the bloody piano till my fingers died,' she said lifting her fingers now to check if they were still a part of her body. 'At first, Don was amused at my renewed interest, considering how much he knew I hated the instrument,' she said. 'I showed signs of making progress, but my tutor patronized me like a child, as though a lollipop or ice cream cone would appease me, and bring me some amount of instant joy. It frustrated me that he chose to ignore what I was feeling for him, but I couldn't really do anything if he didn't want to ruin the teacher–student equation. He didn't want me in the same way I wanted him. That was it. Proximity without intimacy spelt hell. Somewhat like a wasted erection,' she sniggered.

It was my turn to keep quiet.

'You know, Zef, it was the first time that I had ever experienced such anguish about unrequited love, and the impending rejection. Looking back now, I couldn't see why he would also want to be with me. I was short, flat-chested, had bamboo sticks for legs, two wires for arms, and a pimple festival blossoming on my face,' she said.

I stared at her. It was so hard for me to imagine her as ugly as she claimed. In spite of all this, her skin was gold, it glowed. Even though her kohl-rimmed eyes were fuelled with liquid sorrow, I remember thinking at the time, that tears suited her face. There was a sense of melancholia in her, which my mother made no effort to conceal.

She told me that after two months of lessons, he came home one day to talk to Don about leaving the job of tutoring her. Apparently, his application to Trinity College, the music school in London, had been cleared and he would be off to study music there, and he would have to leave right away. Of course, Don was delighted because his discovery had won a place at a great music school, but he was also sad that the mirth that my tutor brought into the house would stop.

The tutor told my mother that he'd be back in maybe a year, or more, who knows how these things go, and that she should keep practising the piano because she had the fingers for it. 'Okay? Promise?' he had asked her. But my mother just nodded her head like an overfed monkey because her tongue was stuck to the crown of her mouth.

'I wanted to tell him so many things, Zef. I wanted to tell him to stay for another second, another minute, another hour, or another day, another forever, but . . .'

'But what?' I pressed.

'I suppose,' she whispered, 'you can only say something when you know the other person wants to hear you out. I couldn't do anything even if I wanted to. I didn't realize that he was leaving in the next two days. I kept staring at the house gates hoping he would come back to say bye, give me a hug, kiss me, take me with him—as it played out in the film in my head—but no such thing happened. He just left. He disappeared into the same haze he came from.'

My mother said that the days following his departure were the hardest. A sense of emptiness, an unwelcome quiet, she said, settled at the pit of her stomach. There was nowhere to go, nothing for her to look forward to, no one to pat her back when she got the keys right while playing a tune, no laughter in the house, no one to give her goosebumps. The clouds remained in a permanent state of grey.

'I didn't know what to look forward to any more,' she said. 'The worst part, Zef, was that I couldn't even tell Don that I wasn't really interested in the piano as much as I was obsessing over my tutor. I was lost in my own silent film, given that I spent my days nursing lusty fairytales. I kept practising my piano like a trained robot. After all, my tutor had told me to practise, hadn't he? Don teased me and said that maybe one day my music will eventually bring my husband to me. I smiled deep down. I actually started to believe that maybe one day my secret chord will draw him back to me, and he would enter through the same gate, assume his place next to me on the piano, and instantly fall in love with me.'

Knowing my mother, she must have probably rehearsed this scene in her head over and over and over again to put herself to sleep; in the same way I do—even now—when I imagine and execute epic plays with real-life characters, all in the cosy comfort of my head, secretly praying that at some point they come alive by the time I eventually wake up. These visions of lust into love that she spoke of seemed to be a solipsistic luxury for her.

But none of what my mother wanted to happen happened.

'I wondered,' she said, 'that if I was missing him and thinking of him so much, wouldn't he be thinking of me too?'

She imagined her tutor mapping his way under the unfamiliar, moody, rain-drenched skies falling all over England, she imagined him walking around in a trench coat that Don lent him with his trumpet in a box, she imagined him lighting a cigarette for lunch, she imagined his face coming towards her in the red rain, she imagined him reading music while standing under the shadows of cathedrals, and busking away to make some money, she imagined him in bookshops devouring books that he couldn't afford to buy.

'I imagined too much nonsense because I was obsessed with him,' she said. 'I just wanted to slice his chest open, and place a picture of me in his heart.'

Don also travelled a lot in those months. 'Business,' he told my mother who was left under the care of friends, 'was growing across Europe,' so he left for short hauls to score deals.

'How much of it actually rallied onto success seems hard to imagine now,' my mother said, 'but at least he was making that effort. I stayed back, going through life with the disdain that usually accompanies a gawky, ugly teenager. The only excitement was when

Don would return from these trips with beautiful dresses to make me look girly.'

But as the year passed (or was it more?), her music man never showed up.

'I began to imagine if he was a figment of my imagination. There was no sign of him at all, no letter, no message nothing,' she said.

Eventually, my mother said that she stopped playing the piano because she couldn't be bothered.

'He wasn't there. Who was I fooling?' she said. 'I was no good. I didn't want to play it for an audience comprising my whisky-loving father. I started painting my fingers black again. I went about life like a cat in a dog suit.'

I smirked at that line but straightened my face before she could notice. But this story didn't end there.

Everything changed two years and twenty-seven days later. My mother had returned home from school and could smell him from the gates.

'It's funny,' she said, 'how we remember people. Some people's smell never really leaves you. It floats right underneath your nostrils, you have to call for it in thought and it will show up in three seconds. At first, I thought I saw the smell of his perfume as I entered the space he had occupied. His smell . . . how can I put it . . . it had a shape to it.'

That smell was reason enough for her to realize that she was *still* terribly smitten with him.

She saw his face as she made her way inside, and her body just convulsed a little bit; her world just stopped as though it had a collective cardiac arrest.

'I felt as though I got shingles all over my body, an irresistible urge to scratch myself like a dog that had eaten his own shit. I ran in to see if he really had returned. He was there, looking like . . . nothing as I remembered him—scraggy, unkempt and unshaven. Standing before me was the clean-shaven face of a god.'

She claimed that he looked like those mixed race curly-haired baby Gap models of today—I imagined him to be the love child of a threesome between Bryan Ferry, Lenny Kravitz and Lara Stone. He had shown up wearing a beautifully tailored maroon-velvet coat, a French-cuff white shirt with a flipped collar, just 'the way they did it at the time in Japan', worn with a pair of handcuff-shaped silver cufflinks, with beautiful grey pants with cuffs that ended just above his ankle, brown brogues, no socks and a Hemingway hat that hid his puffed mane. From what I understood from my mother, her old tutor suddenly possessed the spectacular swagger of someone supremely confident and well-fucked.

'My tortured genius vision of him longing for me under lonely skies flew right out of the window,' she said wistfully. 'What was I thinking? He seemed to have some sort of a personality transplant, and so out of my league. He must have been bedding a series of nymphs and flesh-hungry flautists at the music school, all of them much older, bigger breasted, curvaceous and exceptionally talented, unlike me.'

When she finally faced her tutor, he smiled at her to say that Don had complained that she never played the piano. My mother stood there in front of the two of them, frozen as though someone had stuffed a boiled egg down her throat, with her sweaty 'coal-miner's hands' (her words, not mine) tucked deep into her pocket. Classes were resumed right away. Don, too, according to my mother, was so thunderously joyous as if his long lost son had returned home.

The tutor told them that he had come back to Madras because

he had got some sort of a grant to do some sort of research. My mother didn't pay any attention to all of that. When I asked my mother how he seemed to waltz back so easily into their lives in the same way he did the first time around—out of nowhere—she said that at that point of time, they didn't seem to mind. The two of them, Don and her, were just so overjoyed that he was back, and with him he brought his huge tennis-ball eyes that bore the promise of life and laughter to this condemned house, in the same way he did earlier, in the same way no one had in the past.

I guess we all do need someone to help us hear the music in the world. To Don and my mother, the trumpet player did just that.

Don had invited him to stay for lunch (drunch was more like it). The trumpeter regaled them—mostly Don; my mother was just an appendage who happened to be listening in—about his days in London, and the whole experience of living, breathing, eating, drinking music. Somehow the whole London experience was good for his ego; it made him come into his own as though he had shed his old skin, to make room for a new one. My mother said that the tutor seemed to be a little louder, a little more excitable, a little different from his earlier shy self.

Soon after, they started lessons, he became a frequent visitor to the house. My mother remembered coming back home from school once to find the gate painted lemon yellow. The exterior of the house was a tomato red. Upon walking inside, she heard Coltrane play the blues, and saw a very inebriated Don slouching on the dining table, drinking what might have been his eighteenth scotch of the day, and the tutor—who had affixed a brush to a pole—painting the walls of the living room a beautiful sky blue. Painting was a mild word. He looked like he was splashing the walls with measured and silent violence, reminiscent of Jackson Pollock. She asked Don if he had actually agreed to all this, given the fact that she had never really seen her father agree to anything very easily—besides a drink—especially when it came to *his* house. But before he could say anything, her tutor jumped in to say, 'You couldn't possibly paint one wall and leave the others bare-naked now, can you?'

So that was that, then.

A few weeks after resuming her piano lessons, she said, the tutor randomly asked her if she wanted to go see a small concert that his friends were putting together at Marina Beach. He said that it might be a good music lesson for her. My mother, too stunned to utter a word, vigorously waggled her head like a trained monkey.

'I assumed he was taking me out the next day but he didn't show up. He suddenly disappeared like a dream. Two days, three, a week, finally two weeks, passed. I thought maybe I had heard wrong,' my mother said. But then he showed up at home and apologized for his absence. He said that he had started to juggle handfuls of research work, gigs and lessons, and was designing the music syllabus for armed forces' bands, among other sundry things—all of which helped him get by way better than he did before. He then asked Don's permission to take her to the concert.

'I was sixteen going on a paralytic attack,' my mother said to me while rolling her Rizla. 'I wore a knee-length, hand-stitched lace cream dress that Don had bought for me from Milan, under an electric blue jacket made by his suit tailor in Madras. The jacket was so tight I couldn't even squeeze a smile if I'd wanted to. I wore a pair of chunky, tan heels with fat leather-buckled straps. They felt like ankle weights. Still, I wanted to look like one of those women who always keep a loving eye on themselves, the kind that makes life seem like a beautiful adventure and whatnot. I still remember that day,' she said half dreamily. 'I was so nervous, I remained as still as a body in a coffin, as someone who was dressed up only to be buried deep into the ground.'

But as the evening passed, she said that she remembered it being impossibly otherworldly. The crepuscular evening sky, the crescent moon, the strains of the string quartet, the smell of his skin, him. She said they walked around a little bit after the concert, a little ahead of the neighbourhood. They saw writers take photographs, painters make scribbles, lovers nibbling on ears, pigeons pecking on peanuts, travellers turned poets—they walked a little ahead of the street, a little on air, a little down the Marina Beach, a little ahead of Madras, a little inside the clouds, a little towards heaven.

'I felt cathedrals growing in my brain,' she said. 'There was no other way to put it. I fell in love with him even more. Maybe I fell in love with the magic that the moment offered. It was the first time I was alone with a man, Zef.'

Finally, they sat down and she took out a bunch of notes and lines, answers to possible questions that he might throw at her. She had scribbled them on paper napkins and had folded them into the shape of ducks. She had carried them with her, and had kept them in her jacket pocket. His eyes gauged her with uncertain, restrained curiosity.

When he saw them sticking out, he smiled and said to her that the boats got flattened out. She remained quiet and fidgety. And just like the music fading out in a movie, a look was exchanged, he crossed the invisible line of intimacy and wrapped his fingers around her, and kissed her.

'I bit his lip. I didn't know how to kiss. He flinched but told me to try again. I did. Kissing him was like eating love,' she said. It seemed like an extended form of embrace, somewhat tenderly punctuating that moment of their coming together. It sealed her sense of longing for him, and of this moment, of her love, which was fraught with a fiery yearning.

'It was too devastatingly surreal. My head was racing . . . I had too many questions, the sort of questions that plagues the insecure—did he do this with most girls, or maybe he decided to start life afresh with someone like me, a virgin with ugly fingers,' my mother rambled.

She said that he must have seen the quizzical look on my face and quickly motioned his mouth to apologize and told her not to tell Don what just happened.

'When he said he was sorry, I blurted out that I loved him. He was quiet and then smiled and said that he loved me too,' my mother said. 'This was the moment that destroyed my life, Zef. Or maybe defined my life. In hindsight, I'm not even sure if he said this to me or if I imagined it. It seems somewhere between truth and fantasy because it defined what I started to give, take, expect out of love—possession, obsession and ownership of another heart.'

That night, she told me, they had lost track of time, as one would if one were lost in the throes of something terribly exciting and inappropriate. Their eyes exhaustively marked and registered the contour of their lust, their hunger for each other played on as their invisible tongues started to lick each other. She said the two of them stared at each other with every inch of their vision, with their veins, with their hearts if hearts had eyes. She recognized herself in his face, in his smile.

At midnight, as the sky extended its velvet cape over them, she said that she felt a fear swell inside her that this was all getting over too soon, as terrifyingly good things do; that this dream was ending too soon and that she had to do something to hold on to it.

'I was nervous . . . of its newness,' she said.

'Why?' I asked her, half amazed at hearing my mother talk like this.

'I thought I would never see him again. I was desperate to hold on to him, this dream of him and me together, so I hesitantly pressed even though I was unsure of what to expect, but then I didn't want to be without asking. I asked him if we will still have lessons and he gave out a full, throaty laugh saying that he wasn't going anywhere, and that he would see me tomorrow.'

'So then you continued classes as usual?' I asked my mother.

'Yes,' she said. 'We continued the classes, I played the piano and he played the trumpet. When the melody put Don to bed and the dogs at ease, we escaped to head to the beach, anywhere where we could be alone, my room, his house, anywhere where we could talk and then some.'

She said that after the first kiss, things moved like Speed Neutrino, as though it was an accident waiting to happen.

'Soon we started frequenting his house, which was as small as a kennel and so simple, stark and so very middle class, nothing like this ghost house I was used to living in,' she rambled like a hurling train. 'It was a paradise of dead plants, feeble light, scattered liaisons. He also had a huge suitcase filled with religious idols and charms lying half open in the corner. The whole room was that corner, actually. Once, I remember, a bat had flown inside through the window and had temporarily turned the room into a sky. When we made love there, sometimes I wondered how he had not one single artwork on his walls. I wasn't used to that sort of lack of décor, you know.'

That sounded like a pretty hilarious observation to me but I didn't say anything.

Everything seemed magical. She said to me that there were nights, and days, and moments in between when she had prayed—let me have him. And now that she did, he provided the heaven that she had wanted all along. Until one day he told her, right after they had sex, that he had been booked for a mini tour and had to go. A booker, one of Don's friend's had heard him on Don's recommendation. A tour was organized with a group that would be travelling to Calcutta, Bombay and Delhi.

My mother cried breathlessly, wondering what she would do when he was away—she clung to the length of his body—but he assured her that it was only for three weeks. Before she knew it, he had taken her home, and it was the next morning and he had already left.

'I walked around like a dog on heat,' my mother said. 'Don was quiet too, going about pretending to work. It seemed as though some dark shadow had descended upon our home, as though all the stars, the entire solar system, had been blown out. I was worried if my delicious tutor was sleeping with someone else during the time apart, you never knew the musician groupies. One day, in between those weeks when I returned from school, Don told me that he had telephoned home an hour ago.'

She said she tried to mutter 'oh' nonchalantly, mostly because she didn't want to parade her eagerness in front of Don, lest he caught on, even though she was dying to know how he was doing, what he had been eating for lunch, how his concerts were going, what he was wearing, did he find someone else—actually, not that. But all she could manage to ask her father was how her tutor was doing. And all Don said was that the boy was attracting the right crowds. When my mother persisted, Don didn't bother replying. She tried again to check if he mentioned any time frame for returning. Don just said that he didn't check, but my mother didn't give up. She still tried persuading Don to get him to say what she wanted to hear but her father just glared at her, and that glare only meant silence from then on.

While my mother was incredibly happy that Don was the man who kickstarted her tutor's career from obscurity and then promoted him among all his friends in the know, who then put him onto various other friends in the know and finally to an agent who seemed to have gotten him all these gigs—she was also just frustrated being away from him. She said that she became terribly sullen at home, picking fights, not eating, the standard woeful routine that afflicts the broken-hearted. Don had noticed but chose to stay quiet.

'I had no choice but to wait it out,' she told me. 'I tried to believe that he was going to come back—well, he came back the first time—but he made no promises. But after nearly three weeks of no news from him, I was angry and upset and felt incredibly let down. I had almost given up when, after a month and a half, he showed up at home.'

In her excitement to see him, she licked his lips with all her love messily spilling out everywhere.

She forgot all about her anger with his absence and got carried away as he regaled her with his stories on tour, the people he met, the adulation.

'He was unapologetic about his absence. Maybe he knew I'd wait. Maybe I knew he'd come back. But even as I told him that I missed him,' she said, realizing something else now, 'I never really heard it from his mouth. I tried telling him that my body ached when I wasn't with him. But, maybe, he was just too excited with the din of his new success and new income to hear me.'

They spent the next ten days together, in some sort of clandestine, forever-picnic haze, at least in whatever way they could—stolen in between his other commitments and away from Don's prying CCTV vision—before he was summoned for another godforsaken performance or research or work somewhere else.

In the days and months to follow, as word about his music spread gradually, the travelling exponentially increased. The two of them would be able to snatch a week, sometimes even less, a few moments together, before he would take off with no return-to-sender stamp. Places to fly, people to flee. That sort of thing. He'd make promises to meet my mother but couldn't keep them.

'It was a pain loving someone who isn't around. I missed him even when I was not thinking of him. I'd keep going over to his house in the hope that I would just maybe bump into his ghost, but . . . no show,' my mother said. But she'd return home crestfallen. 'The time apart from his skin was what haunted me the most,' my mother told me. 'He was my world like any man you love ought to be. When he'd be back, I'd break down only for him to tell me that he was working hard so that one day when I turn twenty, we'll get married and settle down together and travel the world. And of course, I believed him. Why wouldn't I? He loved me, I loved him, what's not to trust? I accepted just about anything—his erratic presence, as long as he came back to me—nothing else mattered. I just didn't want to ever let him down by behaving my age. Why would I do a thing like that?'

It made me wonder if my mother had any friends at all who knew about this non-general-type lover/romance. It was an odd case of love and/or pagan chemistry.

'No,' she spat back. 'He had told me not to utter a word to anybody. He didn't want us both to get into any form of trouble. So I wrote everything down in a diary but then again, sometimes I felt even that was not listening,' she laughed.

One day, he picked my mother up from school, or wherever, and took her to his house. But he remained silent on their way home. When they got there, he showed my mother a calendar with all the dates crossed out. There were dates for gigs in universities, cruise liners, and maybe even in the bloody spires in the sky for the next few months.

In a soft, persistent, eager voice that seemed to wrap itself over her ear, he told her that the new job aboard the cruise liner will help them sail into another life somewhere, away from here, and that they can make it together on their own. My mother felt scared. She said that Don wouldn't hear of it, to which the tutor told her that they needn't inform Don. She contemplated escaping for a few seconds but very soon the vision was marred with a violent Don killing the two of them with his bare hands before they headed out into the tropical sunset. My mother cried, hating that she was still sixteen, and wishing that she was much older.

As his career started taking shape, my mother had to get used to the idea of his prolonged absences, and his capricious schedules. She said that she didn't really have a choice, he was on his way to becoming someone relevant, doing whatever it takes. At least, that's what she started to say to mollify herself. And just when she would start to worry about his impending return, he'd show up with some presents, many stories, new adventures, new earnings—take her to naked slumber when Don wasn't around. Maybe in her brain, she thought that this was how grown-ups had romances: between busy schedules, hurriedly in between life and its hectic ties.

'But before I knew it,' my mother said, 'two delirious years of my life had been vacuum sucked out of me. I was going to be turning eighteen in a few days and he was away in some godforsaken country with no news for a month. And, Zef, we *had* made a plan for my eighteenth birthday. At least I thought we did. We had planned it almost five months earlier. But my birthday came and went, and there was no sign of him. I went in and out of Don's study the whole day, just in case he called. But nothing. In some bizarre fairytale plot in my head, I thought he'd surprise me by showing up, but I was just left with all these unsatisfactory, empty thoughts, nothing more. I had planned on a picnic with him, picked a spot so secret that it was out of a Monet painting, but he hadn't even bothered to send even a telegram. I spent the day by myself, in my room, with Katrina stirring up inside my veins. I had no choice but to live through it, sulking in private, crying into my pillow, talking to a yellow moon drunk on loneliness.'

Instead, what she did on her birthday was a yearly ritual that Don had started. He would take my mother to his friend's photo studio to get her pictures taken. The idea was to chronicle a photo for every age. But a few days later, Don received a phone call from a gentleman who produced the local news and owned a film studio. He had seen a picture of my mother blown up in the studio and had called to enquire if she was conversant in English and if she could come in to read the news and maybe for a screen test for a (Tamil) film. Don was aghast at the absurdity of the question. 'What sort of a barbaric world do you think we inhabit? My daughter even sees her dreams in English!' he told the gent. So it was a 'yes' to read the news; 'no' to the screen test. Don declared that he didn't want his daughter being the coquette for every pocket.

'I wanted to inform my lover about my new job but Don just let out a grunt when I asked how to reach him. I knew that Don's friends knew his agent but sometimes it was hard to get my father to do anything, given how boozy and untrusting he'd become. I tried every trick in the book to make my need to get in touch with him seem a little more genuine—I didn't want to miss out on my lessons, I needed help to practise the piano, I too wanted to apply to Trinity, I had to write a musical composition. Don mumbled something indecipherable, which reminded me how clumsy he got when he was drunk, and also prone to dangerous outbursts.'

My mother was nearly finishing up at school at this point. So, for two hours after school, three times a week, she'd go to read the news, but she also made time to practise the piano.

She continued, 'In the romance in my head, I thought that maybe he would watch me on TV somewhere and then he would come rushing to me.'

'Happy ending?' I deadpanned.

'No,' her face fell. 'One month stretched to sixty days of complete silence. I became worried. That was very unlike him. I thought he was lost at sea like the stories of relatives of acquaintances you hear about. There was no news. I was so anxious . . . I was what you would say as a child, a paranoid android.'

His absence haunted my mother like a smoker's old habit. She missed him and there was nothing she could do about it. That emotion had set inside her skin and there was nothing she could do to get rid of it, except wait for him. 'Sometimes, we have no control over the emotion that grips us, it mixes with our blood, and as much as we want to get rid of it, we can't,' she said. 'But that's the thing with men, they can't multi-task, multi-miss. They don't get that there is somebody wondering how they are breathing, what they are doing, even as they go about their daily work. The wait killed me. I didn't want to mourn my lost love already. He had filled himself all over my heart so that there was no room for anyone, anything else. My asthma reappeared as I started smoking Don's cigarettes to keep me calm. Almost three months had passed and I had not heard from him. No matter how busy I kept myself, I still managed to think about him.'

My mother said that she tried telling Don that they should send out a search party, or register a missing person's complaint but he would just laugh it off saying musicians were like this, unpredictable and very busy touring from one time zone to the other.

'I tried to plead as subtly as I could,' she said, 'but Don would just shush me with some weird logic and I wouldn't know what else I could do. I told him we should try the agent but Don was livid to even hear me suggest this. He yelled at me for appearing so eager and desperate—that was true, I was eager and very desperate but so what. All I said was that I didn't want to miss out on my lessons.'

Finally, after four months of excruciating silence, my mother said that she couldn't take his absence any more. She started stalking his house every evening after work. Every day, she went hoping against hope to be surprised to see the lights on inside. I wondered if he was invisibly staring at me through some hidden window. But no such thing happened. 'I think a part of me thought that if I went every day, he might feel some sort of karmic connection and come home sooner,' she said. 'With each passing day, I felt a sense of helplessness descending to the pit of my stomach, a feeling akin to not knowing the answers at an important test, a sense of sheer dejection crippled me. I tried to get him out of my head but the more I tried, the more he stayed trapped with memories inside my face, under my skin, between my veins. I think I wanted him because I couldn't have him any more.'

Still, she didn't give up. My mother thought the last resort was to try her luck by calling Don's friend who had put him in touch with the agent and who would then help her get the details of the cruise liner he was on. Even if it meant defying her father's orders. It was a long shot but she was desperate. And she had to do this without Don's knowledge.

She waited for the time to be right, which meant that she had to wait until Don was asleep or out of the house. So one afternoon when Don had gone to the bank—which wasn't the bank, of course: he had gone to his local liquor dealer—my mother entered his study, a sacred ground accessible only by invitation, to open his desk and raid it.

'When I managed to open the bottom drawer, I was amazed at how fastidiously Don had preserved everything. It was a feast for the eyes. There was a beautiful diary where he maintained a meticulous, calligraphed record of people he owed money to (but obviously never returned any to them because he never had any left); there were a pair of old cufflinks that his father had given him; an antique silver spoon with my initials engraved on it—he must have got them made when I was born; address books from his days as a cargo boy in the army; my report cards; a few wine corks. I kept staring at all this, Zef,' she said. 'Then I noticed a package of papers, postcards and bent photographs, all of which was bundled up tightly with a ribbon. I took it out, didn't think much of it, having assumed it to be something that Don had collected over the years, and then I put it back inside.

'My objective was to find the number of the agent, the cruise liner, anything. I didn't want to lose focus. But just as I put this package back in the drawer, the hair in my nose stood up. I smelt my hand. I recognized that familiar smell, the mix of cinnamon and clove. Then again, I thought it was my imagination. I took out the package and smelt it again, and it *was* there. It *wasn't* my imagination. It was real. The same smell hovered about. As my eyes furiously poured over the little bundle, I realized my heart was palpitating out of control. Five seconds later, I noticed the handwriting on the package. I saw the familiar manner in which the letters were beautifully, and eccentrically, cursive. My legs were shaking in fear, Zef. I thought there were forest fires underneath my feet. They were all letters, postcards, photographs from him. He had written from every part of the world he was in, Zef. He had sent dried leaves; he had sent photographs of himself laughing. How could he laugh when I spent sleepless, tear-filled nights thinking of him? He had sent pictures of himself at the Trevi fountain, standing in front of the Royal Albert Hall, of his performance on a cruise liner, of him outside Sacre Coeur, of him with his band mates, and of him wearing a tuxedo. All these things that I saw came out at me like a series of unending bolts of lightning, the kind of lightning that you see out of an aircraft's window, shaking the plane to the core. With each streak of silver, I felt my insides shuddering. There were postcards and there were telegrams informing us of his every move; there were little notes; there were receipts of his fees at Trinity. Don had been godfathering him the whole damn time. There was his life for the past three years, and more.'

'Why didn't Don say anything?' I asked her. But she ignored the question.

'Before I knew it,' she said, 'I could hear Don entering the house and in my nervousness I put everything back in the drawer and ran out. In hindsight, I wished I had taken the bundle and run. And I didn't even manage to get the details that I wanted. That was just bloody brilliantly depressing.

'The next few days,' she said, 'went by in a haze.' The anxiety killed her. She wanted to confront Don but didn't know what to say. She was scared. So she continued living in the same silence that a child does when he discovers his father is addicted to porn, and doesn't tell anyone out of fear, out of respect, and to not let him know that he has let him down.

But then, sometimes, silence's side-effects become a suppressed rage that, when unleashed, can set the sky on fire.

'Every time I saw my father behaving as though he had done nothing wrong, I'd start frothing with fury,' she said. Eventually, when my mother couldn't contain her fury any longer she confronted Don, before the anxiety of discovering those letters permanently paralysed her. 'I still remember the day,' she told me. 'He was sitting in his study, glasses perched on his nose, one hand holding up John Gunther's *Inside Europe*, the other dangling a whisky glass. He looked delectably vague, like Lady Marchmain, all he needed were some curls rolling down and a black veil.' When she asked him why he didn't tell her that the tutor had written, he said so very calmly that he didn't see the point to keep her informed.

My mother summoned the courage to tell her father that she was in love with the tutor. Don let out a smirk. When she told him that they had planned to marry when she was twenty, Don let out a deafening laugh. She started to fidget around in nervousness. Don looked at her sternly, with cold sobriety, his eyes pierced through her skull like an X-ray machine, and he told her to deal with the fact that she was nothing but a passing infatuation for the trumpeter. Before she could open her mouth in protest, he said that he had lived many more lives than she had and warned her to not cross the line on this one.

'He told me to get out and he blithely went back to reading his book. He didn't even flinch at my violently shaking body. He didn't care,' my mother said. 'I felt as though he hit me in my stomach with the butt of a rifle. It was claustrophobic living in the house after having this discussion with Don. Left to me, I would have been rowing my own boat to Vietnam right away but I was so physically weak, Zef, that I considered switching on the light bulb as the hardest thing in the world. I just didn't want to live at home and see my father. But I had no choice. I still had one more crucial semester of school left, and my job at the TV station was just a hobby that could barely provide me with three meals, two fruit juices and the five cigarettes that kept me alive on most days. I had no choice but to reluctantly push my feet homewards, and stay there and wait it out till . . . I finally grew up, till he finally shows up,' my mother rambled on.

But then she said that the only thought that comforted her was the devious logic (uncared for by reason) that he was true to her. 'He had written, Zef, he had thought of me. He wanted me to see him enjoy all the things that made him happy. It was my alcoholic, senseless father who was playing devil's advocate. I was just happy thinking that he had thought of me. I knew he was going to come back. He always did.'

She said she kept herself busy in the days to come by drowning herself in the mundane. Occasionally, she would stop by to see if his house had some sort of movement. On one such stalkerish trip to his house, she saw all the lights shining bright inside, which made her a little excited, angry, nervous and confused at the same time.

'I hadn't passed by the house for a week, so the chances were that he must have just come in between those days,' she said half trying to reassure herself. 'It was nearly at the end of four months but I did wonder why he didn't tell me that he was back. Between the time it took me to summon the courage to ring his doorbell, a thousand thoughts ran through my head—maybe he had just returned, maybe he was unpacking and thought he will call me later, maybe he . . . no he couldn't be . . . he was honest, he told me he loved me. He had written home. Finally, when he answered the door, he appeared sheepish, and said that he had meant to come over and call me and that he was sorry he didn't tell her that he had arrived. I didn't care. Of course I believed him. I loved him. I just reached out to hug him. And he hugged me back, but with some hesitation that, I realized much later, often accompanies guilt. Zef, in the past, we had thought nothing of raping each other, thought nothing of tearing our way to get inside the fabric of our skin, but now he just took me home that night and it was only when I got home much later did I realize that I didn't allow him to talk. Oh well, he can talk tomorrow when he picks me up, I thought. I was just excited that he was back, Zef.'

But he didn't come home the next day.

She said that she gave him the benefit of the doubt. Maybe he got busy. The best part was that he was back. That's what mattered. 'So I made my way to his house instead,' she said, swallowing her shaky voice, as though she was trying to stifle the vomit rising up to her mouth.

My mother got up, went into the kitchen. My eyes followed, panicking. I thought she had gone to throw up, but she came back with two glasses containing three massive pegs of whisky. She handed one glass to me, and sat down.

'Drink up,' she said.

I had a little bit. It was too much for me at 11 a.m.

She swallowed what was in her glass, and then in mine.

And then she spat out the words.

'Just as I was rushing my way up the front yard, and burst open his front door, I saw him passionately kissing my father, on the mouth. Don.'

'The two of them, Don and him, were so lost in their moment that they didn't see me staring at them. I didn't know what to say, or what to do,' my mother's voice shook. 'I felt hot tears coming. I thought I died. I thought the sky had crumbled into darkness and fallen into pieces. I felt my heart constricting. I felt asphyxiated. I felt a fog descending right inside my eyes. I thought I dissolved into my own shadow. Then everything crowded in on me until I blacked out. The next thing I know I was being taken into the emergency room with one female doctor and one excessively ugly fat-cheeked, triple-chinned nurse who treated me with the indifferent kindness of someone who was accustomed to heartache. Blobs of her sweat drizzled on to my skin. She somehow morphed into a pug for a second. I couldn't see straight. Because I had been crying, I looked like I had boiled my head in a pan. My asthma had gone out of control, which made me pant like a long-distance runner. I was shaking vehemently, uncontrollably. The doctors couldn't diagnose what was wrong with me. One of the doctors thought that some ghost of god had gotten into me, something which was quite the norm here, used very conveniently by devout women who wanted to skip lines to get to the deity in a temple much quicker than the rest. They tested me for all sorts of things, all of which came out negative. Finally, when I found some strength, I clutched the doctor, my nails digging into his elbows, and told him with whatever voice I had left: "The crisis is in here . . . in my heart. I can't find a beat there because it's been shattered into a billion pieces."'

Chapter 5

The incident had set my mother's life on fire. Imagine losing your first love—the first man to start a riot in your heart, enter your body, lick your lips, bite your tongue, swallow your spit, eat your teeth and trace your naked body with his fingers—to your own father?

It makes sense now, a little bit. I was trying to understand all this from my perch of sanity, going with my mother to a place I didn't want to go. The idea was to try to ground her and if I failed at that, then at least thinking about getting to where she was. It was, in a way, an attempt to understand the place from where the quiet anger crawled into your sleep. Like trying to find the small pieces of a big jigsaw puzzle—you know you saw the pieces somewhere right now, three seconds ago, it was right here, oh no, where did it go, just like the words that vanished from the tip of your tongue into thin air with that last sip.

A deep-rooted hate for Don occupied permanent residency in my mother's wounded heart. It was all the cumulative life experiences of a not so normal and unpredictable childhood that still lived as dark atavistic forces within her psyche. But do you really blame her?

By the time her conscious mind fully grasped and processed the significance of what she saw, she felt a hurt that was stripped of any thought. It was in that split second where her world crumbled.

'The whole thing may as well have happened an hour ago,' my mother told me, flinching at the toxic memory.

My stomach lurched with disillusionment about what truth would follow from now. The truth is that we despise what we know because once we know it, it becomes a part of who we are, and then we despise ourselves.

My mother said that she woke up in the hospital with a jolt. Sweat trickled from the nape of her neck. The room was stark, bare and was burning like a furnace. It was dark outside. She saw an impeccably dressed Don ('the monster had the time to go home and change as though he was heading out for a fucking cocktail party') lost in a haze of amphetamine slumber. Next to him was a cold cup of tea (no milk), which she was sure was laced with some whisky. There was an empty packet of pills too. He was still holding on to her hand. She shook it away from his grasp. That woke him up.

'Good morning, darling,' he said with embarrassing chirpiness, kissed her forehead, and started to fidget around with some accelerated urgency. The quartz in front of her blinked 3 a.m. The stench of a whiskeyed kiss lingered on her head. He got up and walked towards a suitcase that was kept in the corner of the room.

'Did you get some rest, dear? Now let's get you ready and cleaned up, so we can both go home. I hate this hospital. It is so terribly depressing. See, I got you this lovely dress, and I also brought you this pair of shoes . . . I thought you might like to match it,' he smiled gleefully and held up a pair of purple lace flats. 'We don't want you leaving the hospital in this wretched attire, now do we? I hope you managed to get some sleep. The lady in the next room was howling like a hungry wolf. I mean, for heaven's sake, we all knew that she was giving birth to a set of twins fathered by her uncle, who is a judge at the high court here. This should be a mental asylum. People are truly crazy here. Oh, and did you know that one of the nurses who attended to you was actually rescued from a brothel?

She was taken in by some convent that trained her to be a nurse. Let me go call her, so she can get you ready. Oh wait, I nearly forgot to tell you I saw peacocks dancing on the terrace just above this room. I was wondering what the thumping noise was last evening, and when I went up, I saw the most angelic white peacocks, one came and started pecking at me, so I sent for some peanuts and biscuits . . .' Don went on rambling for a bad ten minutes in the same way the guilty and the drunk do. His voice was slurring at the edges. He kept shuffling all over the room like a rabid dog that has just escaped a kennel. He avoided any sort of eye contact.

'I tried to interrupt him so many times, Zef, but he just wouldn't let me get any sort of word in,' my mother said. Confronting him was like a big joke with all her panic-stricken words and questions, drooling out of her, spilling messily all over the phenyled floors. 'I thought he would owe me an explanation or an emotion but he steered away from even remotely mentioning what happened. He didn't seem to even have the urge to discuss what had happened despite my persistent needling questions. But the bastard . . . he must have been drinking his mind away, hoping that what ensued must have been a hallucination so inappropriate that it could not have been real,' she said.

He couldn't think it was a mere hallucination, I thought, but didn't say it out loud. You poke eyeballs by accident but you don't get naked and kiss a man by accident.

Eventually, when Don decided to give in to my mother's questions, he gave a publicist-approved smirk, one that showed off all his teeth, and flicked a thumb on the corner of his lips, just as an actor would before he says everything else besides revealing the plot of the big blockbuster he was starring in, and said, 'How about we double up on the piano lessons to make up for the lost time now, huh?'

That was enough for my mother to resort to violence. She

tumbled out of the blanket, plugged out all the drips and wires that her body was connected to, flung the tea cup at Don, upturned her bed, hurled the suitcase at him and destroyed whatever it was that came in her way, and cried and screamed like a banshee, as loud as her lungs would allow her to, 'I hate you, I hate you, I hate you. I don't want to live with you. What sort of a wretched father are you? How can you even do what you did and expect me to come home? You are the worst kind of human being there can be. How can you do this to me? How can you be this way? And how . . . how can you do this . . . with someone . . . I loved? With someone I loved so much. You knew I loved him, yet you . . . you . . . and him. You are such a fucking bastard,' she started crying and hitting Don.

Just then two nurses came rumbling inside, and Don took over the situation, clasped my mother by her arms, apologized to them, and said that all was under control; his 'daughter was merely having a tough start to the day'. After they left, he turned to my mother and spoke like a cardinal: 'I draw the line at swearing, young lady.'

'Well, I draw the line at . . . at . . . lying . . . and cheating . . . and being the way you . . . and . . . and doing what you did,' she spluttered, not able to describe what she saw.

Don remained as calm as a man walking on a wire over two skyscrapers—best to look up and keep traipsing ahead than be bogged down by the ungodly low-life noise surrounding him.

'I did not lie to you. I did not cheat. However I choose to be, it just doesn't concern you,' he said serenely.

'Doesn't concern me?' my mother screamed, ready to throttle him.

'Well, it never came up, darling,' Don said in a sing-song manner as though he merely forgot to tell her about a cancelled picnic.

My mother couldn't believe her ears. Neither could I for that matter. I couldn't even imagine what havoc that level of betrayal must have played on her angry and confused teenage brain. It must have been some irrational emotional earthquake.

'Well, now it has. So tell me, tell me now,' my mother yelled.

'I like men,' he said.

'That's it? That's all you can say?'

'Well, what else would you like me to say? It's the truth. I'd like to get on with my life now. There are some people waiting for me at home. So can we please get a move on? Chop chop, sugar plum.'

Don kept sashaying about in the room tidying things up like a drunken clown on stilts, avoiding her gaze. He was far from apologetic. He didn't care about what she found out. It seemed now that he had become even more self-assured, relieved even, confident that a part of him that he had kept alive within himself was no longer a secret, the two of them (him and my mother) would and could continue to live as they did earlier. The truth was that Don treated his daughter's witnessing what she did as some kind of a *fait divers*—like some major incident that appears as a tiny fleck in a newspaper, as a mere footnote to his expansive, outrageous and deceptive life. She told him that there was nobody waiting for him at home and that they couldn't leave this room till she gets some answers from him.

'Answers? What answers could you possibly want? Stop being such a cry baby, for heaven's sake,' Don laughed. 'The person who has all the answers is that teacher of yours. He was the one who lured us both. He is the lecherous creep! He is the one who . . .' Don was trying to find excuses for his behaviour by indulging in a ridiculous blame game.

'Can you believe the man, Zef? This was my father,' my mother said. 'He just didn't seem to get it,' she said. 'He betrayed me and he didn't seem to care. It didn't even occur to him that he should be ashamed for having an affair with my lover. *My lover.* That man was my first, he was my life at that point of time, for heaven's sake. Don knew how much I loved him, and yet he couldn't stop himself,' she said to me. A tear stung her eyes. 'It was not in Don to be ashamed. That bone didn't exist in his bloody body. He treated the incident as something as flippant as stealing my candy and I was making a huge deal about it.'

Don continued trying to coax my mother to come home. 'Let's get you home now, come on now. You can recuperate there. Everything seems scary at night but in the day it will all make sense, I promise. I'll even buy you a box of those mille-feuille that you really like. And then we can go shopping and get some new clothes stitched for you and me.'

'In his brain, everything, whatever it was, was as clear as the light of day,' my mother said. 'And he must have thought that since he wasn't so confused, why should I have to be? I realized that my father had been a mad lunatic. I had to leave. I couldn't go back home,' she said.

'Is, not had been,' I corrected her.

'What?'

'He's not dead yet,' I reminded my mother.

'To me he is,' she said.

Don, it seemed, had absolutely no sense of guilt, remorse or any morality at all. He didn't know that he needed to feel any of those emotions. He simply couldn't be bothered with trivial aspects of counselling his daughter once she had discovered his sexual proclivities and the affair with the trumpeter. Good God no. That would be a full violation of his Don-ness. It must have been all those years of alcohol—it took over the windiest part of his brain and spread quickly from head to toe and everywhere in between. It must have filled his nerves with rancid nonsense.

Don continued to babble about buying some new art for

the house, and that the gardeners were waiting to manicure the landscape, and that he was thinking about having a garden party, and that he needed to do this or that.

My mother started to cry. 'I didn't want to go back to that hell. I felt every part of my body constricting. It was as painful as . . . stigmata . . . stigmata, yes, that's right. I started to scream that I couldn't live there. I just wanted to leave. I held on to the leg of the bed because I didn't want to leave. Don tried to drag me while I yelled at him, calling him so many bad things. At first, he tried to calm me down gently. But then when I bit him, he gave me one tight slap,' my mother said.

Don had caught hold of her arms, steadied her up and said with a tone of steely finality in his voice, 'Darling, calm down. Stop threatening me like your mother did. It is my house, my rules. Make it work for you. You made it work so far, you can even now. Trust me, you can. So stop all this rubbish about leaving . . . Where will you go? Where can you *even* go? Let's go home and get some rest and then we'll go out for a picnic tomorrow, okay?' He let go of my mother when she froze.

The man clearly treated the entire incident like a minor blimp in their picket-fenced idyll.

My mother stared at her father. He stared back at her. Maybe even he could see the hurricane inside her eyes and how he was floating inside it so listlessly.

In that second, my mother decided to run. Away from this room, this life, and this monster of a father. She ran so fast that no one could keep up behind her. That's when it also fully made sense to her why her mother, Sancho, *really* left home. Her husband drove his wife out of his house in the same way he drove out his daughter. Her husband had destroyed her mind in the same way he destroyed his daughter's.

Don was such a whip lasher according to my mother. He drove her nuts with what to wear, how to wear, how to sit, what to do, how to love, how to pretend. And now he was lying half dead in the next room, all his beauty erased by the lines of fear, scorn and cheap alcohol.

'I thought I forgot about this rage that I had because Gravy calmed me down,' my mother said. 'But now that I am in this house, I can feel the stirrings in my chest, it builds up like an acidic burning sensation. I want to claw my hands through these walls, these blue bastardized walls, all these memories greet me like unacknowledged feelings at every turn. It's like being buried alive, Zef.'

I could feel my mother's fury piling up like angry clouds that threaten to lash out but they just hover above and put you in a depressive mood, and disappear.

'Then why did you come here?' I asked.

She was quiet for a while and then spoke so softly I could barely hear her. 'Because sometimes we are our own jailers,' she told me. 'Because no matter how much we may hate our parents for all the dreadful things they have done, they are still *our* parents, after all. Gravy tried to make peace between Don and me but the idea of coming here just filled me with so much dread. But now . . . now in his death, he is doing just that. It seems as though he willed it for me to come here and look after Don.'

The dead have their own ways of bringing some order into the lives of those still living.

Coming back to what happened, my mother said that the months and years after her running away were the worst days of her life. I guess because once you learn the truth of something as ghastly as Don's sexual hunger, it's hard to unlearn it.

My mother basically tried to orphan herself in the only way she could, emotionally and mentally.

'Didn't you want to find your mother?' I asked her.

'For a minute just when I was contemplating leaving home, I thought I should . . . but that urge lasted only a minute. I wouldn't even know where to go, what she would have looked like, where she would be. She didn't make any sort of contact in so many years. She . . . she had abandoned me as a child . . . she chose to leave me with a lunatic, she could have taken me with her, yet she . . . she chose not to. At that time . . . I was just so terribly upset and angry that she too, like Don, had failed me as a human being, as a parent and had left me . . . with this monster.'

'Maybe she had tried taking you with her,' I said.

'Who knows? Growing up at that time . . . with Don being the way he was, I believed him when he said that he *had* tried looking for her and that she didn't want to be with us . . . I was so incredibly naïve to have believed that bandicoot. The truth was . . . that Don raised me in such an all-pervasively peculiar way that I forgot to even miss my mother. He . . . just filled up that empty noise, he smothered me with so much love, so much madness, so many gifts that I didn't remember what it was like to even have had another parent. He never . . . never really let me feel her absence . . . or her presence.'

The nurses at the hospital helped her enrol at the YWCA in Madras.

'It was one horrible room—as big as a bed—which burnt bright white with one tubelight,' my mother remembered. 'There was no closet, no desk, no anything. When the girls would come in for a chat or a secret smoke, they'd stare at all my beautiful intimates, in lace, satin and mercerized cotton— all thrown around the floor. I wondered whether if they stared hard at these pieces of private vanity it would help them know me better. There was one bucket, one mug and one common toilet. It was disgusting but anything was better than living feeling guillotined in my childhood home. I did a nightly course in English Literature at the local college and during the day I did odd jobs at the TV station. On the off days, I'd go sit on the beach. I was barely making any money, I was losing my mind. Staring at the beach and confessing to street dogs to stave off my hunger was better than nothing,' she went on.

Soon after, my mother then proceeded to engage in a steady destruction of her twenties in a frantic, urgent and athletic pace. The lethal mix of a nervous breakdown, anxiety and sexual betrayal were all the important motifs that led to the sort of synaptic burst that pushed her over the edge. It was raw emotion, as raw as freshly cut meat with the stench of blood and the metallic tang of the butcher's knife all over it.

'The first thing I did was cut up all those nauseatingly sweet dresses that Don bought for me; I felt choked in them. I didn't want to belong in my skin any more. I wanted to put on new skin. I didn't know how to live in my body. I wanted to get Don out from living inside of me,' she rambled. 'I pierced my nose on both sides, and bought men's clothing to wear. I don't know what I was trying to do but I wanted to look as unladylike as possible, as far removed from vulnerability, as far as possible from the way Don had wanted me to dress. I wanted to forget who I was and how I was raised. I took that rejection by its horns. It pushed me to new extremes, emotionally and physically. I wanted to be wanted even more so than ever, I wanted to be a part of someone's core. I was mourning for a lost love and I thought that if I replaced the absence of the five-foot nine-inches of the trumpet player-shaped hole in my life with someone else, then I would be fine. Because . . . because it was ghastly waking up in the middle of a lonely night and breaking into a cold sweat, a sense of fear and abandonment and a searing heartache, with no one to reach out to even when daylight breaks. So I thought that if I was pursued and loved by a better man, then I would never feel so rejected, and I could forget the misery that I was waking up to.'

She went quiet for a brief while, collecting her breath. Perhaps she was choosing her words for the next round of lashings because she was nowhere near done.

'For a long time I tried to seek validation from everyone . . .' she started to say.

'Who is everyone?' I interrupted.

'All these men. We always seek validation from men—it's a female instinct, and you'd be lying if you say no.'

'How many were there?' I asked so quickly that I wished I didn't. I hate that sometimes my mouth reacted quicker than my brain.

She had the presence of mind to not tell me.

'But what happened afterwards?' I pressed.

There was a long pause. She spoke in the manner a stutterer looks at his speech and blanks out of helplessness, knowing that he has to start but not knowing how to start because the tongue seems to have gone on a holiday and is unreachable. I had to be patient. Anxiety is the death of anything.

Finally, she spoke without stopping because if she stopped then she couldn't start again. She was attempting to give me an anatomy of her heartbreaks by fearfully arranging the information in some sequential order, somewhat like piecing together a crumpled paper after it has been through the shredder, trying to make sense of the chaotic rambling of her messy emotions.

'It was about love, a willingness to love, and being loved, Zef. I fell for every mediocrely-sketched demon of a man who crossed my path. I was hungry for romance. They say you never quite love anyone with the same levels of passion, intensity and innocence, the same besotted way you loved your first love . . . the first person who touched you . . . but that wasn't the case with me. I fell in love a little too easily, a little too much and one by one . . . they all left me even faster. I thought a relationship would shield me against the world. It would make me feel safe. So I played the part, now in hindsight, rather too desperately—I tried to be clever, funny, smart, dishonest; I pretended to be happy, I told them what they wanted to hear without ever speaking my mind—because if I really told them what was driving me or haunting me, they'd think I was too intense, too needy, too clingy, too crazy, too demanding. When they said they wanted to meet me, or take me dancing, I'd jump at the chance, and hold on to them like a lifejacket. I was just so scared that they would leave me. I wanted them around me. I played along. I was always available. There was no limit on how far I would go, no boundaries, no length. I had no confidence. I would stigmatize myself for them. I shaved my hair, I drank like a fish, I snorted everything I could, I waited for hours because they said they would come ten minutes ago. I moved to Ooty and lived on a boat for a month because that man took me to the movies and bought me a couple of nice skirts, I made uttapams and sold them to honeymooners there. I hitch-hiked to Rameshwaram because another man I met said he was going to show me the sea that had no waves there, and when I got there he was nowhere to be seen . . . I later learned that he fell asleep in some fake Buddha temple there and then disapproved. Then there was another man who seemed so much in love with me that he spent all his time with me till the hour of his engagement.'

'What?' I interrupted. That was a little funny, even though it wasn't meant to be.

'Yes,' she let out a little laugh. 'I didn't suspect it at all,' she told me. 'He seemed like a conservative four-eyed student who was rushing home to study for an exam. He said he was just leaving for an hour, and when he didn't show up three days later, I went to look for him at his usual haunts. I thought he died. But I met his friends who told me that he had gotten engaged the week before and how come they didn't see me at the ceremony.'

She was piling up heartache like old newspapers.

'I don't know if you were plain stupid or naïve,' I told my mother.

'I was desperate,' she offered as an explanation. 'The truth was that they all made me happy and unhappy at the same time, and I thought that was *normal.* I ended up believing their actions, their porn-taught precision when it came to scissoring my insides—all of which I thought suggested love but did not pay attention to their cold disclaimers. Maybe I should have read the fine print. None of them realized that I was just a girl, not an object, not a loverbody. I crossed every line and when there wasn't any, I made sure I set the bar at lunacy. I would have set myself on fire only if they asked. It's ridiculous how one rejection makes you go off the deep end instead of making you stronger. I loved everyone like they were the love of my life. They'd pursue me to no end and once they had me, they wouldn't want me any more; they would have every excuse in the book as to why we won't work, they had to leave town, or abandon me, or marry someone else, or turn out to be a convict, or just . . .'

'Not interested?' I mumbled, wishing I didn't the second it rolled out of my mouth. 'I am sorry,' I quickly added. Her long-suppressed separate life—filled with drugs and a confusion of lust for love—was egging to come out of its cobwebbed box. Truth be told, there was an inherent human need that grew inside my mother—a sense of fear of being left alone, the thinly marked hunger that made her stink of desperation and made her hang around men like a human barnacle.

No one likes that.

'They didn't want me in the same manner as I wanted them,' she said. 'They'd sway me with the corner of their eyelashes and would enter and exit my body when they chose to but they just didn't want to be near, near enough to my heart. In the end, I'd be up crying and looking like a raccoon. One can go to any length to make something work but sometimes even that doesn't seem to be enough.'

'It seemed like a revolving door of madmen,' I said.

'Maybe that's why I liked them, because they were mad,' she smiled a bit. 'Gravy included.'

The irony wasn't lost on me. The woman can talk. She had/has a mad heart, which is so fraught with fiery yearning that no rain can douse it. Her brain was a swampland that suffocated me with its hidden secrets. But then I had to stop her from disappearing down the plughole of her inner soul. It was disturbing to hear at many levels. But then again as some class of a masochist, I had asked for it. Her love had lit my way, my life, but now it darkened my horizon.

'You know what the silliest thing was, Zef?' My mother sounded like a teenager nursing a broken heart.

'What?'

'The worst was telling someone you love him and he thanks you for it—as though you just passed him the bread basket. I never understood why one would trivialize the intensity of the emotion and say yes, I care for you too, as though he was doing you a favour by sharing the same pillow, same plate and same toothbrush,' she muttered.

'But did you really love them?' I asked.

'At the time, I thought I did,' my mother said. 'I just didn't understand how people have no qualms undressing and caressing each other but can be terrified of exposing their vulnerability, of being emotionally naked. What was the worst that could happen? They'll fall in love—what's so terrifying about that.'

The one bloody trumpeter and her father had made her a basket case. Some moments—ghastly moments like these that accord that strange change of fate—ring like church bells, high over the sky, as big and wide as the sky, as loud as the sky. So they end up haunting you every second of your life.

'With each rejection, the slap on my face just got harder,' she said. 'Every time my heart would break in so many unnecessary ways, I'd piece it together only for it to be broken again by men who only knew all too well what they don't want. Eventually, I couldn't piece it to make it whole. The heart isn't like a liver, it doesn't grow back. Maybe there were warning signs but maybe I chose to not look at them,' she said. 'I think, Zef, men are wired differently. Women, we, find a sub-level to any level of emotion. I know I did.'

The more she was saying, the less I wanted to know. These were all the little waves adding to the massive emotional watershed.

'How could you keep humiliating yourself like this?' I spat out the words. I was a little disgusted with her life so far. How could one not be?

'I don't know,' she whispered. 'I kept relinquishing all my emotional energy onto these people, thinking that they would bring me happiness. But they didn't. I had no one, no direction. It is the temperament of humans to love, then destroy, then love again. That's what makes us humans, right?' she mumbled.

'So then?' I asked.

'I made my bed and I needed to lie in it,' she said.

'But it was a broken bed,' I said.

'The metaphor fits,' she hid a grin. 'Eventually, I learnt,' she added.

'When?' I asked.

'Being chronically hurt wears you out after a while,' my mother said. 'I realized that I was waiting for someone who'll never come. It was like . . . like . . . gumdeath. You don't realize that you are eating your own blood when it stains the bread you are chewing. I think my heart just threatened to give way if I didn't stop. Maybe it did. I don't know but it made me somehow understand that in the end, love or the want of it, is a terrible destroyer. Love made me erase love,' she said. 'I learnt the hard way that no relationship is worth chasing, if you have to chase it, it doesn't exist. And nothing really prepares you for heartbreak because each time you think you are used to the pain, it seems so new and hurtful all over again. But the trick is to never love too much. There has to be a limit on how much love needs to be allocated per person, remember that Zef.'

I just nodded my head. We were quiet for a while. We were both processing all of this. She seemed like a vulture of madness, like her own worst nightmare.

Slowly, I asked her, 'After all this, then what . . . ?'

'Eventually, I gave up on the idea of love itself. I burnt my heart. It seemed like a prerequisite to life. Sometimes your body has the wisdom that your head doesn't have. Sometimes your body tries to accept what the heart rejects. And sometimes, unknown to us, our body knows even before our heart does on how much to give in, and when to get out. So I started . . . using sex as a tool to vent out the aggression, the anger, the animosity, the insomnia, the paranoia of not being wanted. I think I was trying to kill something inside of me to bring something else alive. It was some cycle of insanity. I crashed into the wall I created. It was easier to have my body loved than me.'

'You went from one extreme to the other,' I told my mother. She had inherited the sense of restlessness and recklessness from my lunatic grandfather.

'You struggle to become someone and in that course you become the person you are,' she said. 'Like an author who is a stalker of characters in real life—in the same way you do as you write all this for your diary, or as a remembrance of your incorrigible parents who are just recovering humans—before you become *you*, there was somebody to influence your ethic. For me, it was the trumpeter and the bastard lying in the next room, who destroyed it. At some level, everything comes from inside of you: what we become because of who we meet and how sometimes we can remember everything even if we don't want to. Every encounter leaves a stamp of its occurrence inside us, even the people who pass through us like some vague spirit in a hurry to get somewhere else. All of them stay inside us for all our lives in some form, even when you think they have long exited our skin, they stay inside our veins, and mix with our blood.'

I heard her out of her verbal diarrhoea. She was carrying these experiences with her for all these years. Poetic memory can drum up a hideous storm, I suppose. It takes your mind places where it has no business going. All these words she was saying, she was letting it all bleed out of her. My stomach just sank in the same way I used to feel when I didn't prepare for a test that was taking place in the next three minutes. It killed me. I could feel a blade of tears threatening to scissor my eyes apart.

Just when I thought that this was all for now, she blurted out, 'Then I realized I was feeling pregnant one day.'

My mother spoke without explaining the transition. This happened. He came. He left. He died. I got pregnant. Time went by. Then another thing happened. She didn't make any attempts to explain the sequence, the order of the transitions, the how and why of them and their impact. She didn't really explain herself, she had her say and it was left for me to understand. She was in a rush, competing with herself to get all this out of her body. I just had to keep up—to ask would be to bump its energy—and if I didn't, I would be the one on the floor picking up the pieces of this stolen jigsaw puzzle.

'Feeling pregnant?' I asked, thoroughly bewildered.

'At first I thought that something was wrong with me . . . my body. I didn't have the urge to smoke any more. I lost all appetite for whisky. That had never happened. That's when I realized I was pregnant. With you,' she smiled.

'By whom?' I wasn't smiling.

'By this man,' she said. 'Your real father,' she whispered.

'Was I an accident?' I asked. 'Were you married?'

'Yes . . . and yes . . .' she said.

'You got married in the middle of all this?' I asked choking on my words.

'Yes, but it was a secret,' she said it so nonchalantly.

'Secret?' Jesus, what is she going to throw at me next.

'I never told anyone I was married.'

'Why?' I asked. 'This was not the marriage to Gravy . . . was it?' I just wanted to clarify.

'No, Gravy came much later and . . . but Gravy and me . . . we never got married.'

'What?' I was a little speechless. My mother keeps changing my life. She keeps confessing to something or the other. She seemed like an oyster—when she opens, she gives out pearls, when she shuts, she clams up.

'Then who did you marry?'

'This other man . . . the one who had gotten me pregnant . . . he seemed like such a good influence on me, at the time. We met in a zoo, and he pursued me incessantly through letters. We wrote letters, strung on by our memory of the smell of our bodies. In a way, he forced me to fall in love with him.'

'Did you?' I asked.

'Did you what?'

'Did you fall in love with him?' I asked curtly, acutely aware that I was sounding like a lousy headmistress.

'I didn't know if, at the time, I had the strength to really fall in love with anyone, or anything,' she offered as an explanation. 'But I remember being at peace with him around. He fed me when I was hungry, and held my hand gently. And love, it feeds the eye. It makes it fat.'

She said that around the time that she had met with my real father, she had fallen off the deep end of the curb, with the drugs and dharma bums and what not. But mostly it was the drugs. She was, apparently, chewing them up like candy, and had gotten addicted to the pure white energy, the constant fireworks in her head, flying next to the stars, borrowing the galaxy before exploding into petals of the night. You get the picture.

'I hadn't thought of him, this man, your real father until now,' she sighed.

Soon after Gravy had entered her life, she said that she had forgotten everything from her past.

Eternal sunshine of all that shit, I guess. Maybe she was holding onto this memory, of this other man, temporarily only for it to be forgotten, or left behind on a park bench, or in a busy street—until fate walked her to Gravy. Isn't that how one ends up losing something? After all, aren't we holding onto things till they are needed somewhere else?

'Your father, for a while, was the warm ray of sunshine on a grey winter day. But it was just that—it was warm for a while, but then the clouds came out. It wasn't a textbook love affair. It was all too true to be good,' she laughed at her own description.

My mother, this woman, was lady death. But this sense of nuttiness was what made my mother so vulnerable. That second, I wished I wasn't her daughter but her friend, a brow-soother. I wished I had met her at the same age she is at right now, or at a bar, at a carousel in an amusement park, where we were relaxed, finding some djinns in our tonics, eating candy floss.

They lived on the beach, the two of them—my mother and this man who sired me—in this hamlet called Ganapatipule. It was a paradise with several exclamation points. My mother had groggy recollections of happy memories—everything was magical.

'That's when I thought I would go ahead and have you. I was always so lonely that it was thrilling that I would have someone to live for, and someone who will always love me back. You do love me, right? I know you loved Gravy more than me but you do love me, don't you, Zef?' she asked me eagerly.

'I have always loved you,' I told her. She seemed so desperate for reassurance. And I did love her. A little more than a little, but lots less than lots.

'Thank you,' she said.

I laughed.

'What did he look like . . . this man . . . this father-person?' I asked.

'A bit like James Joyce sitting and reading in a park,' she said.

'That's what he looked like?' I smiled.

'A little bit,' she said.

'But where was this man . . . why were you alone when you were pregnant?' I asked my mother.

'I don't want to get into that today,' she said a little airily, finally, as though to mark the end to this conversation. 'Not right now, just remind me some other time, okay?'

This was ridiculous. She didn't want to get all Rashomon on it now, it seems. *Now!* After telling me half the story! Have you ever heard of a child who has to remind her mother another day to tell her who her father was?

Even though I was dying of the curiosity that accompanies concern more than anything else, I realized there was no point in pursuing this if she wasn't going to spill it right now. I suppose eventually, every piece of information, every feeling reveals itself to you at an appropriate time, when you are ready to receive it. I had to wait because I wanted to know before memory fashioned my childhood into something I chose to believe rather than what ensued before.

Patience was imperative while dealing with my mother. I listened to everything she spoke—all her unrelated nonsense—with feverish concentration that came from a fear inside me about what would happen if I let my mind wander by itself. Some sort of a darkness had crawled and stayed inside my skin like a chill that couldn't be cured with Crocin, Grappa or a distorted father's warm hug. I have to admit, though, that I felt like an emotional dustbin, like a nanny listening to the fantasy tales of a child who pays her bills while her own child sits at home alone with no one to talk to. I was tired just hearing her out and she lived through this. And she still hadn't told me about the father who sired me. God knows what that story will entail.

An awkward interlude descended upon us, a silence that often comes when you have just revealed your life's misery tale to a stranger on the bus and now that his stop has come, he leaves you saying, okay, take care, hope things get better for you soon, and you feel like you've been slapped on your face for nothing.

'Don was around when I was born?' I asked mainly because I couldn't handle any more silence.

'Yes,' she said.

'But how did he know you were here, and pregnant on top of it,' I asked, trying to do the arithmetic of their unnatural relationship.

'He's Don, he knows everything, he is awake even when he is sleeping, he has eyes at the back of his head,' she said. 'But I didn't see him at the time. I was just told that he was around. I didn't want to upset myself seeing him when you were given to me. It was the most monumental part of my lousy existence.'

'Isn't it tiring hating someone for so long?' I asked.

'I am here now, aren't I? We may be related by blood but for him it is cognac that is more important,' she said.

'But he's half dead now,' I said.

'I am here when he needs me the most.'

Still, she sounds like such a confused child, I thought.

She was quiet for a brief second before she said, 'When you were born, I cried a lot, tears of anger that stemmed from what Don did to me, from being incredibly lonely. I wanted to make sure I never let you down like my father did. But I was lousy. But I think now . . . I did let you down.'

'You haven't let me down,' I told her.

'I have. Maybe we didn't save Gravy,' she said.

'We tried. He's been trying to die for a while,' I said.

'No, maybe we . . . I . . . didn't try harder.'

'Try harder for what?'

'To . . . to . . . he just died . . . he shouldn't have. I am so angry . . . with him, for dying . . . and with me for . . .'

'It's not your fault,' I told her. It really wasn't anyone's fault at all.

'It is . . . I . . . you don't . . . under . . . stand . . . I wish . . . we . . . that . . . bottle . . . how could he die . . . he shouldn't have . . .'

My mother sobbed in between her choked breath and whispered stammers. I hugged her.

Growing up, one of the only reasons I had contact and some compassion for Don was largely due to Gravy's efforts in making it possible. He understood Don's desperation and longing for company. Before (he lost his mind), my father and me would often come to Madras and spend some time with Don, so I could nurture an independent, private equation with the man.

'Your mother has her reasons but they shouldn't be yours,' he had told me when I asked him why my mother seldom (read: never) accompanied us to meet Don. He was amazing like that. Gravy. He had that oddball generosity of spirit that came from outside this world.

The few—three, actually—times my mother accompanied us, there would be an awkward silence that would neck out of Don's house. And when the silence got suffocating, Don would turn into the loudest showman around, fuelled by several mind-altering substances. Now I realize that the noise comes from vocal chords laced with guilt. Don and my mother made no eye contact and they'd be as incongruous as a pregnant midget amidst a sea of glamazons whose legs were ladders to heaven.

The emotional distance between them was immeasurable.

At the time, I didn't dwell on their awkwardness. I didn't read too much into it because I didn't want to or I must have internalized it in the same way a child instinctively understands the immense power of keeping quiet during the exhausted silence that descends after a heated fight between the parentals. Nothing was said, but everything was understood. My mother would often make excuses to leave just as soon as we had entered. Eventually, she stopped coming with my father and me.

Every holiday I spent with Don was a lesson in life, via books or booze. It was the most glorious form of miseducation that I always looked forward to. He read a lot, and drank a lot because he was the king who was married to his solitude. He'd put me through various challenges of reading Tolstoy, his favourite writer. Most of the times, he'd hand me the Russian's book of short stories, ask me to read them, make a précis and do an oral test.

'Try and understand this now, when your brain can be stretched like a chewing gum because when you grow up and you need to answer life's most evil questions, you know where in your head you can go to look for solutions,' he'd say.

I am not joking. I was ten. I wanted to go out and swim in the backyard. It would make sense if all what I had read had made me some class-of-a-mind reading champion or an under-aged, hyper-aware genius by now, but alas, I am now just nothing but a less-than-zero, college dropout with a spelleing problem, and someone at the edge of despair, at the edge of an edge, holding on to the thin thread of lost love; someone who has an unhealthy fixation on nostalgia, who spends her nights reading erotic literature not so clandestinely, her twilight reading obituaries clandestinely, her days trouncing solitude by furiously scribbling journal entries of my family's buried, broken lives, and the in-betweenness dealing and drinking with the lives loved, lives betrayed, lives ruined, lives fantasized, lives unfulfilled, madness, destruction, deconstruction, and family members who were either dead or dying any second now.

It had been over three years since I had last seen Don. Strange, I didn't realize it had been that long until now. Perhaps dealing with the rapid-fire deaths of my uncle and aunt, and my father's gradual descent to the dark side before he took his own life did ensure that time went by at supersonic speed. The last time I had come to this house, a dilapidated smoke-scarred mansion that seemed to be suffocating its concrete lungs, was the first time I had come by myself, unaccompanied by my father.

Gravy had taken me the year before on our biannual jaunt but a terrible fight between Don and him made him vow to never come back to this house again. But that didn't stop me from coming. Why should it? It wasn't my fight.

And, Don, ah. Where do I begin? The man would dress like the Prufrockian hero of his own film. That swagger was imperial. He never wore a watch because every time was a good time, and all days are nights really. He used to say that he didn't like time strapped to his body. Besides, the clock was always stuck at quarter past rum for him. His voice carried inside it a hot wiry breath of cigarettes and scotch, a smell I grew to love and now crave in the men I fall for. He would manage to wake up any time between lunch and dinner, depending on the amount of sunlight creeping in from the curtains, eat when he was hungry, shower when he was sweaty and get dressed as though he was expecting Mandela in the next five minutes. He would wear a crisp white shirt with just half an inch of cuff peeking out from his perfectly fitting linen suit, with the collars up. It was accessorized with tacky yet lovable cufflinks that had tiny oval photo frames—he placed a picture of me, dressed as a monkey and clinging to a fake plastic tree on his right, and my mother in her bell-bottomed glory on his left. I don't understand the logic but with Don it was not what you wear but how you wear. There was a serious amount of peacocking but it fit him like a glove. Think of it as carnality with a twist.

How can I put it—clothes, for him, were a weapon, a vehicle to transport us someplace else. He wore clothes like an envelope, and he was the letter magnifique.

Don's bare feet never touched the floor as he chose to wear his handmade wing-tipped shoes at all times. The pants always ended an inch below his ankle to reveal drastic neon-coloured socks. His silver hair with a middle parting was fluffed up lightly. He saw his whisky-vodka-gin-laced world with his thick, square glasses, which made him appear like an ageing hipster. It was a look that was mimetic of a certain post-war era, quirky only in the way a formerly debauched grandfather connoisseurs his clothes onto present-day consciousness. But sometimes, especially now at the time of this writing, when I think back, maybe he was so well-dressed, only to hide the glorious mess inside.

He gambled for a living, he spent for a living, he drank for a living, he read for a living, he just did too many vague things for a living after his leather business went bust. Don did contemplate opening an alligator farm but he spent the money on a bottle, or a crate. He went through life with a sense of disconnected hedonism, always ramblingly hungry for adventure and sensation.

Compared to Don's archetypal Wildean dandy, half-man,

half-sex-machine, my father looked like a kind, mild-mannered geography teacher. Like Oliver Twist's older, sombre brother. He was a delicate man, my father.

I remember one summer in particular. I was twelve. I remember it vividly because it was the last time my father accompanied me to meet Don. Don came out to greet us. He was shirtless, and wore a pair of cheetah-printed shorts. He still had a pair of neon socks and his shoes on. His eyes sparkled when he saw me. He lifted me up and kissed me on both cheeks twice. He kissed my father on both cheeks once. The he lifted me up and kissed me again on both cheeks, to remind himself that I was really here.

'I am so happy you came,' he said happily.

He never let go of my hand. 'Shall we read?'

'No, I just came,' I wailed.

'Okay, then would you like a pant stitched?' he asked me.

'No'.

When we went inside, we found a mini army of tailors standing at ease. Don said 'one minute' and then went and stretched his arms like some type of living Cristo Redentor. That was his signal for them to resume work. The work was to take his measurements for a pair of trousers, leather trousers did I say?

'They are making it here for me, would you like anything done. Last chance, what do you say?'

Gravy and I both said no.

The days were great. Idyllic, even. My father would take pictures and cook potatoes. A healthy diet of happiness. It was a routine of very hectic vegetation. We, Gravy and I, would start cleaning Don's house the second we got there, mainly because it was usually covered in mounds of cobwebbed madness. Don never cleaned anything, he never did anything, except for filling up his bar. But we wouldn't touch the closets, we couldn't enter his study in his absence (he'd lock that door if he was out—he had three places, besides hanging it on his belt—where he would hide the key: 1) inside the right pocket of his white suit hanging inside his cupboard 2) between the pages of the 1923 edition of *War and Peace*, and 3) underneath the mattress of his four-poster bed), and we couldn't enter my mother's room. We respected that, aware of the consequences of crossing Don's orders. At one point, I saw a family of rats scurrying their way through the glass cabinets in between the clothes, the books with their yellow pages crumbling into powder, and the curios. But we let these rodents stay there. They were a part of this soulless montage; why ruin their happiness?

Usually, Don, in his excitement for my arrival would have something ready for me. A few years ago, he gave me an old TV, except it wasn't a TV. He replaced the screen with water-tight glass and turned the old idiot box into a mini aquarium. The other presents included a View-Master where the slides were mostly naked men sunning themselves on Waikiki beach in Honolulu; a pillow the shape of Africa that glowed in the dark with secret pockets; some rum encased in a dagger-shaped bottle—('Some tonic for the soul,' he called it); staplers because I left all my pages of writing everywhere ('A practical gift, for you, child,' he said); his expired passport as a souvenir ('I fly in my head now,' he wrote on a little note with it); a disco ball that was soaked in psychedelic passion; a scratched oval watch with a frog-leather strap that seemed to work only if it was under direct sunlight; a hip flask filled with chocolate milk; small bronze Jesus-shaped paperweights; Buddha and a temple; a little opium box with chilly in it because he said that if I travelled to Europe the food would be bland and I might need something to spice it up; an airgun; a little cape with a silver lining (yes, really) so that I could 'ride on the back of sand and storm', and a meat cleaver in case I wanted to murder someone, I suppose. But my favourite present was a compass that Don had broken open, written the word 'Home' and had sellotaped the axis towards it.

'I may have no moral compass, darling child, but this compass will always get you to me. I will be the hot water on a cold, winter day for you,' he wrote.

This time, he had built a bed that hung from a tree for me. It was a scene out of a Tim Walker photo shoot. He always found cool ways to extend my childhood. Yes, I know, never trust a drunken carpenter. I climbed up, sat on it, rocked a little too much, the bed dangled, I fell down and broke my nose, and my knuckles.

Don collapsed on seeing blood raining down on my face.

My father rushed to the local chemist. He was worried sick that I had gotten so terribly physically hurt. His patience with Don was beginning to wear off, partly because my father never touched alcohol in his life and Don touched nothing else.

By the time I got out of the haze of the medication, the blue skies had given way to a velvet amphitheatre that was littered with orphan stars speaking everyone's worn-down names. Medication makes the poetics come out, perhaps. The house was quiet. My father was sitting next to me—with food, with ice, with medicines, with wit, with comfort, with bed-time stories, with dinner, with potatoes, with some deep-fried love.

'Where's Don?' I asked Gravy.

'Ha,' my father smirked. 'Gone for a "smoke",' he grinned, as he gestured the inverted quotes exaggeratedly with his hands.

As if drinking during the day wasn't enough, just as night fell, Don would disappear. He'd often say that he liked wandering the streets at night because it was about escaping and dreaming at the end of the day. I think he wanted to escape to a place where the noise outside was louder than the noise inside his head.

He once told me, 'As day turns into night, the night turns

into whatever I want. Sometimes drinking at night pushes me inwards . . . somehow, as though I am walking towards this dream, not those dreams to realize or accomplish, but just to live in that dream state that comes over you like a halo, you don't get to do those during daydreams that come to you when there is still the sun outside. Drinking at dusk makes me see things that I cannot see during the day. I like the mood at night, everything becomes more funny, you see more, dead flowers come alive at night.'

But maybe he went to hunt for the breeze, get a midnight drink, indulge in late night lust. Who knows? He was a night soul. The truth was that he never really dealt with his alcoholism because he was too inebriated to think there was a problem.

While we were there, Gravy would wait until a little after 1 a.m. just in case Don didn't amble his way home, to go look for him. (I'd often wonder what would happen if we weren't there to bring him home.)

It became a pattern. Gravy would go out, rely on the power of his intuition to find Don in the darkest of all places.

'I find beauty there,' Don once screamed when my father muttered that he was embroiled in a brawl at the Tambaram train station covered in motor oil for some inexplicable reason. When my father brought him home, wound him down, Don was still flying like a badly lit rocket.

'How did you get to the station?' my father asked.

'I don't know,' Don said. 'I am sorry that I had too much to drink . . . actually not that sorry, hahahaha.'

'How did you get into a fight?' Gravy asked Don.

'With that horrible man?' Don asked. 'The one who wanted to throw some acid on my face, slit me with a broken bottle, break my legs, shoot me in the kneecaps, and shove an electrical rod up my rear.'

'Maybe,' my father said.

'It's a blur. Are we talking about the fight that just might have happened or the one that is happening in my brain right now?' Don asked him in all seriousness.

'I think you need some rest, Don,' Gravy said curtly.

'Rest is for the poor, and wretched is for the weak. Rest, wreck, rust, wreak, repeat?' Don sang.

'Go to bed,' my father spoke like a good matron.

'Are we in England right now?' Don asked. (Guess being so intoxicated didn't require getting on to any planes to travel anywhere.)

'No. In Madras,' my father said.

'I think hangovers have lost their sweetness, they have become sinister. I feel like someone is breaking my brain. Oh, how will you know?' Don mocked Gravy. 'You've never had a sip in your life.'

'Why don't you sleep for a while?' Gravy tried to pacify him.

'I feel I need an elf to wash and comb my hair . . . it's a valid necessity,' Don said.

'We'll talk about it tomorrow, now get some sleep,' Gravy said.

'Being alive gives me a headache. Get my coat dry-cleaned,' Don ordered. 'Sorry, I meant please.'

'Sure,' Gravy said ever so sweetly and started tucking Don into bed like an epileptic child. He untied his laces, started removing his socks but Don flinched. He never liked his bare feet to touch the floors.

'My week never ends really . . . it just continues, rolls from one into the other, stretches like a languid day, tumbling into another, sort of like a never-ending cinnamon roll . . . What were you talking about . . . ?' Don spluttered to himself.

'Yes, every day is a weekend, every day is a Sunday rest, for you, you live Monday like Sunday anyway,' my father said.

'Don't patronize me. I don't reside in the land of cockaigne,' Don screamed.

'Did you do some cocaine now? Oh goodness, please tell me you didn't,' Gravy screamed.

'Not that cocaine you stupid man. Cockaigne . . . a world so far from here, an imaginary medieval mythical land of plenty where there is nothing but pleasure . . . have you ever read a book in your life?' Don hissed condescendingly.

'Not the books you do. Now please go to bed,' my father tried telling him again.

'And now don't you dare steal from Auden,' Don mocked Gravy. 'Sunday rest, you know that poem . . . my working week and Sunday rest.'

'Go to sleep, Don.'

'I hate you,' Don screamed.

'Nit, Don.'

Just when Gravy would manage to calm the old geezer down, remove his shoes, tuck him into bed, place some dried, extremely salty lemon for him to chew on in case he felt like throwing up, and a bottle of water, Don would wake up like a beaten-up boxer before the count of ten, and stride into our room, pace up and down like a toothless tiger, and start sermonizing like those television evangelists, his booming voice spilling through the crippled mosaic.

The sad bit was that he would blinker out my father. Gravy, the poor man, would be standing there like a mute spectator, like those underpaid extras working 24-hour shifts for just being blurry bystanders in movies, or like those bouncers in clubs who watch the debauchery but can never be a part of it because they have to clean up after, breathing the same air but still feeling choked. But given my father's ungodly amounts of niceness and decency, he remained quiet.

Until this one night.

'You know, Zef, today I met my old friend,' Don started.

There was no stopping the man. He was high as the man on the moon, and just needed someone to hear him.

'Let her sleep, Don. She has been awake for more than a day,' my father said, knowing very well about my fear of sleep since I was a child. I remember telling my father that 'sleep is not coming to my eyes,' and he had laughed at the syntax.

'Please don't interfere when I am talking to my grandchild,' Don said to my father but he was staring right at me. My father didn't retaliate. He was relying on the power of silence, and maybe a prayer, for sanity to come descending.

Don sat at the foot of my bed. He put my feet in his lap and scratched them because he knew I liked it. In a way, I liked to hear him talk. It had me in hysterics. It was the same sort of joy that comes when listening to a song that you know you are going to love the second the beat rolls on.

He started. 'Zef, there are only two types of honest people in the world—toddlers and drunks. So let me tell you a story. I met this man, the other night, He was a real character, Zef. He had ears that were clipped in the centre. We used to be exactly, and approximately, around the same age. But not any more. Nobody seems to be their age any more, let alone act their declared age. I seem to be the only one growing older. Do you think it is because I don't colour my hair?'

I didn't say anything. He wasn't looking for dialogue.

I presume most people when drunk aren't looking for banter. Neither did my father say anything.

Don went on unabated. 'Here is the funny bit. He went and dyed his hair a shade of midnight blue, which may have taken fifteen years off his face only if he hadn't dyed his entire body the same colour as well. He looked like some class of disco fighter.'

He saw the look on my face.

'Yes, I know,' Don burst out laughing. 'I felt bad for him the other day so I gave him my white shirt, and a tie. He had to go back to the card table and they didn't let him because he didn't own a shirt. So I gave him mine. I also gave him my hat, and my glasses. So today

I told him, give me the shirt back, it was the last of my tailored ones. I told him to keep everything else. He didn't say anything. Just sniggered and pointed to the shirt. The rat bastard had dyed my shirt blue. I was so angry but then I found it all so hilarious. Men are just mad. He said that it matched his blue mood, because he was just too sad, his wife had left him, his children left him, and he had no money. Sounds familiar. But then the blue got him luck. After winning at the tables, he went to the races, bet on the horses and made a killing. He has promised to buy me a nice white shirt. Isn't it a glorious story? But you know what is better is how he was skilfully steering his luck. Remember this, my darling, so that when you grow older, you can write this and make some human travel far, far, far away from his family and laugh at this blue man.'

We started laughing, Don and me. My father didn't.

Don continued relentlessly, 'I was just about to ask him if I should also start dyeing my body. We all know I could do with some luck, given the static I seem to live in. That was when your father came and took me away.'

'That night, Don, those goons were ready to kill you,' Gravy intervened. 'You were on their table and they realized you had no cash. They had thrown you outside. But you won't remember anything because you were pissed on nuclear waste.' My father said all this.

'I don't know how your father manages to find me, every night. It's a skill,' Don looked at me and said.

'It's called concern,' my father retorted.

'I never asked you to come after me,' Don said, finally looking at my father in the eye.

'I know. I have a conscience, unlike you,' Gravy said.

'Conscience, man, you kill me. You . . . you are teaching me about conscience. You. You. You must be delusional. You are cunning,' Don spat out the words. 'You like to temper decadence with prudence.

I don't. It's one life. You want to play God so you can be a hero to my grandchild and my daughter.'

My father kept quiet.

'Go to sleep, Don. It is late,' he said.

'Ah, listen to him, "go to sleep" he says,' Don mimicked Gravy.

'Calm down, you've had too much to drink,' Gravy said.

'Don't tell me to calm down,' Don screamed.

My father remained quiet.

'Ha, look at you. Trying to be a hero in front of this child? You've already taken my daughter away from me. She despises me, thanks to you and your messiah complex, and now you want to make my only grandchild hate me.'

'Watch your mouth, Don. Don't cross it. I have tolerated enough,' Gravy said in a cold, stern and collected voice.

'I have class, and it's called third,' Don laughed. 'Threatening me, are we? The only reason you are here is because . . . well, let's not go there. I am drunk but certainly not an idiot. You ensured that there was no space for me in my daughter's life. And that wasn't . . . anyway . . . she hates me . . . and you didn't do anything . . . because of you . . . and your so-called goodness. If only . . . she . . .'

'She despises you because of your selfishness,' Gravy interrupted. 'Being a father doesn't mean handpicking frocks and shoes from expensive stores for your child. I had nothing to do with what you did to her,' he said.

'Stop pretending to be who you're not,' Don screamed. 'Get out of my house, and go tell your saint to fuck off!' Don screamed, his eyes bloodshot red.

My father and I left the next morning, we walked into the thin, tight air. I kissed Don on his forehead. He was slurring away in a deep amphetamine slumber. He twitched a bit when I kissed him but didn't wake up. Maybe he realized that I kissed him goodbye when he woke up. I left him a note saying I will come soon and that I love him. I wanted to tie those words like a string around my neck, close to the pulse of his throat, and to the thump of his heart.

I felt so bad. The next round of dismay rumbled like a bunch of clouds in my throat. I could still smell the stench of smoke from his old window, last night's smell, this morning's distance. It was sad. I took such painful strides walking out of this house. My hands were shaking.

My father sensed it. 'Don loves you, Zef,' he said. 'He loves you and your mother more than anything in this world. But if he had to choose between you and the alcohol, he would choose the alcohol. It's not because he loves it more. It's just that it comforts him in the way we cannot . . . in the way ordinary people cannot. That's selfish because we are there for him. I can only tell you that you and your mother will be the only ones who will end up looking after him,' Gravy spoke those words so premonitorily. 'I will never come back here again but I won't stop you from coming. But I am done. I have tolerated his spite and hate for far too long. He is a mad man who doesn't want to be saved.'

Both these men, both of whom I loved, had slayed their relationship, and left it like a carcass on the table, bleeding with all its broken veins.

For a month after Gravy's death, an oppressive silence came over our home. But home seems too strong a word. Its charm started to wear off the second my father left this life. He made it a home, a treasured sanctuary that we ran to for company and comfort. It was built by him when we had decided to anchor ourselves in Delhi. But the idea of *this* home came to him in his dreams. See, when we had bought this piece of arid land, it came with a typical house, a lateral structure that, according to my father, 'lacked in thought and humour'. So after a month or more of living here, he woke up one afternoon saying that he had dreamt of the home that we should be really living in. He quickly sketched it on the palm of his hand with a felt pen, called in the most easily available contractors and by the time I came back from school that day, he started to build it even while we were still living inside it. My mother and I were just silent witnesses to this madness. 'He is happy, he is consumed. No need for any interruption,' she used to say.

In an attempt to build it quickly, the house turned out a little incomplete, a work in progress. But now when I look back, I feel as though the house planned itself over the years. It feels like an architectural autobiography of sorts of my parents' lives, lived so hurriedly, so whimsically. From the outside, the house had an austere geometric pattern, which resembled a Jenga game. It was an experiment in vertical living. Three lopsided floors placed so haphazardly on top of each other that it seemed as though a hurricane might destroy it. But our home stood valiantly, held together by luck—in a colony teeming with sudden-money (hardware-business money; Gulf-returned money; Ugandan-returned money; patent lawyers'-salary money) and houses that remind you of stale, ugly, florid cakes—our house held on through all these years, in spite of the inferno brewing inside the inhabitants.

We had a garden, which was brief but beautiful. It was green like an autumnal park, like the colour of progress. There, we kept a white, plaster-of-Paris, life-size Ambassador, which had mannequins of faceless little children, wearing only bubblegum-bright shorts, placed inside it, some with their hands up in the air, some with their heads bobbing outside the window, as though they were going for a joy ride in it. It was a hilarious sculpture that Gravy had commissioned from a friend of a friend at the capital's art school.

We also had a fake plastic life-sized banana tree with a fake plastic monkey clinging on to it with all its fake plastic strength.

My father had placed an open-to-the-sky courtyard right in the heart of our home so he could sit there and watch the rains. If desperation had a colour, it was the colour of rain, he used to say. Our walls, all conservatively painted in shades of vanilla and cinnamon and post-it yellow, were brought alive with portraits of our friends and our pets and portraits of spaces that were once occupied by someone, or a memory of someone. The photographs, they seemed like an open diary of our fragile, hazy, private lives, offering some sort of a scrutinizing reconnaissance brimming with such great accumulated history. All of them were taken by my father with cameras that he assembled with his own two hands. He was good at constructing complicated items, and eventually destroying them out of ennui. None of them were coloured images, mind you. They were all dripping with sepia-tinted memories, revealing the secret unrest that was lingering like a shadow, so silently, and only if you looked to observe them a little longer than necessary. When I look at them now, they seem like a series of evidences fashioned and moulded by some fabric of memory, a memory drawn out of some form of yearning. If I stare long enough, they seem to come alive like a thought catalogue. I feel they might emit some form of oxygen to help me breathe better.

Breathe in, breathe out. See, stare, survive. Repeat.

He seemed to take pictures like some type of permanent tourist who was visiting us for a little while, and partaking in our version of reality. And then his time ran out, and he had to go. I never knew the exact moment when these pictures were taken by my father. Because he always took them on the sly when nobody was looking. It matched his quiet personality. Perhaps he did it in the same way I scribble notes, every second of every minute of my life so that I never forget the words I want to use. Perhaps these images were little records for me to see them later when he has crumbled away into the cerulean. On a day like today. These pictures offered me some minutes of serenity, and centred the little part of me that was willing to stay still.

There are several pictures of my mother—one with her smoking a hand-rolled cigarette, the tobacco had fallen off a little on her white capris, the only garment on her lithe body. It was taken in our garden; she was leaning against the plaster-of-Paris Ambassador. A bandana with prints of moustaches controlled her unruly lusty lovelocks (Gravy's words, not mine). A cluster of bangles covered the length of her hands while eight of her fingers were encased in mirror-bright silver rings, leaving only the tip of her (nearly) nailless fingers visible. She looked weirdly gorgeous. There is another one of her sitting in the corner of the courtyard, inside a huge blanket that covered all of her, the shape of her hands inside gave off a silhouette of her being on some sort of a secret phone call (maybe to the KGB?).

There is a family portrait of the three of us wearing leopard masks on our faces, and a tail affixed to our backs. A water bottle without a lid seems to be hanging from my neck. My toy gun is resting at my feet. There are some pictures of me: one with an eyeless toy monkey I was obsessed with when I was nine; one where I was wearing a Peter Pan-collared shirt with matching collars and boy-shorn hair that my father used to cut every Sunday morning until I turned twelve.

There are, oddly enough, pictures of panic, all the various nuances of it: of silent screams frozen inside the thick paper, of anguish-faced strangers running behind the last bus that has left them and trotted off; of empty medication bottles (my father's; my aunt's); of my aunt wistfully wiping the dust off her maimed bald doll that was seated next to the mirror in her bathroom just above a glass jar of cotton wool; of a dead pig run over by a car, with its intestines sprawled all over its body; of strange lovers in fairytale costumes farewelling after a brief interlude; of a child's fearful eyes (mine) scanning the reptilian army at Madras's snake park; of Gravy's mother staring sadly at a crumpled, blurry, tear-stained photograph of someone. Maybe my father was curious about capturing that sort of fear, of what it is like to lose a piece of yourself when you are most vulnerable, a fear of what it is like to be left behind—the innate fear of abandonment and its traumatic after-effects.

There are creased pictures of us—my mother and me—sprawled on the bed, rebelling against the effects of afternoon sangria. It felt that I remained in that moment. Time didn't move, it was patient with us.

There are pictures that were crowded with the invisible and brimming with the secret memory of lives that once filled up that spot, and now the walls wait sullenly for their return. These are pictures that were meant to be sent as postcards to another human, perhaps a love, to say I am thinking of you, me, and maybe us, and longing for your return to fill up this space. There is a picture of the bus stop where my parents met, a moment that drew sky and earth together, that is a portrait of them without them really being in the frame. There is a picture of the staircase where they often made love, apparently. There is a black-and-white picture of my parents—perhaps the only one of them together—where my mother is standing to the left-centre of the frame, as though she is perched on a cloud, with one hand on her hip, the other let loose next to her. My father's smiling head and floppy sun-bleached hair juts into the frame from the side. That's all there is of him in the picture, very little, and in real life.

There are only a handful of pictures of my father because he was the one taking most of them. He was the one painting these memories. These pictures seem a lot more real than he was. It was almost as though he was never there, like some sort of a phantom-lover that some nuns (at least the sorts of girls who convert to the habit because of a broken heart) become delusional over. There were all these pictures everywhere hanging haphazardly all over our chipped walls, on the floor, inside drawers, inside Ziplocs, inside boxes, inside books, inside pockets, inside our hearts (pasted, and now nailed).

I have this memory of my mother taking a photograph of me and my father.

It's a picture that never leaves my wallet. I must have been six years old and about two-and-a-half feet tall. Wait, let me rethink.

Yes, that sounds about right. I am/was/always have been a short human.

The picture was taken during our weekly Sunday picnic by a small lake just a little outside of Hyderabad, where we were living in boxes for an inconsequential period of time, temporarily because we thought we'd leave today, tomorrow or yesterday, back to Delhi. Gravy had taken a part-time consultancy there for some obscure development bank.

We'd go, no actually fly, there every Sunday on Gravy's dirty-blue Vespa (he rode like a maniac to scare my mother), me standing in front of him, in the little space that a scooter provides, my eyes shrieking with the sharp air knifing my pupils, my mother sitting behind him clutching on to her life, camera, food and bags. We looked like a campaign for middle India's funday in the sun.

Once we were there, we'd find a sweet spot, open our beautifully packed lunches and spread them on a red checkered table cloth—a moment of deep playfulness architected by Gravy. Buttered bread and boiled eggs for me; curd rice for my parents. We'd eat quickly; the long ride would make our appetite as ravenous as a Somalian pirate on a hunger strike for three years. After lunch, Gravy would take a nap, I'd be busy with my imaginary friend Shyam, a mullet-haired boy with a Travolta-esque swagger, who wore white shorts and a hound's-tooth-print navy-blue shirt with vampiric collars.

I remember this one day in particular. Gravy, a happy camper with a serious addiction to life, back then, came from behind me and swooped me over his head, threw me up in the air in carefree abandon, and just as I fell right into his arms, he lifted me again and repeated it all over again. I was laughing hysterically with my eyeballs rolling inside my head, giddy with the adrenalin rush the activity afforded me.

That was the picture my mother took—of me mid-air, my eyes shut, and Gravy's hands extended like some kind of Moses, waiting for me to fall into his arms. It was a good picture, one that seems to have trapped, sealed and shut the blissful goodness of the moment in polaroid, one that captured the comfort, the reassurance that my father will always be there for me.

One photograph and the day was history.

I kept thinking of that image, the happiness that it held, reliving the sequence of events in my head, this empire of dirt, assuming that if I think of it hard enough, desperately enough, the moment, the time, the place, the space, the face, the bread, butter, boiled eggs all wrapped in a silver foil, that it will all resurface in front of me and I can jump inside the frame, and live it all over again, and live better than I had lived before, gluing my father to that spot, stitching that smile on his face, and locking it all up till kingdom come. I kept thinking of it over and over again, being thrown up in the air, falling into my father's arms, up and down, laughing out like an owl in the silent surrender of the night, playing the dream, the memory on loop, the old laughter ringing into my ears, the thrill of being suspended into a space so high, flying as high as the eagles, falling into his arms and then being thrown up again until my father stopped laughing, his face uncannily changing into a clown with an upside-down smile, and he was crying, sobbing with all the make-up washing away, until he let go of me, and before the startling realization that he was not going to catch me as I came crashing down, I fell hard on the ground and my brains splattered on to the floor. There was blood on my shoes, on my face, on the grass, on the sky, on my father's clown face.

The dilemma was waking up or opening my eyes first.

Isn't it cruel to make me dream of you, I wanted to yell at my dead father. The choir of furies in my head was playing on full volume. My body ached, my legs shivered out of fright. There was so much playing on my mind that I thought it was spilling outside and when I tried to check if my head was okay, my hands were so numb it rejected any form of movement. I had a cold sweat from this tired, haunting dream. Everything was hazily surreal enough for me to wonder if it just happened or if it was all inside my head. Even my dreams now seemed to have despair and desertion and fear as the main theme running through them, and now there was blood and gore too.

It wasn't just the photograph that I was carrying around in my pocket. It was all these years of memories that were sown in my blood. I hadn't spoken to anyone besides my mother yet about what I felt. It was all her, her, her, I hadn't even spoken to Don in his current avatar. A part of me wanted to talk it out with some of my best friends but I was afraid that once the dam of my vocal chords burst open, then I wouldn't be able to hold back on the emotional odyssey. It was best to keep quiet and process it quietly, internally.

The more I write, the more I revisit memory like this, putting pen to paper, ink to blood, the more the dots seem to connect, and the silences speak. Words became the only instrument I could play with to make sense of everything, to remind me of the reason I was hanging on. Writing became a way to escape from the edge of despair, occupy my body and soul by resisting adversity or preparing for it.

I wanted to explore everything on my own, slowly, gradually, building it up with the slow delicacy that a sculptor of glass employs. Like a delicate coroner of characters. A part of me had all these questions but the other part of me didn't want to hear the answers. This was a journey with no maps—just scars spread like bubbles of water on a body burnt by passion. It was like getting into a car to go on a long journey, but then when you get to your destination, you want nothing more than to stay in the car and breathe the same stale air. It was like being taken to a river to drown.

Gravy kept saying that he had to leave. 'I have to go, Zef, I really do.'

'Where?' I'd ask.

'My sister needs me, my brother too. He . . . my brother is being persecuted by those guys . . . you don't know them. They are staring down at us. You'll be fine but they are too weak. I didn't raise you to be weak.'

Maybe he was starting to die, maybe he was practising to die.

I didn't quite fathom the extent to which he was so troubled and why? My uncle and my aunt were both dead, ashes to dust. Why the hell would my father be so affected by what happens to them now. Sometimes the tiny pieces of bones never really burn away. They rise up from filthy ocean beds and come back to haunt you after taking a life of their own. Were they just being psych-pomps conducting souls into unknown territories? Maybe it was a sibling connection, when one twin itches, the other scratches—that sort of karmic connection, something I wouldn't ever know, being the only child of my parents.

Why did my father kill himself? He was getting better, or was I just assuming that because I wanted to believe he would. Did he really miss his brother and sister *that* much? Was he trying to shepherd their souls into an afterlife. It seemed a tad meaningless to find out now, considering the man was dead but still . . . I started to wonder if he really loved me. I didn't have his blood coursing through my veins. Was it all a play? Was that all it took for him to be gone?

One bottle of pesticide.

Dead and done.

Maybe I loved him for dying before the imperfection overwhelms.

CHAPTER 6

I was lying in my mother's room in Don's house with all these thoughts raging in my head. This was the first time I ever stayed in this room. Only Don cleaned it, and then locked it. My father and I were never allowed to go inside, let alone stay here on our previous visits. Don would only let us occupy the guestroom. I only took the risk now because he was lying comatose downstairs. This room overlooked the empty pool. If there was water, I could have dived straight in from here. It was built that way. The bed was shaped like a bird's nest.

It made me aware of the homeyness of this space, which smelt strangely like my mother smells even now: a mélange of turmeric, saffron, stale jasmine, cigarettes, sadness, whimsy, impulse and heartache. A chest of drawers with two eyes painted on the top two drawers stared at me from a distance. The crinkled paisley wallpaper was scarred by blotches of rainwater that must have seeped in over the years. There was a photographic print of a huge kohl-rimmed right eye—around nine feet huge—with green pupils staring down at me from the ceiling. There was a relatively realistic head of an elephant with only half of its trunk mounted above my mother's desk. Stacked against the wall in the corner of the room, perhaps pushed vehemently by the anguished teenager who once occupied this room, was a lace-cushioned cane arm-chair with the strangest, most inconvenient headrest I have ever seen: it was a basketball-sized, pancake-flat, pixie-faced cushioned doll with a pair of small beady eyes that were stuck too close together for comfort, a lying Pinocchio nose, and an inverted moustache that was split in the middle.

There was an intricately carved antique trunk that Don must have got from some of his travels. When I opened it, I found all these souvenirs of my mother's childhood. There was a church made of matchsticks, a packet of sanitary pads, some dried leaves, a bronze thimble, a bag with a bit of human hair (weird), three pairs of cufflinks, a script of that day's news presumably when she was working at the news station, a beautiful map of India that I felt was burnt by my mother's constant stare, a half-filled diary of teenage emotion, nine vapourized bottles of black ink, a man's full-sleeved shirt, a pillow case with the smell of cod liver oil, and some sheet music for the trumpeter's part. It was some sort of a retro heaven incomplete with unfinished business.

All of these charms have a power to explode in my face like a chilly-filled tomato splat. I shut the damn box. It made me realize that closure is too slippery. Do we really, ever, get over something? Doesn't everything blend into the brown of our skin and remain dormant within the folds of our body?

I wanted to run through the pathways of this house for some sort of sweet pancake-smelling retribution. I think even my thoughts were becoming as oppressive as the numbing, pale-shadowed landscape that I was a part of. There was that familiar, overpowering smell of dried leaves burning, one of Don's favourite smells. These smells become a part of the scenery, even if they are not physically pervading the atmosphere, they come alive with a touch of memory.

It was the home that my mother had escaped to but it was the darkness that she was living in. The last time I was here, three years ago, everyone who was relevant in my family was alive. I had come here because I had failed my exam. I knew that this trip would be my time out from the rabbit hole, the drudgery of school, and reality in major parts. It was also the first time I had travelled alone.

Back then Don seemed to have that swagger, that arrogance of sweeping in and out of various lives, out of rooms like the tornado that brought him in; a swagger that was reminiscent of that Carly Simon song: you walked into the party like you were walking onto a yacht. Now, the man we thought would outlive life itself, had one foot in the grave, and the other on a rotten banana peel.

The last time I met him, I had made the trip here myself. He came to the station to pick me up in his local handyman's van. He wore a cape, he had grown a beard, he carried a sword that he bought at an auction because it would make for a 'charming little accessory'; he looked like a magic-potion maker, he had his hip flask next to him, and a sorry cigarette hanging on his lips. At 6 feet 4.79 inches, he looked mythical. He's my grandfather but with a small see-through hole in his kohl-heavy conch eyes, he had a certain alluring Tolkien-character radiance that one can feed off on, and be seduced by. He seemed possessed by the soul of a fat, underemployed magician. My father must have told him that I was en route, a brief three-second phone conversation must have ensued.

When Don spotted me in the crowd, he came running to hug me and swooped me high up in the air. Kissed me twice on both cheeks. As he brought me down, I noticed that a little child, all of four, was clinging to his cape. A moustache was drawn on her face with a black marker.

'Who is that?' I asked. I wasn't surprised that Don had brought someone (my years with Don had taught me to hope for the best, and expect the worst), but at the sublime, unforgettable beauty of this child. Her skin was the darkest shade of hazel brown, her eyes glistened like a dense forest, and her hair—she had jet-black hair with a zigzag streak of grey running right through the centre. She looked as though she was discarded by the angels.

'Oh this little thing,' Don spoke of her as though he picked her out of his back pocket. 'Say hi to Moses,' he told me.

'Moses?' I smiled.

'Well, I asked her name but she didn't talk, so I just named her Moses.'

'And the painted moustache?'

'I thought you only like playing with young boys . . . even your imaginary friend . . . what's his name . . . is a boy.'

'Shyam,' I said.

'Yes, Shyam, the old chap. How is he? Have you brought him now?' Don asked me in all seriousness.

'Not sure, yet,' I said, also in all seriousness.

'Well, now you have Moses,' Don said. 'And Moses will be a boy.'

'Where did you find Moses?' I asked him as we made our way out of the station.

'Well, Moses found me,' Don was grinning like a lunatic. 'I was sitting on that bench there waiting for you when she, I mean, he came up and sat next to me. I tried speaking to her but he didn't say a word.'

'Oh.'

'So we will take him home, yes!' Don declared.

'What about her parents?' I asked.

'She is a boy, Zef.' Don fake admonished me.

'Sorry, what about *his* parents?' I fake corrected myself.

'You might get bored with me alone and your father isn't here either, so . . .'

'Okay,' I said. 'But you know it will be sad if someone comes back for him when we get used to him.'

'That is true. But it is okay, I have another friend at home,' Don said as though he had left something out in the sun and forgotten about it.

'Who?'

'Just this friend.'

'How old is your friend?' I asked.

'Must be around fifty, actually younger. Don't know, don't care, you never ask old friends their age, remember that. Nobody is their age any more. And if they do tell you their age, just add another four years to it and that will be just about right. Anyway, I think with Moses, you and Shyam around, it is going to be a full house.'

I laughed.

Don seemed to have everything sorted in his head. But then if you are fuelled by copious amounts of alcohol in your body, you are bound to be floating right through the unreal. This was going to be an interesting fifteen days or more. Just as the thought went through my head, a lady came swooping in on us and started to kiss Moses.

Don whooshed her away with his cape, and we continued walking with Moses in tow. She didn't stop. She kept running behind Moses, but when she dragged him away from Don's grasp, he got angry. The woman didn't pay any heed to Don. She kept walking away at a furious pace with Moses. Don chased her down and she started beating him up. He grabbed Moses from her and we started to run. A crowd gathered behind Don. We didn't understand what was going on. Finally, Don stopped. A police van came, took us all to the police station, which possessed the overwhelming stench of a putrid public lavatory. All the cops seemed duller than grass and wore crotch-exploding khaki pants. All of them looked ten months' pregnant. I didn't know where their breasts ended and stomachs began. A wiry man whose ears hung heavy like a basset hound's, wrote Don's details down as we were brought in and then took us in to meet the head inspector who registered the FIR, and mumbled something under his breath. Don's anger started to surge. He told the cops what he told me: 'The child came wandering and sat next to me, so I decided to take her home. End of story.'

To tell you the truth, it was hard to believe Don. If he wasn't my grandfather, he looked like those dodgy old men your parents warned you about.

'Why am I here?' Don asked, his voice bellowing through the rundown station.

'Because of the commotion you caused, you old bandicoot!' the cop screamed back.

'What nonsense! This lady is the cause of all this noise.' Don said pointing to the mad woman like a schoolboy passing the blame over. She was applying lipstick—on her cheek—and braiding her hair. She was also furiously scribbling on the wall.

'That lady is a mad woman who sleeps in the station,' the cop said. 'Get her out of here,' he addressed his elves, 'and lay out my lunch.'

'How the hell will I know that she is a mad woman?' Don screamed.

'Well, you look like her uncle,' the cop said.

Don remained silent.

In the meanwhile, the junior constable rolled out a massive banana leaf on this cop's desk, and started making a mini-mountain of rice, lentils and spinach with his dirty hands. The cop sat down and started first squishing the rice between his hairy, sweaty knuckles. Then he made table-tennis-ball-sized lumps of rice, and threw them inside his mouth like he was playing a ping-pong game with his tongue. He was slobbering away like a glutton as the rest of the watery lentils ran down his elbow. I swallowed my spit, and felt my stomach churn in revolt as though I had consumed poison.

With his mouth full, the cop spat some food out as he asked Don in a muddled rice-filled voice, 'So what are you doing with these two children?'

'You should be thanking me for saving this child,' Don said.

'How would we know you are saving this child?'

'How sick are you?' Don seemed livid. 'I am a decent human

being. I went to pick up my grandchild from the station, and I found this child and we all became very good friends immediately.'

'Very good friends, you sick bastard. I know you perverts. The next thing you'd be doing is taking them to lunch and then to Candolim.' All the cops laughed at us.

Don spat on him.

The cop got up to slap Don with the same hand he was eating with but thought better of it, so instead ordered his minions to handcuff him to the chair.

'And this is your granddaughter, you say?'

The lecherous cop asked him, looking at me.

'Yes,' Don said, exasperatedly. 'Don't you dare touch her?'

'I need proof, child,' the cop told me. And then without me or Don noticing, he pinched my cheeks. The ones on my buttocks. I baulked.

'Come sit on my lap and tell me, is he really your grandfather?' he said.

I got scared and my right hand started . . . well, as a reaction to my nervousness, my right hand would keep moving unconsciously in the air as though it was painting on some invisible canvas or tapping some beat playing in my head. It was a childhood condition, which was often triggered by a reaction of nerve impulses to a worrisome thought or moment, and arrested, only to some extent, by medication.

Don saw me do this and got even more exasperated. 'Stop moving your goddamn hand, child, borrow a pen and a paper and write something!' he screamed at me.

'What do you mean proof?' Don then asked the lecherous cop. 'She has my blood, and can you please give her some paper, her hand will drive us all nuts if it starts moving like a ghost's.' Don's voice was shaking.

'Prove it, then.' The cop was King Leer, staring at me, and

relishing our agony and discomfort. I guess he was looking for a good bribe, or a blow job.

The irony was that no matter what sort of bodily evidence Don or I would give or secrets we could share to prove that I was his grandchild, it would all seem sick and twisted right about now.

Finally, Don pleaded. 'Please believe me.' His handsomeness was tinged by grief and/or anticipation.

'Why should I?' the cop asked.

'Why shouldn't you? I am a decent person.'

'Me too,' the cop sneered. 'That's why I ran away with two children from the railway station. Be prepared to spend the night in jail then,' he threatened Don.

'Can you please come to my house? I have pictures of my family so you know I am not lying.' Don tried to plead.

'Yes, sure, why not?' the cops mocked. 'We'll have tea and talk about life too. Asshole, shut up.'

After that, we just gave up. We didn't know what to do so we all just sat there in this damp room. Some six, seven hours passed. When the cops stepped out to change shifts Don asked me to open his hip flask from his back pocket and pour some drops in his mouth. 'It'll help me think of plan B,' he said. I was too tired to argue.

I think the cops had sent out a missing-child report for Moses. Finally, as the late afternoon was closing in on us, a young couple who identified themselves as Moses' parents came and hugged her breathlessly. Clearly, they had all the proof that we didn't and they looked like what average parents should look like: they wore decent clothes and didn't run around with a cape, hat and hip flask in the middle of the ominous summer.

Don told them that he found Moses and he didn't mean any harm and if they could please ask the cops to release us so we could go home. In their excitement and gratefulness to find their child, thankfully, they did what Don told them. That was nice of them. They also gave that cheap policeman some bribe.

As we walked out of the station, with our shadows moving long and blue, Don told me, 'I miss Moses, we really connected. If I had money, I would have taken you both to Rio.'

'You didn't even know him. You knew him for fifteen minutes. He got us into so much trouble,' I told Don.

'I know,' Don said. 'But what a lovely adventure we had, no? Remember to write this down in your diary. It will add a little colour to your pages. But please don't tell your mother all this or she won't let you visit me. Promise me? Please? If that cop had touched you, I would have lynched him. You are too important to me, Zef.'

This was day one. I had fourteen more to go. How much more 'colour' can I take with this man, I wondered. It was almost as though he read my face when he said, 'Come on, let's get you home? I'm sorry, darling, you know I was only trying to find you a friend to play with in case you get bored of me.'

'I know, Donna.'

Poor Don, he *always* meant well. He never plotted or thought through anything in his life. Whatever happened, happened. Whatever worked, worked. And whatever didn't work was not questioned, rethought or dwelled upon. He didn't have a concept of time and space. He was never in a rush. He never paid attention to his movements, especially if he was thinking, and walking, and drinking at the same time.

When we got home, to his isolated universe, Don introduced me, rather indifferently, to his friend, Roger, who had a thick, long, black ruffian's mane that looked like it was severely braided in a serpent weave last year and had never felt the tooth of a comb since. He was sleeping on top of the dining table when we came in. He woke up on our arrival and flashed a 'V' sign.

At the time I wondered how Don knew this man—the realization hits me now as to exactly what sort of friend he may have been—but pondering over it right now doesn't really serve the need of the hour. Or maybe it does. In the past I had seen many of Don's companions come and go—for drinks or to say hello to me and my father—but there was no mention of anyone who had stayed beyond an afternoon or an evening. Well, at least not that I know of. Maybe he cleared his companions out like cobwebs before we came. Who knows?

Anyway, I settled in as quickly as though I had never left. Don was brimming with the greedy happiness that his only grandchild chose to come to him, the maddest of them all.

'Why didn't you go to Gravy's parents' home?' Don asked me without hiding his sly contentment.

'Because I didn't know the way to their house,' I said, pointing to the compass I had carried with me.

It's true isn't it. Sometimes you go somewhere because your feet know the way. It was just so easy. My feet knew the way here even if I was blindfolded and spun around. Even then, my wobbled body would be able to thumb its way here.

'Oh, well, I am so glad you are here. You just made my month, my dear child. So what do we do? Shall we dance?'

'Okay,' I said.

'Okay. But it's still daylight. Shall I put out the light from the sun?' He laughed.

'Make it night already?' I asked.

'Yes, every day is darkness for me anyway. All days are nights really. But then again, it is always better to deal with melancholia during day time than at night,' he said. I'll put out the light from the sun, so we can skip straight to a night of fun . . . I've been a puppet, a pauper, a pirate, a poet, a pawn and a queen,' Don did a little Sinatra skip.

'You know, frankly, the forecast calls for clear skies and many, many gin and tonics. But I am out of spirits like that, metaphorically and really.'

'Water is fine, Donna.'

'Never say those words in front of me, child.' He sounded aghast. 'Do you know what water is made of?'

'No.'

'It is $h_2 0$ which is actually hungry, horny and obese. It is meant to be served at funerals in case the tears stop. Then you can splash some on your face and pretend to be sad.'

Don went to his bar, a French tapestry cabinet, and lifted a full bottle by its neck as though he was carrying a rabbit, and poured me a little something in a glass. It looked like a strong version of apple juice. It was cognac.

I remembered hating the taste but loving the sensation.

Then he gulped a third of the bottle down without pausing to breathe. He came and sat down. He started sipping it slowly, savouring its taste now that he had already reached the heady equilibrium. After a few sips, Don told me, 'Cognac and me . . . we are long-time lovers. There is a sense of being hyper alert, but then you are not really being here or there, just an unencroachable feeling of floating through in-between thoughts. There is something about it in my blood that mixes well, as though I am floating on a waterbed.'

He rolled the drink in his mouth like he was doing some sort of alcoholic yoga, the art of relishing every sip like it was his last and becoming fully conscious of the phantasmal sensations therein. Don was good at life. He liked to enjoy and destroy. An energetic transporter, he was always tipsy and spoke theatrically with his hands, eyebrows and disco-ball eyes.

'Have you ever made love?' He asked.

'No way,' I said.

'I forget that you are fourteen. Forgive me.'

'It's okay, Donna.'

'They say when you make love, oxytocins are the hormones that release. Well, it is a little like that for me. I get a little dangerous in my head. Only in my head though. Never in reality. I live in a parallel universe, which is a way happier space than when I am not intoxicated. It helps me leave the world for a bit. It keeps me in a haze of happiness. Anyway, how is your father?'

'He is okay, a little quiet, a lot mad these days,' I said.

'Why?' Don persisted.

'I don't know. Must be work,' I said. I really didn't know. He was possessed by some kind of a floating rage. Something kept eating him up like silverfish, gnawing at him in his sleep and his waking hours, like an unattended septic cut. A cancerous part of him would eat up any strength he had left, trapping him in a cage, yet allowing just enough of himself to remain, so as to watch his own emotional suicide. He was on the edge and somehow never quite returned to the equilibrium he knew earlier. We, my mother and I, tried to make sense of his paranoia, somewhat like two mathematicians who couldn't add a lunch bill. The harder my mother—with her fake-brilliant tensile strength on tackling all this trauma—and I tried being his spigot, the more Gravy just retracted inside himself, nestling into a world of his own by excellently pleasing the left-over demons that drove him inward. He kept prancing about like an explosive spider.

'He's not what he used to be, Donna. Something is bothering him. He hides in his room all day and night, and . . . feels that he's being watched. He keeps apologizing to us,' I told Don.

'Does he still like using commas?' Don asked me instead.

'Not as much as he used to. He's pretty much anti-all things and anti-everyone,' I said.

'Commas are just stubborn full stops,' Don remarked.

'Ha.'

'Is your mother fighting with him . . . that girl needs to calm . . .'

'No, they are not fighting,' I interrupted.

'I always liked your father. He should have been your mother,' Don declared.

I kept quiet, I think I was wired to be silent. Perhaps that happens when you come out of a noisy womb. I only seem very talkative and highly verbose when I write. Otherwise I have been a pretty silent child, always have been. I do feel for things very intensely, but I never really show it, preferring the option of scattering the pieces inside of me. It's only my mind that races faster than a feral Formula 1 circuit, it has never known to stay still, it only parks for a little while, it never speaks what it really wants to say, so it stays quiet. Maybe that's pretty unhealthy, maybe it isn't.

Don took my silence as a cue to keep talking. Remember, that point I told you about filling up the emptiness with noises. Or maybe he just needed someone to talk to.

'Is he still angry with me?' Don asked.

'I don't think so,' I lied. My father was very hurt with the way Don spoke to him. He told me that but he also told me not to discuss the fight in front of my mother because it might give her a chance to say 'I told you so, the man is a selfish harebrained goon, I don't understand why you need to mingle with him,' and my father will have to argue saying that I, as a grandchild, needed to have an 'independent relationship not marked by her (my mother's) prejudices'. He wasn't in the mood for any discussion these days, anyway.

'It's okay, Donna,' I said. 'I am sure he will come again.'

Don smirked. He knew I was lying.

After a few minutes of silence he said, 'Your father . . . you know, he didn't have to be this nice to me.'

'What do you mean he didn't . . .'

'No reason,' Don interrupted almost immediately. 'He's a nice man like that. Never judged me, never was once embarrassed by me.'

'Why would he be embarrassed by you?' I asked.

'No reason.'

'Okay. I am not embarrassed by you as well, Donna,' I said.

'I know.' He started to tear up.

I didn't understand why he had tears. I presumed it had to do with the alcohol.

'You know,' he continued, 'if we had left it to your mother, you and I would never have met.'

'Why?' I asked.

'I don't know. We had a misunderstanding. It'll be fine. When things have become so bad, sub-zero negative, the only way forward is up, right.'

'I guess,' I murmured, not quite following what I meant.

'Your father told me that line. Is he reading anything in particular these days?'

'I am not sure,' I said. 'He is very quiet these days. Spends his time thinking in his room, mostly, and not talking to us. He talks a lot to himself, and makes all these notes that he sticks on his room's walls.'

'Maybe I should apologize to him,' Don said.

'That might be a good idea,' I said. I hadn't even been here an hour but I missed my father around, his comfort, his matronly voice calling out 'lunch is ready'—the most glorious words in the English language—and feeding me a double whopper of potatoes.

'Shall I get you the phone?' I asked innocently.

'No, not yet. I will eventually. I don't understand people on the phone.'

'But you have been speaking about him non-stop so maybe you should actually *talk* to him. I think the distance between you and him needs to be . . . thinned down.'

'Yes, I will. Not now though. I have too much going on.'

'Like what?' I pressed.

'Just some things I need to take care of.' He smiled, knowing that I knew he was just making things up.

'Like what?' I persisted because I had never seen Don work a day in his life.

'I have to write letters.' He made this up on the spot.

'To whom?'

'To my friends,' he said.

'You have friends?' I almost choked. 'As in real friends? People you don't owe money to?'

Don laughed. 'Child, you need to know that sarcasm is a body's defence against stupidity. Good one. I have some friends, anyway, I don't want to talk about it. Not now. Now I want to spend some time with you. Hey,' he said quickly changing the topic, 'do you remember the time . . .' Don started with that familiar glint in his eyes.

And I started laughing. I knew what he was hinting at.

When I was about six or seven years old, Gravy and I arrived in Madras for our bi-annual jaunt. Don rounded up fifteen eunuchs—gave them a photo of Gravy and me—and dispatched them to the railway station to welcome us with a signboard that said 'Welcoming party for the President of the Bore Association'. Once we got off the train, the eunuchs threw themselves on us, clapping away like turbo-charged Duracell bunnies. Gravy burst out laughing; I died out of fear. After an hour of following us and not allowing us to leave the station, my father, like a conservative, straight man who doesn't want to be felt up by these transgender terrors, offered them money, but they threw it back on his face saying Don had already plied them enough money and had given them clear-cut instructions that they were to harass my father for another three hours at the least. It was one of the most hilarious moments I would ever witness. The memory makes me hysterical.

Time slid by easily when I was with Don. I watched the contemplative sky deliberating whether to bleed to a full-blown orange dusk or linger in that eerie milky-blue lightness of wistful summer. The cognac had made me ravenous. I told Don and he went scurrying inside the kitchen to find some food for me. Don couldn't find anything that was even remotely edible. I don't think Don knew how to light the gas. There was never enough food but there was always great alcohol. I don't know what Don did but his bar was always immaculately stocked.

But that is the paradox of this madman. Don was chaotic in the sense that he wouldn't know where he was last night, or where the sugar was kept in the kitchen, or when and what he last ate, but that didn't mean he was disorganized. It just meant that those things were not worth caring for. Instead, every book in that house was kept alphabetically with the precision that accompanies a librarian—he'd know exactly where each book with its various editions was kept—the coffee-table books were arranged based on topics. Don ordered some food from his mechanic friend's wife for me, him and the house guest—who I was told had an ETA of anything between two years, thirty minutes and/or three days, at which point he'd return and plonk himself in the house and make himself completely at home.

As the night arrived dip-dyed blue, we headed to the terrace to sleep. The stars trembled across the moonlit sky. Some vicious bats or fireflies came to attack them but disappeared straight into the darkness. I thought I heard some amount of howling between the chipped moon, but then Don said anyone can become a wolf at night. The coolness of the air hung over me like a lover. The day had passed us by in a state of bright blur. Don didn't go out to get drunk. He mumbled something about how having grandchildren was far better than having children. I asked him how he knew this friend who was staying over and had disappeared somewhere.

'Oh, there is some gaudy breeze.' He stuck his neck out like a gazelle hoping that the slow terrace breeze would have some fun with his silver mane. 'Now I just need to coordinate my right arm to deliver cold *cerveza* to my face,' he said.

I thought he didn't hear my question.

'How do you know your friend?'

'How do we know all our friends . . . through acquaintances, of course.'

'Okay.'

'Old friends from the war,' he said.

'Which war?' I asked confused.

'The one in my head.' Then, he started, 'Darling . . .'

'What?' I asked, assuming he was going to tell me something.

'Can you hear that?' Don asked me.

'What?'

'The faint smell of lilies from the outside,' he said.

'How can I hear that smell?' I laughed.

'Yes, you can. Just shut your eyes. And you can hear the rustle of the gentle breeze bring in the smell of lilies from outside.'

I tried to do as he said. I could smell nothing. He felt it.

'Just close your eyes, and allow your nose to wander. Let it go for a walk. There is a lot that you can see with your eyes shut. You can hear the smell coming ever so delicately as a feather falling on the ground. Just try to focus.'

'I am trying, Donna.'

'Shhhhh. Not now. No talking. We need to put today to bed,' he mumbled and just like that he passed out.

I lay awake, staring at the stars moaning overhead. I still couldn't smell anything. A bat flew past. I shuddered. I tried to wake up Don but he was in a netherworld. He was sleeping like a warrior taking his rest before summoning his strength at daybreak to head for another battle, another adventure.

The next morning I woke up first.

I was/am always the last to sleep and the first to wake up. The whole world would be asleep and I would always be the one to see the night sky crawl back and push the sun up above, bright and early. I woke up, walked around. I tried to go inside Don's dust-laden study but he had locked it. I knew he didn't like me pottering about there without his supervision. I always wondered what he hid inside those cabinets but never ventured to open them. I was scared to get caught. I saw pictures of my mother and me spread out everywhere around the house. Some of them were shot by my father. The houseguest woke up after a while, and flashed another 'V' sign. I didn't know when he had slid back home last night.

As he shuffled about the house, collecting his things, his hair and himself, that's when I noticed Roger. He looked like Jim Morisson's dirty, primal half-brother. He had a two-dimensional body frame, almost wiry thin like a streak of rain. His body possessed an unnatural thinness that must have come from spending half his youth on over fifty-thousand pills of MDMA. I thought the weight of his unkempt hair might just squash him. His T-shirt hung on him as it would on a scarecrow that was made of one stick of bamboo. He must have been fairly pleasant-looking once upon a time but now his beauty seemed ruined—maybe by the drugs, or deception, or just lack of care, or purpose, or lack of a permanent bed. He had a flat, blank matchbox of a face that had a pair of cucumber eyes gleaming like a rat's, and a nose that seemed painted on it with sketch pens, complete with a black outline for the beige colouring inside.

He looked so ridiculously asexual, and harmless, like someone who was too busy dealing with the demons flying in his head to care for small talk. But I was wrong. Just as I was making a mental note of him, and thinking all of this, he surprised me by making me breakfast (he cut up a banana), which was very nice of him and spoke to me.

'School holidays now?' he asked.

'Yes,' I said noticing how incredibly thin his eyebrows were. I was acutely aware that I must have looked like those shifty-eyed weirdos who talk to you while staring at your forehead.

He ignored my stare. He must have been used to people noticing his lack of eyebrows. 'How is Delhi?' he asked.

'Where do you live?' I asked.

'A little all over the place at the moment, here these days; I am going to Pondicherry now, and then I'll figure,' he said.

I kept quiet and ate the banana.

'Don speaks of you and your mother constantly. You look like her.'

I was about to ask him how he knew that but he quickly added, as if he had read my mind, 'Your father . . . he takes a lot of photos.'

I nodded. 'How do you know Don?'

'What did he tell you?' he smiled a thin, kind smile.

'He mumbled something about meeting you at war,' I said.

'Is that what he said?' The man laughed.

'Yes.'

He let out another laugh but didn't bother clarifying.

'Do you come here much?' I tried again.

'Not as much as I used to earlier,' he said.

A silence descended in between us, the sort of silence, where you rack your brains to hurriedly say something or be interrupted by someone else.

'Well, I am going to have a shower and head out and let you and Don spend some time together by yourselves,' he said, as he unhooked his hair and let it fall like night. He scurried off while I took a book and started to read.

When Roger came out of the shower, he saw me and said, 'Why don't you sit over the other side?' motioning to a chair facing a regal 100-year-old Tanjore painting of a white Krishna glistening with rubies and pearls that Don had bought from a temple, or a poor cousin, or somewhere else that he had made up, which I cannot remember.

'The view is better than what is in front of you now, don't you think? It's not about how you see the painting, it's how the painting sees you. It's ogling at your ignorance,' Roger said while holding a black marker pen in his hand.

I didn't know what to say to that, so I thought it was best to smile, agree, change seating position, and keep reading. The truth was that I was so engrossed in reading that I didn't realize that what was in front of me was a six-foot-tall painting of one of Don's long-dead pet bulldogs, Brutus.

I continued to read but I was distracted when I saw a vision of Roger fixing his face in front of the mirror, drawing his eyebrows in one sharp streak with that permanent marker. His hands shimmered with silver nail varnish that glimmered like a dandelion splitting the night sky, the length of his middle finger was covered by a serpentine gold ring.

He saw me staring at him in absolute amazement.

'New day, new drama,' he grinned.

I didn't know what to say. I had never seen anyone like him. To be honest, he looked like an over-caked prostitute from whom you would extricate services and secrets and not pay at the end of it.

He winked at me and told me to let Don know he was off to Pondicherry for a few days.

He left with his hair gliding behind him, with a small backpack and a beautiful weather-worn leather suitcase that didn't seem to have clothes in it. It was just a thought, I could be wrong. It looked like a prop box of some new life. I watched him walk away, rushing like a cyclone in the afternoon rays, like a bat into the darkness.

When Don woke up, he sent me to the store down the road to get some ice for his whisky. I told him that Roger had taken off to Pondi. 'Who is Roger?' Don growled in his sleep-stained voice.

'Your friend, the one who was sleeping on the dining table when we came in yesterday,' I said.

'Oh, that's Robert, dear. Was he here? Did you meet him?' Don asked me.

'Yes, but wasn't his name Roger?'

'Roger, Robert—same bloody parasite,' Don said.

That was another thing with Don. You'd never know when he'd fall in and out of love with people. One minute, he'd put them up on a pedestal, and the next he'd crush them like a bug under a shoe and swing straight ahead with his life; the third moment, he'd still continue to welcome them into his heart as though nothing happened. He was a mass of contradictions. He loved madly, but hated venomously, and sometimes he did both together. It was never easy to understand, but it wasn't that complicated to figure out either.

'How do you know him?' I asked him.

'I met him here in Madras, years ago. I don't remember. I was standing with my head down and lighting up a cigarette. He came up to me to borrow a cigarette and we have been friends ever since.'

'You have strange friends, Donna,' I teased him.

'I know, they destroy me,' he slurred.

My stay with Don without adult supervision was interesting to say the least. Everything had an air of laissez-faireness to it: rest, wreck, rest, wreck, repeat. We chatted like a couple of 70-year-old bats sharing the last dregs of what life has in store before either of us cops it. He taught me to make a coffee table with all his classic bound books; he bought toy swords so we could pretend to fence inside the empty pool at the back of the house. We would go to sleep at odd hours, maybe around seven or eight in the morning and wake up in time for breakfast at night. Cold cuts for me, cold lines for him (I'd imagine). He was a savage beast but he took care of me like a hospital matron, bringing me the right amount of nourishment and adventure. The man opened up a lot, but I was quick to realize that he didn't tell me everything. I know he wanted to but there was some voice in his head that told him to stop where he had to. There were pauses, hesitations, resistance but that's when I also realized that he was not a regular grandfather, who was married to a bench in a bank and had a steady life, steady wife, steady income and steady children. He was a one-man industry of insanity.

One day, Don shook me furiously awake from my afternoon slumber and said we needed to rush to the hospital because he'd got a message that one of his gambling buddies had been admitted. So just before rushing, Don took out three of his whisky bottles, made me hide one underneath my T-shirt, he hid two under his (multi-purpose?) cape and we left. En route to the hospital, we stopped at a liquor store to buy some more alcohol.

'I thought we have enough,' I said.

'It can never be enough,' Don reasoned.

When we got to the hospital, I realized that we were heading to the rehabilitation section where his steroid-faced, bone-idled friend was admitted for alcohol abuse. He had sent word with a nurse-boy to Don to supply some to lift his spirits, quite literally. We saw Don's friend lying like a skunk on that metallic bed with his hand chained to it. There was a string of garlic hanging by his bed to ward off vampires or something. When he saw Don, he asked him to open up the windows a little bit.

'What the hell for?' Don asked, genuinely flummoxed.

'So I can see the wicked view of the clouds, you idiot,' his friend said sarcastically, while leaning into Don's cape to nudge him to take out one of his cigarettes. 'Now put it in my mouth, and light it. Hurry,' he said. Don did as he was told and then made me stand outside the door to keep an eye out. After his friend puffed away on three cigarettes, Don took out a straw and placed it inside a bottle of whisky and fed it to the gentleman. With each sip, the man seemed to get a new lease of life. Later, Don and he shot the breeze for well over an hour, and just as I gave him the sign that his friend's son was coming down the pathway, we wished him well and quickly left.

On our way home, Don held me, and pierced into my slit eyes and said, 'Please don't let me die in a hospital like that, promise me, Zef. Make sure you give me a roaring funeral, a great party, there should be no presence of water. Just . . . just don't bury me with a tombstone and all those creeping vines around . . . wonder how they grow anyway, surely the dead can't give them life, can they?' Then after two seconds he said, 'I think I would make for a better ghost than a human anyway.'

I promised him.

It gave me the chills thinking that he was going to die one day. Wasn't the plan for him to live forever?

It wasn't a few days until we got caught for what we had done.

That man, Don's friend, escaped from the hospital and came out to hide in our house. He brought with him a stolen traffic light—I don't even want to know that story—as a present for Don. This man had escaped from the hospital by bribing one of the nurse-boys, which meant that he brought the nurse-boy to the house for Don to pay him off. Since Don didn't really have any money (at least the amount that the nurse wanted), and the nurse refused to leave till he got what he wanted, Don gave him the beautiful Tanjore painting that was hanging in the living room, and a pair of emerald cufflinks, and four bottles of whisky. He told the boy to sell the painting. This behaviour was not unnatural to Don. He didn't care about all this. Nothing affected him. He didn't allow it to affect him. Don treated his friend like he was expecting him anyway. He just longed for people, and then dismissed them when he got bored. There was no love lost, it was just love interrupted for a while.

After all this was settled, Don returned to look at his friend, who had already made himself at home by lying down on the chaise longue, like an enchantress from an impressionist painting, with a bucket of ice on his eye.

'Please don't waste the neighbour's ice on your face, I need it for the drinks,' Don told him very, very matter-of-factly. His friend didn't react indignantly. He, too, must be used to Don's getting his priorities right. He didn't react at all for a long time.

Don tried quoting Keats in a highly exaggerated voice: 'Oh, ye! Who have your eyeballs vexed and tired.'

He moved towards his friend to examine what had happened. Apparently, the man had run out of the hospital in such great speed that he had tripped against a stretcher. Don saw a huge violent cut just above the man's right eye and pushed his face back in absolute revulsion.

'Let me go get you some tea,' Don said, heading straight to the kitchen. He came out some twenty minutes later and fed it straight to his friend out of a beautiful tea cup that had handles in the shape of a woman's legs. The man spat it out first but Don wasn't surprised.

'Okay now, come on, gulp it down. You'll feel a lot better, soon, I promise,' my grandfather said. He sounded as compassionate as the Dalai Lama.

After all this was done, I went to my room for a shower and Don had fixed himself a drink and took his place under the tree inside the house. About an hour later, as I came out, I saw the man feeling up the new traffic light as though it were a seductress in the throes of simmering passion. His wound looked like it was burning his brain up.

When he saw me he asked me, 'Child, why do you look like a vicious panting mix of a Rottweiler and a wooden table?'

I didn't know what to say.

Then he asked me, 'Do you think this is a constellation that is waiting to burst?'

'It is a traffic light that you brought,' I said.

He kept playing with it a little too disturbingly for my own vivid sexual imagination. But eventually, he got an electric shock, promptly froze and fell to the ground. Before I could react, he was recovering; he sat up and spat blood, took off his clothes and ran to the backyard to hurl himself down the slide. But his bum got stuck midway and refused to move forward. Friction must have burned his bare bottom. I wasn't sure if I was going to die of laughter or of fright. After forcing himself all the way down, he dived into the empty pool. After a painful fall on the green mosaic, he regained his composure, and saluted me like he was the chief of army staff. It was hilarious. He started pretending that he was in the midst of a war. After pretending to duck a few shots, he fell backwards clutching his heart. He looked at me and said, 'Did you see the last bullet come? I think it has stung my eye. It's bleeding glass. Hurry, call the paramedics. What are you staring at? I am dying. I don't want my bastard son to collect the medal when I am dead and dining with Lucifer.'

I was in splits.

I went to Don who was engrossed in reading a book on logic and told him what his friend was up to.

'Let him be,' Don said coolly, without even looking up at me. 'I am busy now,' he said as he directed his hand towards where his whisky glass was located at the foot of his chair, took a sip of his drink and continued to read.

'But Donna, he is rolling all over naked,' I screamed.

'He really must have been restricted in the hospital,' Don winked at me.

'Shouldn't you do something?' I asked him.

'No, he'll be fine tomorrow whenever he wakes up,' Don said nonchalantly.

'How do you know?'

'Because the side-effects will wear off in about eight hours or so.'

'Side-effects?' I asked, completely baffled. 'Of what?'

'Of the opium tea I gave him.'

'What?' I spluttered.

'The man wouldn't shut up about his agonizing pain so I thought the opium tea would eventually put him in a state of cloudiness. A little off planet . . . as they say. He might be chasing alien kittens. Let him do his thing. It's a pain reliever, he probably won't even feel his heart breaking. He won't feel a thing when he eventually gets his brain back tomorrow,' Don reasoned.

I was stunned into silence. With this man, I learnt something new every day.

Don's friend finally went to bed in the empty pool. Don went and put a band-aid above his friend's eye and placed his clothes next to him so he wouldn't be embarrassed when he woke up stark naked the next day. The man woke up by dinner the next night. Neither of us said anything about his antics the previous night so we pretended like it didn't happen. The man had no idea anyway. So things went back to normalcy. The two of them drank themselves silly destroying the lithium in their brains, and eventually, when they were flying, they started shedding skin like an anaconda. Don would put the music on and then we'd all start dancing. There was never a dull moment. The two of them kept losing themselves in the labyrinths of gossip, as though they were in some sort of an exile from reality. And when it got too hot, they sat in their underwear and continued doing what they were doing without any interruption: taking several white rocks the size of jagged sugar cubes that were all overflowing from a Dresden bowl, heating them up in a pipe and taking a hit of the vapour, one by one until the two of them were sprawled on the floor. That's what I remember. All Don said was that it would help him drown out the noise from his mind. His friend said that he could feel every atom in his body lightening up. He also said that Don was a great friend to have when one wanted to forget about the rest of the world.

It was a relief, in a way, to hear these two bats talk. They gave flight to my imagination, and extended the constricting territory of my brain. They were old but they didn't really care about morals, or the lack of them, or their influence on me. By the end of the week, Don's friend just wrapped himself in a bedsheet for the rest of his stay. 'Freedom!' he yelled. Eventually, that man's son found out where his father was staying, came to our house, and took him (read: dragged him) back home. The man rolled out and dragged himself by the end of that same bedsheet—horizontally—like a convict, without saying a word or even making eye contact with us. On his way out, he gave me one clove of garlic. 'It'll protect you,' he mumbled.

I asked Don if the son didn't have a voice. He didn't even make eye contact with us, let alone say hello.

'Maybe he is afraid that if he starts talking, he might start crying,' Don offered as explanation. 'If I was a father like my friend here, I'd be pretty broken too,' Don said.

Ha, I only wish I'd understood the paradox of what Don had said then.

A few days later, his friend sent a hand-delivered note saying:

> Thanks for saving my life on a repeated basis. I am sorry I left my goodbye manners after all those bottles of scotch. Can you also please send my morose son some of that tea?

Don sighed wistfully. He must have been used to this. Anyway, soon after that, Don realized he had no money for more alcohol and food. So he took me to the races because just reading couldn't satiate his urge to make some quick money to spend.

That way Don was an anomaly. While he loved the material strength that money rendered, he quickly realized that with him, it wouldn't stick. So he made peace with the fact that, as long as he had someone to borrow money from, he'd be fine, and when and if he had money, he would lend it, drink it, or gamble it away. And on the days he didn't have money, he was just looking for company. In a way, his desperation to be with people was somewhat similar to my mother's constant search in her youth to be loved. It is only a reversal of fate, and karma, that Don was doing now what my mother did when she was much younger—looking for a friend of some sort.

He would often start deep and meaningful conversations with random strangers, store clerks, people on the road—whoever had ears and was available. We spent one afternoon photocopying a book because Don didn't have money to buy it. 'So pleb,' he tried to justify, 'but what's so bourgeois in buying a book?'

He kept talking non-stop with the man who managed the store, about so many things that I had switched off after a while. On our way back home, Don stopped me and asked me very diffidently, 'Did I sound rich to the photocopier?'

Huh? I didn't understand what he meant.

'No, I meant, did I sound like a rich, arrogant man. I used to be like that when I had money—the residue must still be there. Right? I am not like that any more but sometimes I might sound a bit vain.'

I didn't understand his stupid realization. So I didn't say anything.

'Come on, let's go back, I need to apologize to him,' Don said.

'To whom?' I whined. What was this man on about?

And just like that we went back to the store and Don proceeded to apologize profusely. 'I am sorry, I didn't mean to sound rich. I am not. I used to be but not any more. I live in this haunted house with my grandchild, but I live in utter penury. I am just a regular person, like you, middle class, and poor. But I am happy. As perplexing as it may sound, one can go without the other.'

He was nuts like that.

On our way home, Don's troubadour tongue told me, 'You know, your grandmother would have liked the fact that I went back and apologized.'

'Sancho?' I spat out.

'Sancho,' Don sighed romantically. 'She was a lady who got the joke before anyone else did—she understood everything.'

I had completely forgotten about Sancho's existence until then. It was like this: if you are careless with something it gets broken. I was careless with my grandmother's memory. She didn't figure in my present or in my past. She died even before I was born. Nobody spoke about her much. Don never did until now. And neither did my mother speak of her until after my father died. While I knew someone had existed in the blurry distance, I never really paid much attention to it. In fact, since I had always seen Don alone, I presumed he had *always* been alone, like those single-celled amoeba, with no debt (financial or moral), without any emotional investment in another human being. I always thought that he stood alone in the periphery of life, when everyone found another human heartbeat to hold on to. So, not even a fleeting thought to enquire about Sancho struck me. I had never seen a picture of her in this house and my mother didn't show me any. Maybe my mother was also trying to block her memory too? Who knows? She was also a strange woman, revealing secrets as she remembered them in no consequential order.

When we got home, Don strode purposefully in. The house wasn't locked. There was nothing to steal, Don would say. He made himself a huge drink and ran to the bench underneath the tree in the house and sat there. It seemed as though there was a great rush to do nothing.

'I miss her. I always did,' Don said a little wistfully.

'I've never heard you talking about her until now, Donna.'

'I don't know . . . I avoid thinking of her because I feel really ashamed.'

'Ashamed, why?' I was a bit surprised, he sounded so mellow, he was whispering like a child found guilty of cutting a girl's hair because it was just so tempting to do so.

'Just because of all the things I did, all my unruly, untamed desires and emotions that I wasn't proud of but . . . but I couldn't hold back, there was some animal inside me,' Don said. 'Some beast that had to come out, something out of my own control.'

'Like what? Drinking?' I asked.

'If only it was as simple as that,' he smiled.

'Then?'

'Not loving her enough,' he said.

'Who did you love then?' I asked.

'People not worthy of being loved. I loved her from a polite place, not a passionate one.'

'Why did you do that?' I asked because I didn't understand.

'Because I was a foolish drunk. Sapphire in my blood. Sometimes I think Sancho wills me to think of her even if I don't want to. Her spirit keeps moaning overhead somewhere. I keep telling myself not to think of her because when I do . . . I feel so broken and sad. So even if there is a fleeting thought that may just crawl into my head, like a rat trying to nibble at something and scurry away, I distract myself. Even when she was alive, she was too scared that I might forget about her, or not think of her, so she was always pirouetting around doing something to get my attention. And today was one of those days where maybe she wouldn't take no for an answer.'

Don was talking about Sancho as though she was sitting in the next room.

'So how did you think about her even when you didn't want to?' I asked him.

'It was strange,' he said. 'Sometimes I think she has the power to see me even when I can't see my own reflection. I had walked into her room, opened a closet to take out some old book which I wanted to show you. It was a closet where she kept everything she collected, she was a kleptomaniac,' he said. 'Guess we were in a way made for each other, huh? I never got around to throwing anything,' he smiled. 'There were photographs, pins, staplers, spoons, diaries, notes, medicines, bubble wraps, old magazines, hairclips—those were the things she wanted to take to her grave I think. Mad woman. But I didn't look at all that. I just wanted to get my book and leave, but then suddenly out fell a milk packet containing a picture of your mother sitting on Sancho's lap, trying to play the keys of the piano. I had just bought it, your mother must have been four or five . . . I don't remember.'

Don stopped talking.

'Donna?'

He remained quiet.

'Donna?' I shook him.

'Yes, she was so bloody good only if she hadn't . . . all became such a mess . . . she learnt the piano from . . . sorry, what was I saying . . . I lost track.' He almost looked embarrassed and stopped talking.

'Sancho?' I offered.

'Oh yes, sorry. So I saw this picture of Sancho, and I thought of her, your mother, and in a way, she got what she wanted, she wanted me to think of her and that's exactly what happened. She was fiercely determined but then I think she . . . lost . . . her will and I let her . . . clearly, death doesn't dampen her determination. Maybe if I think of her hard enough, she will show up, which I need to avoid at all costs. She was the same when she was alive, she was persistent.'

'What do you mean?' I asked.

'I didn't want to marry her when I met her. I was twenty. I wanted to get out of Madras.'

'How did you both meet? Was it love at first sight?' I asked.

Don told me that he had met her when he went to take that equine Trojan statue that was placed at the entrance of the house. Her father had said that it was meant for the man who marries his daughter. 'I thought that if I say yes, then her father will stop talking. His voice had the same gnawing effect as that of a mosquito's, highly irritating. I thought I'd disappear after taking the statue, I gave them an incorrect address, I thought I had them fooled, I thought I had Sancho fooled, but she showed up. And I don't even know how she did it. It took her three months but she made her way to me, Zef,' Don squeaked and smiled at the memory. 'She . . . she told me that she loved me and I told her that it was just an infatuation on her part, and that I didn't love her back.'

'That's a little harsh, isn't it,' I said.

'But why lie?' Don said.

True.

Don said that he had gotten a job as a cargo boy in World War II and—at the time—was getting ready to leave. 'I didn't think I was ever going to return here for another ten odd years or more. That statue was safely kept in a warehouse and she could have it back. I told her that,' Don said.

That's the thing with Don. It was always about wanting something absolutely, desperately, immediately, and life-threateningly necessarily. But then, as soon as he had it, he'd lose interest in it. He was just an overgrown baby with an unruly emotional index.

But that didn't stop Sancho. She didn't care about that statue. She had a full-blown love affair with Don in her head. 'She was persistent then about making me think of her, as she is now when she is dead. You know what she did? For the seven years that I was away, she would send me little love notes and pictures of herself every month, or every fortnight. So even if I wanted to forget her, I couldn't. She would find out what part of the world I lived in and every month she would make her brother take a photograph of her wearing the most outrageous clothes. At one point she wore a hat comprising two wires with an egg in the centre, an orange flamenco skirt, a plastic overcoat with nothing underneath, and a pair of cloth shoes. She carried an umbrella and a knapsack that looked like a coffin. It was a hilarious image that made me write back to her asking her what she was doing with the thick plastic overcoat because it's too hot for that in Gokarna. She wrote back saying that it was a part of my ensemble, and it was supposed to catch the sea breeze but there was none on that sticky day.'

Those photographs must have had immense power, I thought, because it made him come back to where he thought he would never come back, and marry her. And fall in love with her. In that order. Don showed me one of them, the photographs. I gasped. She looked like a savagely Promethean beauty: ferocious, savage, heart-destroying, eloquent even.

She was wearing a man's shirt with capri pants, a burning cigarette between her lips with ashes falling all over her, a gun in her hand, a polka-dotted scarf rolled under her chin, with the waves cascading over her shoulder, and her face pulled back into a severe stare.

Just as I was about to ask Don, he said, 'Yes, it was a real gun. She was ready to kill somebody that day.'

'Who?'

'Your grandmother was a maverick. She was conceived on a train.

She would shoot rats, bandicoots and rabbits from her bathroom window with a cigar in one hand. She was a very good shot, for a lady with a weird jaw. But now I think that the jaw was one of the best things about her. She had this mole on the side of her neck that kept growing. She named it Bastard,' Don smiled.

We stayed quiet for a while. He must have been lost in a haze of Sancho-ness, smirking at her invisible ghost.

'So then what did you do after you left Madras?' I asked Don.

'I sailed to the Middle East. As I was a part of the British troops, I was stationed in Egypt for three years. I was a cargo boy. I did everything: transporting food cans to the front, shovelling mines, packing bodies, collecting shrapnel, witnessing the cutting of spies' fingers, sleeping with nurses, cleaning toilets.'

After the war ended, Don embarked on becoming some kind of Christopher Columbus, and kept searching for islands visible to his eyes alone.

'I went to Algeria with a bunch of comrades, and when I got bored, I managed to take a boat to Greece,' he said. 'I wanted to study the New Testament in Greek. It was an urge, something that I thought of one night when I was sleeping on an empty stomach, some sort of fear—the kind that hits you only in the darkness—got hold of me. I did a hundred other things in between, but as the sky lay out like a pathway, I didn't know what route I was taking, but I followed my legs. I sold biscuits, underwear, and found my way to Warsaw.'

'And all this time, Sancho kept sending you her photographs?' I asked.

'Yes.'

'How?'

'I told you she was determined,' Don said.

'Did you respond?' I asked.

'Occasionally. But I had my hands full. I didn't care either, honestly speaking. Because I knew she was there waiting for me. Where's the chase in that?' Don said.

My grandfather looked too beautiful and damned to have had only one lover.

He was an amoral, sensual, manipulative bastard. I just took a while to accept it, admit it and finally not be ashamed of it. He wasn't.

'So who was the other person?'

'There were many. But there was one that destroyed me for a while.'

'Who?' I asked.

'We met at the staircase of the same building we were living in. I fell in love before we even said hello. But I kept denying it to myself. It was wrong.'

'Why? Because Sancho was in the back of your head?'

'No, because it was an emotion I wasn't used to feeling. It was out of my body.'

'Love does take courage, Donna,' I said.

'Where did you learn that?'

'My mother, surprisingly.' I laughed.

'Yes, but . . . but . . . this was different,' Don said.

'How so?'

'It just was. I thought it was a phase, something that came out of sheer loneliness. I thought I loved that person accidentally because at the time I had no one to love, really. But it wasn't. It stuck on. I was happy.'

'So then what happened?' I asked.

'We spent the days living in the right, and the nights sleeping on the left. Lust soaked with a lot of love. Well, that's what I thought. We didn't see the light for many days, we claimed each other's bodies, owned each other's breath, and counted each other's heart beat, we built caves in the air, spoke our secrets into our palms. We were together for three months, no . . . one year or more, or less, it's all a blur. The earth below my body shook.'

'That must have been some love, Donna,' I said.

'*Some* loves are like that. They are a particular brand of toxic, soul-demolishing, cannibalistic sort of love that requires a few lifetimes to finish, but then it gets buried alive,' Don said.

'What happened then?' I asked.

'One morning I went to buy some breakfast, and when I returned, my flat was empty. No sign of two lives beating as one inside. It was over even before it had begun. I didn't understand how people can snip other people from their lives. I became a victim of my own philosophy. I walked around the city, searched for my lover's face among the crowded sighs of strangers. It was . . . it was like in the movies, you go tapping onto some stranger's back assuming that when they turn it is the person you are looking for and when it isn't, you say a sheepish apology and move on, embarrassed. That's what happened. The guilt must have gotten the better of love, for my lover.'

'Why guilt?' I didn't understand.

'Not guilt, maybe the risk? I don't know, whatever it was, it wasn't easy being lovers like that in that era,' Don explained.

'Why not?' I persisted.

Don remained quiet.

I knew he was hiding something but he couldn't voice it. I suppose, what happens in vagueness, stays in vagueness.

He remained quiet for a while before continuing.

Finally he said, 'I didn't know how to recover from such terrible, burning love. It was a rare romantic downer. All it takes is just half a heart to destroy another. There are some bodies that haunt us, that we want to devour and drink up, whose smell intoxicates our veins. I couldn't sleep for days, for months. There was perpetual gloom, which was only lit by the fear of abandonment descending on me. Every night through the naked window in my room, the moon would cast its ugly yellow streak and I would cry to myself that I lost the first and only person I loved.'

I kept quiet as he continued speaking. Honestly, what could I have even said.

'I stayed in that flat for two months hoping that my favourite person would come back to me. Instead, I received a letter from my lover stating the cause of disappearance. It was crisp: Had to leave, my brothers found out. They were out to kill you. So I escaped. Take care. Zef, I would have expected 'love' instead of a 'take care'. How impersonal was that? I mean won't you not expect that from someone who you have been stark naked with for days at a stretch, with someone who has told you that they slit their wrists four times in an attempt to come to terms with reality and still survived it, someone who opens up their scars to you, the type of scars you can't see with your naked eye?' Don went on.

It was a little poetic, even if he was recounting his heartache.

'Well then what happened?' I asked.

'Eventually, I heard that my lover had settled down into a charmed suburban life. That door had been shut on my face. It all translated into the same thing to me. The ownership over another human, it was gone. I became a loose cannon. We only want what we don't have. I was angry. I drifted into a netherworld. The abandonment made me heartless in many ways, ashamed too . . . Everything became sex or death. I'd put more emotion in a handshake or a hug.'

In retrospect, the similarity between the way Don and my mother led their lives after their heart was first broken was uncanny and eerie.

'Why ashamed, Donna?' I asked.

He hesitated for a brief second. 'I think . . . I don't know but maybe because I was way too honest with my emotions, too raw. It got me nowhere.'

'Oh.'

'I was living through hell. It takes a whole lot of strength to regain your ability to laugh with your friends and be seriously happy, and not claim that you are happy and all of a sudden a random smell will send a tear down your eye and when they ask you, "What happened? Why are you crying?" You'll say no, it's just the smoke from a cigarette that's boiling your pupils,' Don said this in one breath.

'So how did you land up here then?' I asked him.

I waited for him to speak. But he didn't. I had lost him to his past again.

'Don?' I tried. 'Donna?' No response. I shook him a little.

'Sorry, my dear child, what did you ask me?'

'I asked how did you get here eventually?'

'Here?'

'Yes.'

'Go to my study.'

'Your study?' I was surprised.

'Yes. See the bookshelf to the right. On the seventh shelf, look at the ninth book. It will be the short stories of Tolstoy bound in red. Bring that book and come.'

'Donna, I don't want to read.' I started to whine.

'Just bring the book, Zef.'

When I went to the study, I followed his instructions, and found it exactly where he had said—the seventh shelf, ninth book. The man was scarily meticulous. I gave him the book and he took a photograph out from it.

'This was the picture I got from Sancho, around about that time,' he said. 'She never stopped writing to me. She really loved me, that mad woman. I don't even know why. It was as though she was riding for a fall in choosing to be with me,' Don said, handing it to me.

It showed Sancho wearing a dress with a pair of brogues. Don said it was the sari that her mother had bought for her wedding. Sancho had cut it up and made it into a dress that just about came below her crotch, sending the entire town into a tizzy because she was what you call a wild child.

'Who does that with a nine-yard Kanjeevaram sari, for heaven's sake?' Don laughed.

Ha. I looked at it. I fell in love. Wonder why he didn't. She was standing on top of a canal bridge in Madras. She lived in a different era in her head.

Behind the photograph she had scribbled this note:

it's a beautiful afternoon.
the aer is still.
i could live. or i could die.
there is silence.
there is music.
there is chocolate, endorphins, shoes to make me run away from myself.
there is everything. but you.
i carry your heart, in my heart. should i let it go? should i let it stay?
i have a lot on my mind, a little in my belly. lot to worry about, little to live for.
but all i can think of in this second, 15:55, is not being next you.
soon, you say. or maybe i imagine you to say that. your silence eats me up. i'm greedy for more of you. impatient too. vices, galore.
wonder where you are, as i suffer in my grotto. i have much to tell you but the words don't add up to what i really want to tell you somehow. my morbid thoughts must be put to rest, with faux goodness from the star's hollow nest.

a wretched fly circles above my head.
i miss you despite the work load and word overload.
there is everything here. but you.

I gave the photo back to Don. He held it against his heart.

'She never wrote in caps. That's a little vain, isn't it?' he asked me.

Unapologetic vanity, I presume.

'So what did you do?'

'I had a vague feeling that if I didn't go back she might jump off the bridge,' he answered.

'Did you go back then?'

'Yes . . .'

'And?'

He looked at me and said, 'Sancho used to say that I should stop drinking so much whisky or there will be none left for my funeral.'

Ha.

'Anyway, make sure this whisky glass is never empty. The second it is empty, that is the second I will stop telling you my story.'

That is precisely what I did. I was breathlessly curious.

Don said that he didn't want to keep meeting her just at the end of these sentences. So he made his way back but decided against telling her.

'Surprise her?' I asked.

'I didn't really know what I was doing. I wanted to have the luxury of changing my mind . . . It was a long journey. I didn't really know what I was going to think at the end of it,' he said.

Ha—Don did know himself better than all of us; he knew how quixotic he was.

Anyway, he said the journey to Gokarna took over six months and he decided to stick with the original plan to head to her house.

'When I knocked, she opened the door and said, "Hello, would you like some coffee?" There was no shock, no surprise on her part.

All she said was "don't speak loudly because my mother is sleeping." I was stunned, Zef. I expected a hug in the least and here she was talking to me as though I was returning home after a regular work day and not seven long years. She brought me coffee and told me to hurry up and drink it, we have to go out. I was too speechless. Was there someone else who was sending me all these love-soaked notes? An awkward silence entered the room like an unwelcome third party, the kind of silence that comes between two lovers who convey everything they have to say via letters but when they come in actual physical contact they don't know where to start, or how to say all the things they have been rehearsing in front of the mirror. Finally she said, "Okay enough with your coffee, let's go out."'

They walked in silence towards the rainy sea for about twenty minutes.

'Walking with her made the city scenic,' he said. 'Then she turned and hugged me as though she was squeezing my heart out of my body. I embraced her as well. She had the smell of dried roses in her hair. It is the smell that I will always remember her by. I still remember what she asked me that second, Zef. She said that my hug . . . it seems less than what it should have been. The intensity is far less than hers. I told her I found her odd behaviour amusing and annoying at the same time.'

Then she proceeded to tell Don that she couldn't act so excited because her mother was in the next room. Her father had gone fishing a few years ago and had still not returned. Her mother still waited for him. She said that her brother had died in a freak accident while holidaying in Ooty. Apparently a gang of boys had dared him to spend a night at the cemetery, and he agreed. He went in, scared out of his wits, and managed to spend a few hours there. But when a lousy wind led to an acidic rain from the heavens, he got petrified. So he started to run for his life but the housecoat that he had worn got caught on the edge of some tombstone, and because it was pouring and he was in a space where the dead lay six feet under, he was too terrified to turn back, thinking that some ghost had caught hold of him, and so he died out of fright in the same spot, in a cemetery. She spoke without stopping to breathe.

'I was shocked and I rarely get shocked,' Don said. 'By the time I could react, she told me she had also been raped by her uncle, and that she got pregnant, and she had a coat-hanger abortion. There you go, seven years in less than seven minutes. She was revealing secrets as though unwrapping a burning wound. The quicker you do it, the lesser it will hurt later. The ground must have swallowed me because I was too stunned to talk. She was the visual shorthand of vagueness, Zef. I asked her which uncle, but all she said was that it didn't matter, he's dead now.'

Don told me that he asked her if she killed him but was too nervous to hear the answer.

Sancho apparently remained quiet for a while and said that she had something to do with it but cannot be fully responsible. 'No evidence can be found, I am safe.'

Don told me, 'Sancho was fearless. She spoke like she was in a French film, you had to understand the nuances. This was not the demure welcome-back party for my new orthodox life that I was expecting, Zef. I had found Clint Eastwood for a wife.'

'We walked around the neighbourhood,' Don recollected. 'It was calm, like the quiet of the sun melting into the evening sky. Then all of a sudden, Sancho turned towards me and asked, "So we will get married, yes?" I was still speechless, Zef. She said, "I've been loving you for far too long to stop now so please don't dissuade me or . . ." What! I interrupted her . . . you will kill me?' Don smiled at her proposal.

Don told me that when she quoted John Donne—'We can die by it, if not live by love'—he was sold. 'So that's what we did. We got married,' Don told me. 'She had the looks, I had the time. That's when I realized, Zef, that women are sensitive, they are the gentler breed, they overthink every little thing and they care more than they should but that's what makes their love so strong. But I also warned her that ours will be a marriage of trial and error. I needed my space and she agreed to it.'

Sancho and him lived in a kind of gentle afterlife, as though they could see each other's wild dream in that glance.

'Did you love her *that* much to get married to her?' I asked Don.

'Probably not. She loved the *idea* of me, and it made sense. Because I remember thinking that she had a great sense of adventure. I felt I had to start afresh somewhere far and new. There was nothing to pull me back into my old life. Sancho . . . was a promise . . . she heralded something that I wanted to try. I wanted to be around her because there was a certain amount of wilfulness, a decadence that made me think that I could love the bones on her a little bit. I saw the potential to love her because she seemed like she might be a good companion to have. And isn't love just friendship set on fire?'

'How would I know? I muttered.

'Convenience, compromise and comfort,' Don offered in lieu of explanation.

He was speaking like a man with an uncontrollable urge to confess. Quite in the same way one often speaks with such desperation (or maybe that is just me) before the final call to switch off all phones before embarking on a 24-hour flight journey across the Atlantic, after which you don't know if you can ever speak again. His eyes were closed tight, stitched shut as though he was groping inside the darkness of his membranes to retrace his hurried steps through his murky, busy and hectic past, as though a small streak of the present slipping into his eyes would shatter the flow of the narrative, as though opening his eyes would be a startling reminder of a life that he wished he didn't live.

I would have been lost in the maze of Don's mess and madness if I hadn't heard the gates creak open just then. Don's eyes were closed. 'Who is it?' he asked me.

'Robert,' I said.

'Who Robert?' Don asked with his eyes still shut.

'Your friend . . . the one who was here a few days ago,' I laughed.

'Oh, Roger,' Don said with his eyes still shut. He tried to sound breezy but he couldn't hide the hint of disappointment.

'I thought you said his name is Robert, Donna?' I said.

'Roger, Robert . . . who can tell the difference?' Don said indifferently.

As he made his way inside, Don saw him and asked, 'Weren't you gone for a few days? Why are you back?'

For Roger/Robert, I thought, it must have been like coming home to eager eyes that were expecting someone else.

'I want to paint this wall again,' Roger/Robert said.

'You've done enough painting for one lifetime, I think,' Don said.

Roger/Robert didn't say anything. I noticed that he was eyebrowless. There were no sketch-pen marks on his forehead. In absolute silence, the kind that one associates with suppressing a scream inside a funeral home before you see the body of your favourite person, Roger/Robert took out his rolling paper and some tobacco, and started rolling. That was also when I observed the faint trail of a red serpent tattoo that was slithering underneath his Rolex. He rolled his cigarette in less than forty-five seconds, lit it and passed it to Don, who puffed it and asked me if I would care for a smoke. I said, no.

To cut a long story short: Roger/Robert (R/R) stayed for a few days. We had a pretty okay time, the three of us. Don and I did our bit, R/R was furiously writing in his notebook, disappearing and reappearing from his room. He seemed the kind to use a lot of exclamation marks and emoticons. Perhaps he was writing, just as I am right now, trying to come to terms with everything. He'd pretty much keep to himself. One day, when Don had slipped into a heavy, drunken sleep, I heard R/R wandering about.

Just when I was about to ask him what he was up to, I heard the wafting strains of the piano floating in. It was beautiful. It was Gershwin's *Rhapsody in Blue*. The music from the other room had filled up Don's study. It was amazing. I always wanted to learn the piano but my mother had banned it, insisting that I play the violin instead.

Suddenly, Don woke up from his alcoholic interlude. He sat up alert. His hair stood up as though it had flirted with an electric current. Something had shaken him brutally awake. Like some fear got hold of him and he had to find the source.

'What is that noise?' he asked me, highly irritated.

'It is the piano, Donna. R/R must have started to play since we thought we will dance and we couldn't find the gramophone.'

'I know it *is* the piano,' Don gritted through his teeth. 'Is your mother here?' he asked.

'No, why will my mother be here?' I asked, completely flummoxed.

'Then who the hell is playing it?' Don screamed.

'Roger/Robert is,' I said.

'What?' Don screamed. 'Who told him to touch it?'

I didn't understand why Don was getting so angry. He stormed out of the room and took his umbrella from the doorway, Sancho's umbrella, the one from the photo she had sent Don.

Before I had time to react, he whooshed in like an eagle and attacked R/R who was blithely playing away, and hit him on his back with the umbrella.

'What the hell do you think you are doing?' Don screamed.

'What the hell do *you* think you are doing?' R/R screamed back. 'Stop attacking me, you psychotic man.'

I tried to pull Don back while R/R tried to resist Don's attacks. But Don was fuelled by some satanic force.

'What's wrong with a little music?' R/R asked. Neither R/R nor I could follow how this venomous fury had taken over Don.

'Don't pretend to be innocent. You know exactly why,' Don said. 'Get off the piano. Don't you dare touch it. It belongs to my daughter.'

'Your daughter isn't here, is she? And she'll never be here. You are dead to her, can't you see that?' R/R spat back.

I didn't understand the sub-text of this conversation and how this man knew all this about my mother. But this was not the time to ponder that. Don kept beating him. It was a hilarious sight to tell you the truth, even cruelty can be ridiculous.

'I only ever told you to teach her the piano, not play it,' Don started to sob.

'Don't accuse me of something that you ruined very successfully on your own,' R/R yelled.

This enraged Don further. He bit R/R.

'Get out of this house before I call the police. Get out right now,' Don said while punching R/R recklessly on the face. He must have distorted his nose. Finally, I somehow managed to get Don off him. The poor chap rushed off quicker than a Jewish man's foreskin. Just before he left the house, he turned to me and circled his index finger towards his brain to indicate Don's lunacy and disappeared in the same way he came. Out into nowhere. I saw faint traces of blood trickling down the back of his T-shirt because of the lashing that Don had given him with Sancho's umbrella. It was ghastly.

I went to get Don some water and whisky to calm him down. On my way back from the bar in his study, I peeped into the room that R/R had occupied. In his hurry to escape from being killed by Don, he had left all his things behind, including his beautiful weather-worn leather case. I debated for a second to open it or not—this box of vague curiosities—but then I found something glistening like shark's teeth inside. It was a trumpet.

Don was sitting on the piano's bench and had put his head against the instrument. He was crying. 'Your mother hated the piano but when she played, she could set the room on fire, she could call the rains with her melody,' he whispered. 'But . . . but after she left . . . I just shut the piano because I didn't want the noise that she touched to leave the room, I wanted it to stay inside this, I wanted to keep it trapped inside forever.'

That was when it hit me. Today was the first time that I had ever heard the piano being played in this house for all the time that I had spent here. The piano lay in the corner of the hall like a grand old dame that everyone passed by, smiled cordially at, and swiftly walked on past lest the hello transpires into a full-blown nutty conversation that will become just too much to handle. I wondered why I never had the urge to lift up the lid and play around with the keys, but I think I knew that I would be asking for trouble. Sometimes, I suppose, children can instinctively understand where not to push the boundaries.

Today was also the first time that I had seen Don sitting on the piano's bench. He looked so broken. I guess sounds come with a unique feverish speed to take you where you don't want to go. The house had become so deathly quiet now. A few hours ago, we were in the midst of a bloodbath. I thought Don was going to bring the house down and we were going to be embroiled in our own Shakespearian drama. My mind raced as to how we would look—the grandfather and the granddaughter arrested for killing a man because he was playing the most magical musical notes on the piano. Reason for murder: brought back too much memory for the old man. I guess Roger or Robert was used to Don's manic outbursts from a past life, a life that would require the oldest torn piece of shoe to walk down that destructive marsh pit.

But the truth of the matter was that Don missed my mother. He missed her more than he could admit to himself.

His eyes were closed as he lay against the piano, the voluptuous Bösendorfer that he got from Vienna for his only daughter. The right-temple arm of his spectacles had broken during the fight but Don still wore them, balancing them on his nose. It looked funny, actually. He was breathing heavily, laced with the filthy aftertaste of cheap scotch, and his face smelt of dried tears. I thought he was sleeping.

'Don?' I called out softly to check if I had lost him to slumber.

'I am awake, Zef. I don't want to sleep because I don't know if you will still be here when I wake up.'

'I will be here,' I said even though I knew I was leaving the next day.

Chapter 7

I finally made my way back to my parents. When he heard the gates creaking, Gravy hurriedly came down the stairs as though he had just risen from deep slumber. He was wearing a pair of shorts and socks, and a housecoat. He had a toothbrush in his mouth.

'I just woke up,' he mumbled.

It was seven in the evening. He looked bloated and strange. He hugged me like it was the single most important thing in the world, kissed me eight times on both cheeks and before I could start to tell him what happened, he said, 'Wait, give me a minute,' and ran back to his room as though he had put Obama on hold. Of course, there was nothing of that sort, he just wanted to lock himself up, watch videos of operations—those that involved lots of gore and blood (think kidney stones, bypass surgeries, liver transplants, lung congestions—you get the picture?) and he didn't want to deal with the reality of the world, or with me, or with himself. He didn't come down for three days after that. He hadn't shaved. He hadn't changed. He hadn't washed his hair.

His behaviour had taken a turn for the worst, my mother said. Oftentimes we wondered if it was the grief of losing his brother, and then his twin sister in quick succession. His sadness didn't seem like an archetypal lamentation; it was some terrifyingly abnormal version of misery, one that we had never been witness to before. It came at him like an avalanche of aggregated suppressed emotions, something that had accumulated inside him through the years. At the time, we thought that perhaps the three siblings wanted to stick together in their afterlife, given how lackadaisical their relationship was in this life. Gravy couldn't sleep and lay jostling about like an owl, he was worried that he would lose himself to his own dangerous subconscious where he might, just might, end up seeing his sister and brother run down the hill, and then up the road, then down the meadow, and then up the air, and then inside the red-lined clouds to never be seen again. That was puzzling and an incorrect assumption on our part—mostly because he wasn't all that close to them. He was cordial, but nothing more. It was a little antiseptic, the relationship between all three of them. All three siblings led separate lives in separate corners of a galaxy of their own making. As they grew older, the three of them just grew further apart. At the most, they appeared like unacknowledged third cousins from two different families brought together by someone who had married a dozen times in between.

My mother said that Gravy came out of his room only once the whole time I was gone. Apparently, when a fire broke out and damaged the neighbour's home, he rushed over barefoot, donning just his housecoat, monkey cap (even though it was a supernova of a blazing summer) and boxer shorts and his camera dangling over his bare chest to take pictures, almost relishing the sadistic exercise of watching something so precious disintegrate.

The truth was that he mostly stopped going out after he had an accident. He had dozed off for a split second on the wheel while driving home. The car flipped over a huge boulder and somersaulted mid-air. At some point through the carnage, he escaped with some bones broken and with half of his left eyebrow missing, leaving him beautifully flawed. His chiselled nose was flattened just a little bit at its tip, leaving a scar that made him appear like a Dalmatian.

Eventually, Gravy stopped going out altogether. He had a growing aversion to sunlight, of the air outside, and had all these conspiracy theories floating around in his head. His room/study was a mess. It was drenched in a permanent state of midnight. Gravy imagined that he was living in a bunker; and blocked out even a slither of light or life that sneaked in from underneath the door cracks. My mother joked nervously that our house looked like a funeral parlour. It no longer smelt of freshly baked goodness. But the truth was that the grey gloom had not just seeped inside the whole house, becoming a chilly dampness somewhat like a fat fungus that authoritatively declares itself to be spread and stained on the walls and chairs and the sheets and towels, but it had also gone inside the rooms of the man of the house. It was like a terrifying houseguest that wouldn't leave.

Having a conversation with Gravy was like going to Turkey with a Russian phrasebook.

Gravy would say that he was going to sleep for a few hours now, then a few hours at a night.

'Because if I sleep a little bit at night, and a little bit more during daytime, then I can be vigilant if they come to get me.' He spoke in a rushed, stage-whispery voice punctuated by long pauses.

'Who?' I asked Gravy.

'I can't tell you now, they might hear me. Some secrets can kill you.' He'd start muttering to himself.

'What secrets?'

'What month are we in now, Zef?' he said instead of answering my question.

'June.'

'Oh no, the rains will be here soon. July I am getting fat, August run, September sleep, October wind, November rain. December cold. January, February . . . Who are you? March . . . the ides of. April fool. Okay, I am going upstairs.' Gravy would go off into his non-sequitured cocoon.

Gravy was choking on those words that were never said. But

my mother stayed close to him, trying to understand what he was not saying, trying to puzzle together all the words that he was not using, trying to be the anchor in his squall. His insanity fell over him like rain, as though some sort of a . . . of a burkha—for the lack of a better metaphor—like a big, black, sweat-inducing polyester curtain that drowned him under itself.

He was caustic, inaccessible and, during the final moments, he was etiolating towards becoming someone who enjoyed behaving like a splenetic lunatic. He moved with stubborn restraint, his scowling, haunting eyes in some faraway cloud. His mood went from normal to a suicidal psychopath's in a minute. There were some sort of vile atomic neutrons that blazed through his veins. Gravy eventually broke the phone with a hammer; he joked about eating pesticides; he chewed on an electric wire and burned a corner of his bottom lip, leaving a dent on his skin; he was perennially upset about everything; he wanted to suffer; his grief hung like a loaded revolver that was always about to go off; he stank of shit and gripe; he cried like a child; he contemplated applying for a gun licence; he started believing in werewolves; he tried to cut his wrists; he practised committing suicide by holding on to the fan and jumping off the stool; he tried to cut his eyelashes; he kept scribbling incessantly on various papers scattered all over his room and in margins of over-filled diaries; he was obsessed with the idea of dying and amused himself in researching the quickest and the weirdest ways to die; he regaled me with ghastly stories like a butcher lacing his meat; he kept apologizing to us; he never made eye contact with us; he fantasized about his funeral.

These are the things I remember. I told myself to forget all the other nonsense that he did.

He was trying to die, and we were trying to make him live. He had made up his mind, now he just needed his body to follow him.

He couldn't bear to live one inch more, one second longer. It seemed as though he was in such a racing hurry that all he needed to do was wear his overcoat, pull up those collars and get into a coffin.

When I spoke to my mother about my adventures with Don, she seemed unfazed, almost as though she would have been terribly disappointed had none of the spectacle unfolded. She knew only too well that Don and drama always went together.

It was all a part of his Don-ness.

'Did he take you to the Theosophical Society?' she asked me.

'No,' I said.

'That library there was his favourite haunt. He'd befriend strange people from there, sneak them some beer, and bring them home.'

'Well, that wasn't so far off the mark from what we did,' I said.

'What do you mean?'

'Well, one day he dragged me to the hospital and made me a watchman—I had to alert him if the warden showed up as he was feeding his friend whisky through a straw. Then a few days later that man escaped from the hospital and came and stayed with us for a few days.'

'Must have been Mani mama, that drunkard,' she said.

'How did you know?'

'He used to do that even when I was a child,' my mother said.

'Yes, I suppose so. But then as soon as he left, there was this other man who played your piano. I actually wondered why no one ever played it. It was so amazing but then Don just ruined that day. He got so angry. I'd never seen him like that before. His face just turned another shade of purple, like some weird version of Captain Haddock. He started beating that man with an umbrella. That man must have known you because he kept saying to me that I look like you. He spoke in a strange manner, some weird accent, and you know . . . he hardly had any . . .'

'Eyebrows?' she completed my sentence.

'Yes! How did you know?'

'Robert?'

'Yes, yes, but Don kept confusing me. He told me that his name was Roger, then he said it was Robert, so I just called him R/R.' I laughed.

My mother didn't. I thought, at the time, that her face seemed stung by some imaginary wasp.

'Don hit him so badly when he played the piano that he ran for his life. His piano playing made Don cry.'

'I hate Don. I don't understand why you and Gravy seem to be so blind when it comes to him,' she spat out. 'He is a liar of the lowest order.'

'You should have seen Don, he really misses you.'

She ignored me. For my mother, hating Don was the most familiar emotion; she used that as a security blanket.

It only makes sense now that I am writing it. It must have been quite a heavy load to carry on her scrawny shoulders, the memories of so many people, all of them wreaking havoc in their own way, taking only what they wanted and leaving. It all must have pained her immensely, in the same way that it pains my heart as I write it—the realization of it all hitting me like a locomotive.

A few days after I returned, my mother called out to me from the garden as I got home from school. She liked gardening in her bathrobe. She had a diploma in ikebana, though I'd never seen her arrange anything spectacular.

I waited quietly because she said being around plants 'centred' her.

She finally threw away the flowers that she had plucked from the garden, disgusted at snipping everything away, and looked at me with an expression that said: well, that's that.

'How was school?' She asked me, more out of courtesy than concern. My parents felt that school was a waste of time but sent me anyway because they felt that I would lose out on friends. I was mostly homeschooled in an unrestricted regimen.

'Dull,' I said.

'Tell me something . . .' she started.

'What?'

'So Don really cried when Robert touched my piano, huh?'

'Yes,' I told her.

'Hard to believe it,' she said.

'Why?' I asked.

'No reason. What else did he tell you?' she asked.

I wasn't surprised at her style of interrogation. She was made up like this. She would always ask pertinent questions long after the moment had passed and the urgency of the matter had faded away.

'I already told you everything,' I said.

'I was a little distracted,' my mother said.

'He spoke about his affair in Warsaw, then how he met Sancho, and . . .'

'About Sancho?' She spat out the name as though I had exposed a ghastly secret shrouded by years of hush-hushness. 'I don't get why he would speak about Sancho to *you*?'

'Why not?' I asked. 'You never talk about her, much.'

'What else did he say about Sancho?'

'He told me how he met her. That's about it. Then Robert came back.'

'What do you mean back?' she asked.

'He was there when I got to Don's house. He left to go to Pondicherry and came back,' I said.

'Oh—do you think he lives there?' she asked me.

'I don't know. It seems like he comes and goes,' I said. 'Why don't you ever talk about Sancho?' I pressed again. 'I had never even seen what she looks like until Don showed me a picture of her. 'You have never even showed me a picture,' I whined.

'She was pretty ferocious-looking, wasn't she?' My mother said, instead of giving me an explanation. 'She applied rabbit's blood to her hair when she was young so it wouldn't turn grey.'

'She even had a gun in that picture I saw,' I told her.

'The gun belonged to her father,' my mother said.

'Oh. It wasn't a toy gun?' I asked, only half surprised.

'No. Anyway, I don't want to talk about Sancho,' my mother said, dismissing the topic.

'Why not?' I persisted.

She was quiet. I think I saw her hold back tears.

In fact, growing up, my mother spoke about Sancho very, very little. Maybe a handful of times. Four fingers-full, actually. Maybe because she only had a handful of memories.

She later proceeded to ask me a million questions: 'Was the piano still maintained in good condition? Were my music notebooks still there? Were the edges on the last page clipped? What song did Robert play? Did he play well?'

'Yes, yes, not sure, Gershwin's *Rhapsody in Blue*, I think so.'

'He didn't play well?' she asked.

'I thought he did but Don interrupted him when he got into the thick of it.'

'Don is such a rabble-rouser.'

'I feel sad for him,' I said.

'I don't,' my mother retorted. 'He lives in the hell he has created.'

'Don't you love him?' I asked.

'I don't know,' she said. 'Right now, it's a no.'

'But he *is* your father,' I urged; at the time I didn't fathom how one could not really love their parents. Ah, the innocence and ignorance of youth.

'That doesn't really mean anything,' she said.

'Why not?' I asked.

'Let's just say that I have limited patience for *mauvaise foi* and Don . . . because of it.'

At the time, I wanted to ask her what that expression *mauvaise foi* meant but I didn't. I remembered trying to find it in the dictionary and underlining the phrase in red when I was writing it down in my diary at the time.

She was digesting all the information I gave her, processing vague memories. She opened her mouth to say something but stopped. Perhaps she was scared to say the things worth saying so she didn't say anything at all.

Then, as if on some silent cue from the heavens, she started playing an invisible piano. Her nimble fingers kept playing a silent melody that only her ears were privy to, her eyes shut in deep concentration lest her focus drift away towards something as irrelevant and unwelcome as reality. God no! Who would want a wretched thing like life to ruin a beautiful moment?

After some ten minutes, she opened her eyes and said, 'That sounded good . . . in my head at least.'

'I thought you hated the piano,' I said.

'I do.'

'Then?'

'I just wanted to know if I remember the keys.'

'Do you?' I asked.

'Yes. I suppose even if I want to forget the keys, I can't. You know what's strange?' she asked me.

'What?'

'We try to forget someone or something so desperately so that we can move on, in life or otherwise, and in that desperation to forget, in that earnest striving, we end up remembering every little thing, every emotion and every unfulfilled sense of longing,' she said.

That was true, I thought. We never really forget anything, we probably just don't think about it for a while. And it was only a little too ironic that the very home my mother ran away from to forget everything and start afresh was the very space where she returned to take shelter when she felt she had lost everything.

You can't escape who you are, or for that matter, why you are.

Two weeks after that meltdown over the phone with my mother, I left New Zealand to come to Don's house. I remember the moment; it was hipstamatic. The day was dark and violent, the ground was cold and there was a rogue wind. The sky was spread like skin. It seemed to be gauging the landscape with a bitter, distant gaze. It was Sweeney Todd weather. It had been three years since I was here and now it looked like this place had been condemned. As I entered the gates, the house was just mired in a bad cloud, with not a hint of sun caressing it. It seemed as though it was a study in loneliness. The garden had grown into a sloth heaven. An awkward silence stuck its neck out of the house. Don's booming laughter did not spill through the mosaic. That tree in the centre of the house, with its thirsty branches, looked like a ravenous criminal in captivity, quite like the owner sleeping inside.

As soon as I stepped inside the house, I knew this time I couldn't just slip back into my childhood here. You could tell something had altered in the same way you can smell a midsummer rain gurgling up a sandstorm in its wake. I didn't want to go back. Who would, when you are trapped between two people, one dying, and one with no interest in living?

The second my mother smelt my arrival, she hijacked me. She came out with two glasses of whisky, because in this house whisky is drunk more than water. Her sari was hanging like a carcass over her shoulder. Her huge dolorous eyes looked wired enough to have a life of their own. She offered me a glass even before I had put my bags down, and started to unleash so many days' worth of secrets for future melancholy.

My mother told me that Don had suffered a terrible stroke. It was a potent cocktail of a failing liver and a weak heart.

She left as soon as she could get her body to move from Delhi to Madras. I think she was just looking for an excuse to leave our house anyway. She was all alone while I was wasting away at the end of the world.

'How did you know which hospital in Madras?' I asked. Seriously, of all the questions, I could only think of asking *this*? I must be nuts.

'There is only one that would have taken Don in, it was owned by one of his gambling acquaintances,' she said.

The doctors had predicted a slight chance of recovery. But, at this point, Don would be dead if he didn't detoxify. My mother said that he couldn't talk, couldn't feel ('could he ever,' she muttered), and can't probably even live unless there is a miracle. She eventually brought him home and managed to arrange her emotions in the same way she arranged his medicines: in a sterile, medicated manner.

I couldn't resist the urge to see Don so I rushed to his room the second I could get away from my mother. En route, I noticed that his study was locked.

'Never enter that cave', she offered immediately. 'I don't have the strength to discover what might be inside. Besides, he's hidden the key. Imagine that,' she sneered, 'even on his deathbed, the old goon has got his tracks covered.'

I didn't say anything, just made my way to Don's bedroom.

That familiar smell of spilled cognac punched me on my face.

Don was lying in his four-poster bed. He was wrapped in a thick quilt made of old Victorian-patterned lingerie in lace and silk, all seamlessly and adroitly sewed up together with the zips intact and oozing with seduction. The pillow cases were padded bras with all their straps sown on top of them. I had never seen anything quite like it. My mother said that Don had stitched up all of Sancho's privates years ago when she'd left. It was a sight that needed to be photographed and preserved in the museum of the absurd: the image of Don's cloudy face, asleep and nuzzled between the sea of mountainous bumps (the labels slyly gleamed a faded 34B). I had to suppress a laugh each time I saw him.

He looked like the frayed hide of some extinct species, ensconced in his own version of a Hollywood boudoir. All he needed was a mirror on the ceiling and one of those frocks that unemployed aristogents wore in pre-war England. He was fast asleep. Or dead. I hoped not. But somehow with him it seemed as though he was merely resting. I put my hands underneath Don's nostrils to check if he was still breathing, his warm prescription-laced breath kept coming out in bits and spurts, while my heart beat furiously outside my chest, lest his stopped. It was short dizzy spells of terror. The Byzantine gold ring that he wore on his little finger on his left hand shone like God's only light in this dull, tragic room. Don once teasingly told me that he had stolen it from a Pope who had inherited it as a generational heirloom. Maybe he did. With Don, you never knew.

Underneath his pillow, I saw a book peeping out of a velvet case.

My mother and I took turns looking after Don, and each other. But it was mostly me who did the looking after. She somehow stopped after I came. But we, my mother and me, we required each other's inertia to remain in motion.

Sometimes Don's faithless body would let out a fart so vicious it could uproot a tree. It was like some bad rendition of calliope. And then the other times he would let out a massive breath, which had a smell so foul—as though tiny animals had died inside his mouth—it could kill a small child. It felt as though his last meal before falling into this coma must have been stale pigeon. He'd start shaking, rocking violently, silently and his eyeballs would rocket up and down like a ghost had gotten in between them. During one such fit, the key of his study slid out from underneath the mattress. I kept it with me.

Those few days were like twilight. I could hear him moan and grunt, even when I was outside in the garden. Maybe the sound was stuck in my ear, maybe I was hallucinating, or maybe it was real. I'd run and go and see him. But my mother didn't. She treated his moans in the same way one who lives by the sea treats the sound of breaking waves. She would walk past him, paying him less attention than the scenery. She treated him as though she was handling a dead rat, with tongs and gloves.

'It serves him right, he made us suffer when he was alive, it is only karma-induced coma that is making him suffer now. Let the clouds come in and smother him in this trance,' she said.

She made no bones of her hatred for the man. At least she was not lying. Maybe George Orwell was right when he wrote that 'during times of universal deceit, telling the truth becomes a revolutionary act'.

'Why do you want him dead?' I asked.

'Why do you want him alive?' she retorted.

'Because he is Don, he isn't supposed to be dead.'

'You know, Zef, for Don, love, home and family didn't mean anything,' she said. 'It was always what he needed, he'd take what he wanted and never think of consequences. It wasn't about his sexual preference or orientation, it was just about the act, the rush of it for that blinding penis-informed second.'

Over the course of those days, my mother spoke incessantly and incoherently, in creepy bits and spurts, in riddles and metaphors. That probably explains the manner in which I have written it all down here. In the same manner she chose to reveal what was not necessary, to make sense of it in the most thorny way.

On one of those days, when I woke up at an unearthly hour, I called out to my mother but she was nowhere about. A panic grew inside me like mystic pain, it swelled like a fat man's belly while he snored the highest pitch he could summon. I rushed through the house looking for her, with my mind racing, wondering if she had also pushed herself over the edge and had died. After I couldn't find her anywhere, I started drowning in despair. Wait, drown. Pool. The empty pool. Yes. I ran.

My right hand had started shaking, taking on a life of its own. I ran towards the pool praying—a series of promises of denying myself everything that I enjoyed—that she wasn't flat, face down in a pool of blood and that if I found her alive, I was going to lock her up forever, and that I would sit her down, shut her up, calm her down and get along with her. When I didn't find her near the pool, I edged closer to it . . . my jaws rattling like a bunch of skeletons in a big box . . . I found her sitting inside the dry pool, topless, with diver's goggles and a rolled Rizla in her hand.

Her hair looked like she had run the comb brusquely through the top part of her head twice, leaving the bottom part straggly, and knotty, like a pigeon's tail. It would have made for an epic photograph, a scene decorated by Lartigue's eye. She saw my shadow rise from the back and cover her up. Without even turning around, she instinctively raised her hand to give me the extra glass of vodka that she had kept for me and the cigarette she had rolled. She knew I would come here. My mother courage; my lady death. I went and sat next to her. I saw the toy swords that Don and I had battled with the last time I was here. They were thrown in the corner, dust laden.

'No one ever cleans this house, that's why the lives are such a mess here,' my mother said. 'This house was such a disaster, sometimes I think I would like to watch it burn.'

She seemed pensive. I had caught her thinking. Oh no, I knew she was preparing to start burying me alive with some additional information. I felt the slow rise of a panic attack. My right hand kept moving unconsciously. I didn't realize it until my mother gave me half a smile.

'Your hand . . . you can never really control that hand of yours, can you?' she asked me.

My hand was still quivering like a jellyfish on sand, beating to some invisible beat.

'Oh, sorry, I didn't realize it was moving,' I said. 'I got a bit worried when I didn't see you inside.'

'You know your father used to do the exact same thing,' she said.

'Gravy never mov . . .'

'No, your real father,' she cut me again in between.

We stayed quiet for a while. Now I understood the vodka.

'He . . .' She was slowly trying to get herself to speak about him. 'He had this habit of unconsciously moving his left hand in the air,' she said. 'He'd be smoking and then start moving his hand as though he was writing some poem mid-air. He'd do it with his cigarette so it was great watching the smoke twirl.'

'Why was that marriage a secret?' I asked impatiently.

'It was too precious. I thought the sun would burn it if I exposed it,' she explained matter-of-factly, getting up and moving towards the house. I followed her in.

'How did you meet him?' I persisted carefully.

'I met him at the zoo here in Madras.'

'At the zoo?'

'Yes, that day, I had read in the papers that there were these tiger and leopard cubs brought to the Madras zoo, so I went to see them. He . . . he was standing there with his pet monkey . . . it had a funny name . . . Theophilus. When I was playing with the cubs, his monkey jumped up, hurt one of them and bit me,' she told me.

So then he helped her clean up her wound and they ended up speaking for a bit.

'It was an instant connection, so effortless and easy,' she said.

He worked for the State Bank of India and was going to be travelling all across rural Maharashtra to set up branches, but said that he would like to write to her. She agreed.

'Over the course of the next few months, your father and I exchanged letters and postcards wherever he went, and later he sent me cassettes with songs that he had composed. Since we couldn't talk, he wrote and sang all these songs for me. He said he longed for me and that sometimes he couldn't breathe because he missed having me around. And that these songs were the only saving grace. To this I asked him how he would know if he missed having me around when I had never been around him in the first place. With his next letter, he sent me a train ticket. At the time he was living in Ganapatipule, this tranquil little beach town on the Konkan coast, hidden and unscarred by the rest of the world. So I went. I had nothing to lose, no one to owe any explanation to, so I left.'

'Okay. What next?' I asked.

'Then what, we started living together. We continued to live cheaply as one,' she laughed. 'Him, me and Theo. Something about his disposition hinted that he wasn't a rapist. He loved poetry, he was ugly but he was quiet and he seemed sincere. We were both scared at the speed at which our romance was progressing but . . .'

'But what?' I asked.

'Nothing, we still dove into each other,' my mother said. And knowing my mother, and her weak yearning heart, she would have plunged headlong into him, swimming into his veins and nerves. But then, I suppose, she was probably the sort who would love the one she lusted after even if he'd only given her a glance, or a kiss, or a handshake, or a nod. I didn't interrupt her.

She went on speaking unabated: 'I thought this was the romance that I was waiting for all my life. That this was the romance that I *deserved.* There was something like love brewing. I imagined that our love story was something like a dance, I allowed him to lead me and I followed.'

Apparently, it was all too bloody magical. They lived underneath twinkling, clear constellations where there was everything they needed. Biscuits, cornflakes, eggs, bread, desire.

'We kissed until our bodies glowed. You know, Zef, he had a way of speaking without moving his lips too much, and had a prodigious stare, just like you do. He would stare at me the same way you are staring at me right now. We laughed a lot, we were comfortable in our silence. I could feel my heart parking itself in a happy calm space.'

'I thought your heart was broken beyond repair,' I said, sounding so evil to my own ears. I don't know why I was feeling so angry.

'I thought so too,' she said so serenely that I wanted to kill her. 'But,' she continued, 'I seemed to fit into his life so easily and correctly. He lit me up from the inside, his actions made me feel like the one. And I was ready to fall in love with him. I *wanted* to fall in love with him, and I did.'

She said that they lived in a house as big as a cupboard, and if a storm visited then it would have sucked their roof off. But because it was on the banks of the beach, they could escape to the sea at a blink's notice. (The man loved to swim and spent his spare time trying to build a boat.) They lived their love to the soundtrack of the waves.

'We were lost to the world, and the world was lost to us. What was the point in finding our way back?' she said. 'He was the stable sort. It seemed like his emotions were as steady and stable as his desk job at the bank.'

He used to mumble to my mother between quiet breaths, 'Where were you all these years? Where were you five years ago when I was a hopeless romantic?'

She told him, 'I am here now, aren't I? He told me that he was so incredibly lucky to have met me and that he was searching for someone as insane as me for years. But in the past five years, he had apparently tutored his heart to never go astray. So I asked him if he still had some heart left.'

He looked at her and nodded his head, he made a small circle with his index finger and thumb and said that he had a little bit.

She said to him, 'I wanted to tell him that I have enough for both of us. Of heart, I mean. But I didn't. I wish I wasn't so messy, Zef, not so apparent. But I was. All I told him was that I'd never hurt him. I never hurt anyone. I knew what a gut-wrenching feeling of despair and helplessness it was to be hurt, so I'd never subject anyone to that.'

He said to her, 'I don't want to hurt you either but . . . but . . . I do have this tendency to go off the grid, to go and hide, clear my head, clear my life.'

'So I told him, don't do it,' she said. 'I am here now. Don't clear me out.'

'It's that simple, huh?' he asked her.

'Yes, really, it is that simple,' she said.

'Okay, I won't,' he promised her. 'I just . . . I just don't know what I want. I know I want you but I don't know about the future.'

'So what, the passion is in the risk,' she said.

'In hindsight, Zef, I should have fled then and there. But I didn't.'

'Why?' I asked my mother.

She said that it was blissful not to question everything, and just be. In that time, in that collective space. With him, she said that it wasn't about the length of time they were together; it was the 900-foot-deep intensity of their relationship.

'I believed in all his valiant gestures of bringing me to come live with him. I thought that the stars had finally aligned themselves perfectly, and that life had taken care of me by proving that there was someone who was attempting to . . . make sense of me . . . and love me in his own way. That this man, this everyday man with an everyday person's job at the bank, that I met by chance at the zoo was whom I was waiting for my whole life. That this man would turn the scales and weed out all the negatives.'

'Did you ever tell him all this?' I asked my mother.

'No.'

'Did you ever tell him you loved him?'

'No. I was scared he might leave if I told him.'

'So then how did you get married then if you lived in such silly fear?' I asked. It was a logical question.

She was quiet for a while. For. A. Very. Long. Time.

Oh no. I thought. There was something else here that she didn't tell me.

'We didn't actually get around to getting *married* married . . . at least, legally speaking'.

'What?' I was shocked.

'The intention was there but I think it was timing. We went a couple of times to the local temple to get married, but the priest wasn't around,' she said. 'So we thought we would come back again another time, maybe tomorrow. But tomorrow turned into yesterday. Anyway, after this happened a couple of times, we realized the moment had passed us by,' she said.

Soon after all that, one day, the two of them went for a walk in that town. It was an in-between hour: 4 p.m. Too late for anything, too early for dinner. It got a bit poetic. All of a sudden the summer sun suddenly gave way to rowdy clouds, which seemed more like a gurgling bunch of students.. The two of them walked slowly but she quietly realized that she was falling in love even more urgently.

They milled the empty streets and that's when my mother spotted an old pawnshop hidden away inside some crooked, filthy by-lane. She tried on an old ring, one that had a secret compartment to store opium. As luck (or fate, or irony) would have it, the ring got stuck in her index finger, and no amount of grease got it out. My real father had no other option but to buy it. While walking back to their human kennel, she told him that she would treat this as a wedding ring. Engaged; married; same thing, different jewellery.

'May as well,' she said. 'We do live in a world where we tell everyone a little something. If this wasn't love, then what is?'

That's when they realized that they had only known each other for eighty-one days.

They saw a white peacock blaze its wings. They celebrated with drinking tea (a sachet my real father, apparently, had carried in his pocket).

She said that, with Theo as a witness, they got married-ish. 'At least, in our heads we were married. We spoke our vows. But he recited that poem by Auden, the one that starts with stop all the clocks, cut off the telephone. It was the only poem he knew.'

'But that's a funeral poem,' I said.

'Maybe that was a sign that I didn't see,' my mother mumbled, twisting her mouth, squishing her lips.

My body froze in anger. My head was exploding. I screamed at her, 'That's not marriage, that's delusion! I am a bastard. And a monkey was witness to your fake marriage. A fucking monkey?'

'It was more human than most humans,' my mother offered by way of logic.

I wanted to kill her there and then with a butter knife.

'Do you know how incredibly stupid you sound?' I said.

'You weren't a bastard baby. I mean, you aren't,' she said.

My mother was floundering with words going all over the place. She must have regretted telling me all this. For all her hippy-dippy behaviour, I am rather conservative. I think the orthodoxness skips a generation. Insert confused smiley.

'What poem did you recite?' I asked her as an afterthought, just before the silence sat between us, as if it were some critical information that I really needed to know.

'The only one I know by heart,' she said.

'Which is?'

'Thomas Gray's "Elegy Written in a Country Churchyard".'

I was about to say that was equally depressing . . . but by then she had started reciting the poem.

'. . . For them no more the blazing hearth shall burn,
Or busy housewife ply her evening care
No children run to lisp their sire's return,
Or climb his knees the envied kiss to share . . .'

My mother said that around that happy time, she still kept up with her morbid habit of scanning through the obits in the paper. That's how she found that her mother had died. At first, she said that the photo in the obituary 'somewhat looked' like an older, more burdened, version of her mother but then what she remembered of her mother seemed almost like some kind of an apparition under the sun. But it was her.

It read:

Sancho
Once a loving Wife and Mother
1933–1981

The obit was released by Our Lady of Sea Church, Gokarna.

'My eyes processed it but my mind and heart didn't seem to care,' my mother whispered almost inaudibly. 'I didn't have any memories of Sancho so I wasn't sure what to feel at all.'

But, strangely enough, it made her want to take the journey to Gokarna to find the life that her mother had lived.

'I think it was just something that my feet decided on doing,' she said.

Some journeys in life are like that, aren't they? You take them because your feet feel a pressing urge to take you there, and you don't know why and you don't have the strength to ask all the whys. You just follow along hoping that the reason is revealed to you, and once it is—you hope that it accomplishes what it is meant to accomplish, and satiates whatever urge it was meant to satiate.

Upon reaching that church, my mother was told by a priest there that Sancho had converted to Christianity a decade ago in the hope that Jesus might just bring her husband and daughter back—given that the prayers to the other gods hadn't yielded any return. So, in a way, the priest was delighted that my mother had come. 'The prayers had worked, after all,' he squealed in delight. So what if she came after Sancho died. Her daughter had *come*—that was the point of the prayer.

The priest took my mother to Sancho's old family home—the same home from where Don took the equine Trojan beast—and said that she had spent a lifetime staring at the gates. In the end, she was tired of living, tired of waiting.

'Entering that house, Zef, it was—how can I put it—like staring at a dead writer's typewriter.'

There were diaries, closets after closets brimming with them, waiting to be read, waiting to be purged into, words wailing out to be understood. Those diaries catalogued Sancho's life from the time she left Don's elaborate universe until she created her own cocoon in that small beach town. It also chronicled how she tried to come to terms with his bisexuality.

'Maybe that's where you get your writing habit from,' she smiled.

On the face of it, the two of them, Don and Sancho, seemed to be living the postcard life, la dolce vita, in Madras. With each passing day, Sancho was falling increasingly in love with the very idea of Don, my mother gathered from reading her diaries.

'The pages were all about Don, Don, Don—morning, noon and midnight. He was her sunrise, he was her shade. Her obsession with Don continued for reams and reams of pages. It was exhausting just reading that,' my mother grunted.

Sancho treated Don like some eccentrically charming museum, and she wrote about him as though she was gaining some kind of doctorate on his quirks. It was all about how well-travelled Don was, and how beautiful his collection of cufflinks and maps of vague islands were, and how he could always predict the arrival of rain, and how he never walked, he just glided into rooms and lives, and his strange collection of hats, his rosewood walking sticks (which he didn't need), first edition books from dead libraries, his collection of bronze paperweights, cinema tickets from some Polish country, odd coloured socks, corks of bottles he dove into, rolled-up posters of Rock Hudson and Sinatra, and how he was such a man's man, how he could hold a champagne flute with the tip of his right index finger, and how he had a revolving door of best friends that he changed like the lamps in the house, almost like flavours of the month, how well he kept her, and how he pretended to be a professional vagabond when he actually punched in long gruelling hours at his leather machinery business overseeing every minute detail from collecting shipments to sourcing deals and every boring DIY stuff in between.

Soon enough, Sancho wanted children. But Don had a bouquet of excuses. He was so busy, he had work, he needed time, he didn't think he'd be a good father, he needed to make more money, he was just getting used to Sancho and a baby would mean additional responsibility, he preferred pets, he wanted some freedom. But

Sancho, being the eternal optimist that she was, had discounted all his excuses. She thought patience would be the key. She always thought that.

Sancho soon realized what Don had actually meant when he said that he needed his freedom. It was freedom from domestication. It didn't require her to be a genius to discover that Don seemed to crowd his marriage with his Galahad ways. 'Don loved me,' she had written, 'but he didn't seem to love *only* me.' It all unfolded gradually—Sancho went to a party only to notice one of Don's lady-friends wearing the same custom-made necklace that he had bought for her the week before. An absolutely livid Sancho confronted Don who didn't deny buying it for the other woman. In fact, he had the gall to say that 'it was similar but not the same. Didn't you notice that your necklace had a few strings less than hers? I thought you might have liked your piece slightly subtle. That woman has a rather gaudy appetite for jewellery.' Once Sancho discovered a present lying on Don's desk that she thought was meant for her but then it never made its way to her. And there was the other time when Don returned from a business trip with some lady's scarf in his suitcase. Don didn't hide the fact that he was enamoured by beautiful women. He had a voracious appetite, and he didn't care if Sancho had caught him on various occasions canoodling women of all ages wherever he could, whenever he could, just because he could.

Sancho stopped writing about Don's flagrant philandering, passively accepting it like a fly. My mother said that it must have hurt Sancho to write about it because she would be recollecting from her memory, replaying it over to write it all down and for what, and for whom? So she stopped writing about that large, vacant period in her life, abruptly, as though the idea came to her one morning. She must have thought that by not writing about it, she could live in a make-believe world. Don was the tempestuous love of her life, and Sancho just accepted whatever version of himself—sometimes that was more intense than a physical relationship, she reasoned—he gave her, and made peace with the fact that the only way she could have him was if she could share him with other women. It was the only way out for her. My mother said that the truth was that Sancho didn't know that she had a choice to get out of this situation, so she stuck around because that's what she thought was the only thing she could have done.

After a year or more of this sort of living arrangement, where the two of them wheeled in their own worlds in the same house, Sancho's constant drone about a baby somehow successfully managed to convince Don.

'He must have thought that if he agreed, then he can pack a pregnant Sancho off to her mother's house and he can continue living the way he always did, like the heathen that he was,' my mother spat out the words.

Okay, one child. That was non-negotiable. Sancho was upset but it was better than having no children. After a lot of huffing and puffing, and a lot of praying, she got pregnant. For Sancho, it was all about mittens and candyfloss, cuddly bears and midnight fairies. Don went the other extreme. He claimed to be excited but didn't seem to have the flourish of emotions that Sancho craved. Don seemed to behave increasingly strange and aloof. He still travelled a lot but when he was home, he'd be ensconced in his study devouring some book, or getting drunk.

She dismissed the prospect of impending parenthood as a case of nerves. 'Who wouldn't be? I am too,' she rationalized in her diary.

Each time Sancho would try to talk to him about building a nursery, or buying some supplies, or just general chit-chat, she felt as though she was talking to a wall. He wouldn't register or at least he'd pretend that he wasn't hearing her. The only time he did indulge in some amount of banter was when he wanted her to organize his clothes, his food, his garden or his usual grand parties. On those decadent nights he'd be the perfect host, the perfect husband, the perfect human being, the perfect father-to-be. But, no sooner had the last drunken guest trickled out, Don would coolly glide out into the darkness without informing her. Or just disappear somewhere in the house and lock the door (oftentimes with a lady companion). Or go off to his bedroom and sleep off his intoxication.

But one night, just as Sancho was cleaning up, she caught Don kissing a young man—maybe a member of the staff—ferociously. Don saw her staring at him and said that he was just bidding him goodbye with a tip for a job well done and fumbled back inside in an elliptical pattern. He was terribly drunk. When Sancho tried to take off his shoes to tuck him into a couch, he blurted out that he had been sleeping with other men—for a while now, for a long while. 'Didn't you know by now?' he laughed.

Sancho was too stunned to speak. Don snored himself to a deep, soulful slumber while his wife walked around the house wondering if she had heard the man right. Everything gets exaggerated when one is drunk, and if it is dark outside. Even if Sancho somehow had an inkling that Don was a rather strange bedfellow, she didn't even once suspect that he could possibly be bisexual. Even the possibility of such a thing had never occurred to her. Agreed that Don lived in a slightly exaggerated universe, but she was his accomplice, wasn't she? 'Together we had made *this* universe, *our* universe,' she had written in a shaky, nervous handwriting. 'With the cursives running with anxiety,' my mother added. No, he couldn't be . . . could he? How *could* one even sleep with men? How *does* one even sleep with a man? He did have male friends but . . . no, absolutely, definitely not. She would talk to him in the clear, crisp light of day and everything would be all right. Yes, it really would. Maybe he was kissing that man as a dare of some sort, she reasoned to herself.

The next morning Sancho tried to work up the courage to ask Don what she saw and what she thought she may have heard. A large part of her didn't want to ask him because she was afraid of what that answer may entail. She tiptoed outside his study where she saw an impeccably dressed Don wearing his starched linen suit, beautiful wingtip shoes, and a cravat, reading a book—his drink in a Wedgwood teacup on a table next to him. He looked like he was posing for a painting, with an imaginary background of children playing in the summer fields behind him, a sharp streak of studio-light-esque sunshine allowing him to bask in the fake halo of golden happiness poking through his body.

'I don't know how long I stood there, watching him read, drink, read, drink, readdrinkreaddrink, his index finger twirling the pages. He didn't look up either. The skin on his face seemed to have shrunk, or maybe his bones had grown too big. I couldn't tell,' Sancho had written. Eventually, Don looked up, and said a casual 'oh hello you' like a passer-by and went about readingdrinking, unmoved from his spot.

Sancho couldn't wait any longer. She just blurted out if he remembered what he mumbled in his sleep, and what he had done when he was drunk. Don said 'yes' in a heartbeat, without even looking up from his book. Sancho let out nervous laughter. 'Oh, stop joking.' No response from Don. She prodded again and reminded him about what exactly he had said. Don said that she had heard him 'absolutely one hundred per cent correct'. 'But you were drunk?' she reminded him. He retorted with a simple, 'So?' Don got up and decided to leave for work promptly, leaving Sancho to her own devices. He remained as nonchalant with her about his sexuality as he had been with my mother; at the end, making the receiver of this information seem more stupid at not being able to handle the outrageous truth.

Still, our body sometimes grasps reality even before we make sense of it in our heads. She felt as though she got punched in the stomach. Sancho's worst nightmare occurred. She suffered a miscarriage. She was three-months pregnant at the time. On their way out from the clinic, Don gave Sancho what she described in her diary as 'a weak, half-hearted, hurried hug; like the sort of hug that you give a host whose party you have gate-crashed and broken something expensive, and now you have to rush out urgently before you get caught'.

But he returned home a new Don. Later that week, he bought her presents, he bought her clothes, he bought her jewellery, he bought a blue chandelier for his bathroom.

'Deep down, the bastard must have been relieved that there was no baby,' my mother said.

Sancho was a complete mess. She was angry, betrayed, confused and hurt that this entire marriage was turning out to be a complete sham. 'With each second, the anger rose inside me like some vomit that I had swallowed,' she had written. She lashed out at Don until she ran out of breath. He remained unfazed. He told her in a calm headmasterly tone that this was the way he was, a sexual savant of sorts, and he thought he could change after this marriage but he somehow simply couldn't. He enjoyed having sex with both women and men. But that didn't mean that he didn't love her. Don had assured her that it was just a physical need that had to be taken care of with his many dalliances that cut across both genders. She understood his attraction, and the satisfaction he may have derived from his affairs with women. What she couldn't fathom was what satisfaction he derived from sleeping with men.

Sancho tried to convince him that this was a bad phase that will pass, and that he can get over this 'inconvenient patch' if he tried, and she was sorry that she had failed him as a woman, and as a wife, and that it was all her fault, and that everything would become all right if only he put his mind to it, and that she was so sorry for being so pushy about having a child, and that they can try again whenever he was ready, and that she will give him all the time he needs to come back to his senses, and that he can sleep with all the women he wants but please not with men, and they can go to a godman in Kumbakonam to get some sort of help, and that he is just in some sort of bored company that lured him to be this way, and that he couldn't be this way, and that it was the influence of alcohol. Don heard her pleas and tried to placate her in the same way one comforts a mother whose child has died—that things will get better when they really won't.

In the days and months that followed, Sancho realized that she couldn't even discuss this with anyone. She didn't know what it was like to live without Don, and without loving him, no matter how impossible he made it. She also didn't have the courage to leave—what would she even say when people asked her what happened to her marriage? It was too embarrassing a secret to share. The shame of it all traumatized her. No, she would stay. She would make Don come back to her. Women seemed to be an easier gender to handle. But men? How does one even compete with that?

She had somehow convinced herself that it was all just a momentary lapse in personality and that the Don she loved would come back to her soon enough and love her the way she needed to be loved. She just had to give him that space. Isn't that what love is?

Instead, she tried to lose herself in a haze of everydayness. She pretended that nothing had happened. Don was uncaring but not unloving. He didn't try to counsel her to come to terms with his sexuality, all that would be too trivial for him. But he continued to provide for her and look after her as he always had. He didn't think that she would be capable of leaving him, instead opting to treat all this as an incidental part of their lives. He also managed to get Sancho a job at the local Montessori so her brain wouldn't run amok.

But in declaring what he did, Don had drawn some invisible boundaries in her life, and broken whatever she had set in his.

Sancho slowly started putting the pieces in her wretched puzzle together: she finally understood his flavour of the month, and became extra observant when Don's hands lingered on men a few seconds longer than necessary (they always did); or why sometimes his male friends never came with any wives or girlfriends. Now that Don's secret was out in the open, she didn't know what to do besides live alongside it like a bench partner she didn't like. Except this was not a semester but a life term.

From her diaries, my mother understood that Sancho tried to accept Don's sexual preferences, and eventually had to realize that she needed to make space for it in their lives, or she would end up losing him completely. He loved the taste of men and women, and her. 'After all, what is the purpose of love when it doesn't contain the happiness of the beloved?' she had written. It was like accommodating a huge elephant inside a cage, and making space for it because she loved it so much and didn't want to let it wander off by itself alone. With him, it was as though she was balancing herself on the tip of a cloud.

There were times that she followed him around the city (fearfully), but it became increasingly painful to see him laugh and look into someone else's eyes with a lingering, lustful gaze while she spent all her time talking to her own shadow. She'd come back home tear-stained and helpless, and retreat to a small, private, dark corner in her head where she tried to make sense of all her negative energy that she was accumulating by just loving this man and monster. It was a terrible, burning love that Sancho had for Don. But she also knew that if she added fuel to that fire, she would be the one getting burnt. But she kept telling herself that she would win back Don the same way she had won him over the first time around: through perseverance. 'Because if you are a good person, then good things will happen,' she had written. It just takes a little extra time.

A year had passed with Sancho and Don living like nothing more than housemates. They were civil and courteous to each other, as though they were the inn-keepers of this huge house whose owners were away. Don went about his life as though nothing had happened. He was having a blast now that nothing was hidden. Sancho strived to be the best version of herself. She felt like she was walking on eggshells, always watching him to make sure he was okay. It was all about meeting his needs. Even if Don noticed it, he pretended like that's what he expected out of her—nothing less. She wrote that she maintained the house with the precision of a nuclear scientist, she organized Don's study like a library, she took care of his food, his clothes, his odd-coloured socks, his cufflinks, his shoes, his watches, his semen-stained underwear.

'The arrangement must have worked very well for Don,' my mother said. 'He didn't need a wife; he needed a glorified housekeeper.'

Occasionally, Sancho would cuddle up with him in his bedroom and fall asleep. She missed him even while he was in another room. She loved him a little too much in spite of it all. She was so lonely even though she wasn't alone. For a few hours of shut-eye, everything would be great, as though the two of them went back drowsy-eyed to the start of their rainbow. But then she'd wake up in a silent panic, and a fear that would run like a bushfire from her belly to her feet, that this was real. She'd start wondering if Don deliberately kissed that man in front of her when she was pregnant so she *could* have a miscarriage, so he could live without a child. Could this man sleeping next to her be that evil? Sancho also realized that no amount of screaming and shouting could do anything in this marriage. She just played herself to believe that at some point, Don would get tired of this charade and all these men (and women—but mostly the men) and come back to her, and they can live normally as Man and Wife, and his many mistresses.

Oftentimes, Sancho tried to throw herself sexually at Don in the hope of luring him away from men, but he treated her body like a brother's. There were some instances when he nearly gave in—to put an end to her nagging—but those moments were loaded with so much heartache that he instantly regretted it. But then Sancho started plying him with alcohol so they could have sex. She knew that Don would never say no to drink and if he drank enough, he would also be too far gone to care what he was doing. Sancho wrote that as much as she got some sort of a (false) reassurance from what she was doing, a drunk Don was better than no Don. This pattern continued till she got pregnant. That was her plan anyway.

Don was livid. Sancho was delighted. She made the mistake of thinking that her womb contained the magic glue that'd bind the three of them together. The years after that ruined her. While Don held his reserve with the child at first, treating it like a neighbour's child who came to stay with them for a few days, soon enough he was delighted with his new walkie-talkie toy. In fact, he was so happy, that he forgot about Sancho altogether. It was like an attention-deficit-love-disorder. His wife didn't seem to exist in his visual frame. She was there in the blurring distance, collecting rust and cobwebs like the rest of the mad accoutrements that made up this home. Still, being a doting father didn't hamper Don from going back to his old ways. He remained unchanged in that department. He seemed to be having even more fun than usual—having smartly put up a fabulous heterosexual smokescreen, a beautiful façade of a family man for the world, but a sexual fiend that didn't hold back from anyone willing to saddle up to him on the inside. For Sancho, it was like fantasizing about living happily in your dream home but when you get to it after choosing every little tile, you are dead by the time you make the space smell like you, by the time the first monsoons seep into ceilings and form disfigured archipelagos on walls.

She kept wishing, praying, hoping for Don to fully return to her because she needed a part of herself back too, the part that he had stolen. But he didn't. 'I think Sancho's relationship with Don existed only in her heart. Only when it reached her head, did she choose to move away from him,' my mother said. She realized that as the years went by, she was worth nothing in this house. She didn't blame Don for loving their daughter a lot more, she knew that was what is expected of a father, and that *was* what she wanted. But she didn't think that it meant that he would love her even less. More so when she saw that he was capable of giving so much of himself, if he chose to.

Eventually, Sancho's heart quietly disintegrated. It became unhinged, like a top that had been whacked to stop spinning. It was not one moment, or one instance, it was an accretion of the futility of her fate. She just wanted a way out. Alone. She couldn't keep fighting for Don's love, and it wouldn't be fair to compete with their child. She realized that he would never really be hers. Sometimes, even when you think that a child will bring you closer together, it will also let you drift into a continent of your own within the same world that you inhabit. Don had been slipping away from her for years and she couldn't do anything about it. In the end, almost after seven years of dancing to his various whims, and hanging on to every syllable, gesture and metaphor, Sancho woke up one morning, decided that she never really did have any fight in her. She went out to buy Don his most favourite book, and disappear from his life.

Sancho had mentioned in one of her diary entries that she had booked herself a small patch in the cemetary next to the church. She had called it the cemetery of broken hearts. Of her broken heart. She had written something she wanted to ask Don but could never get herself to ask. 'I wanted to ask Don—does he love you as much as I d. . . ?'

My mother said, 'I think Sancho couldn't say "did" or "do". Sancho hadn't made up her mind if she still loved him . . . or if it was a love in the past. I suppose, Zef, the more you say, the less you hold on to yourself. And the only place you'd ever want to be lost is in the arms of someone who truly loves you. Don didn't care who he was betraying.'

'Do you have any of the diaries?' I asked.

'I have some, I couldn't carry all of them,' my mother said.

Among the many entries, I found this poem that Sancho had written a few weeks before her disappearance. I cried a little when I read it.

do you know what it is like to
go back into a memory
of 30, 40, 50 minutes ago
when we were scribblers of silent words
on each other's backs?
when I, lying alone, in the darkness
play with the history of shadows that we
have now become

do you know what it is like
smell the stale warmth of skin
that has been left behind in this room
all I have to hold onto are
sheets scarred like crinkled souvenirs

is it a game of ghostly imaginations
and of frightening magic
were you really here?

so I try to listen to the voices
that we never spoke in

and then
everything goes back in reverse
i dial the digits
till you race across the
bridge with broken lives
under the crimson moth lights of 2 a.m.
isn't time a disconnect?

answer me
do you know what it's like
to go back
into a
memory
by
yourself?

When she told me this, and as I am writing it down, I remembered something that Don had told me when I had met him last. I didn't understand it then but it makes sense to me now.

He told me, 'The truth is, my dear child, when you meet someone, actually it is never one, it is many. But only if you are lucky.'

'Lucky?' I asked.

'Ah, luck. It's a great skill to know how to guide your luck. Even while waiting for it,' he said.

'You sound like a fortune cookie,' I giggled.

'I am a cookie with no fortune, I am afraid.' He laughed. 'I squandered it all away. As I was saying, love is what you want it to be. The next, the now, the always. And for as many hearts are there, a love will eternally be born. You must know that it is never one human, one life, one love. When you grow up, you will realize that you will never end up loving just one person. There will be many lovers, some that you will love similarly, some differently, some intensely, some patiently, some passionately, some hurriedly, some greedily, some anxiously, some sexually, some heartbreakingly, some defiantly, and some foreverly—Sancho was my foreverly. But I don't think she believed me. She wanted to but she couldn't.'

'Why?' I asked.

'Because of my behaviour.'

'What did you do?' I asked.

'Many many things that I wished I could take back. But that's a story for another day and another drink, not now.' Then after a while he added, 'She was good to me, good to this house, she used to wipe the leaves at night so they would glisten under the moonlight,' he murmured.

A stern shadow crowded his face which meant that I couldn't really press any further.

My mother said that Don was Sancho's bad habit. Sancho loved Don for who he was and what he was changing into irrespective of who was at the receiving end of the love that she deserved. She could only give him the kind of love that he didn't need. She loved him even when she wanted to hate him.

But Don loved Sancho only because she loved him more. He loved her in a particular way, not too much, not too little, just the right amount to keep stringing her along. It wasn't the love that he kept returning to in his dreams. But it was a love that was never quite enough to keep it together and see each other through till the end.

Which was why she left.

There is only so much heartache a woman can take (before she joins a convent).

They say to stop the war, you lose the war. That's what Sancho did.

After that, her diary entries were all about trying to reach out to Don to allow her to see their daughter, and that she had made a huge mistake by leaving, and how he made sure that she didn't succeed. He had written back to her saying that she had made her choice to leave, and now she was not entitled to know what was going on in their life. She also knew that he did that to spite her—just because he could.

'Why didn't you tell me all of this earlier?' I asked my mother completely shocked.

'I thought by not talking about it, I would be able to forget the horror of the situation. Sometimes there is no point remembering anything. But I do, even when I don't want to. Why do you think I hate Don so much?' my mother said.

On her way back from this new reality, my mother discovered that she was pregnant with me.

Chapter 8

My mother said that she took her pregnancy as a sign of sorts.

'Sign of what?' I asked.

'My mother,' said my mother matter-of-factly.

'What do you mean?'

'Maybe the priest was right. Sancho kept praying that I would come to her when she was alive, and I didn't. So I went to her when she died, and she came to me through you. The timing was uncanny. I suppose this was our version of a mother–daughter bond in an afterlife. We started over again. She and me through you and me. I suppose when the soul wants, it waits. What she couldn't will in life, she willed in death. What's that movie we watch where the dead mother accompanies the family everywhere?'

'*Volver*?'

It was a movie that my mother took to so easily when we first watched it one afternoon, years ago. Maybe it reminded her of Sancho, who was in a way trying to fix all the meaningless situations that she couldn't resolve while she was alive. Or maybe it was the chronic Almodovarian dismay that sometimes love is never really quite enough, which must have struck some sort of a secret chord.

'Wait, where was my real father through all this? Why didn't he come with you to Gokarna?'

My mother embarked on a fantastical story about this man, my procreator, who was all set to be with her, but not before he met with some sort of a swimming/diving accident, his brand-new boat capsizing, and his being stuck amidst some rocks, the weight of which destroyed all sensation in his right hand. He was lying like that—washed up on the shore for a few hours, until someone spotted him and took him to the hospital. Apparently, Theo the monkey died of starvation waiting for his master's arrival.

'It was a terrible loss. When I went back,' my mother said, 'I saw his right hand dangling like a limp rope. It had no sensation whatsoever.'

'So you became his Florence Nightingale?' I asked sarcastically.

She ignored my comment and continued. 'I embraced his pain and made it mine. I told him what had ensued in Gokarna but he listened with detachment, as though I was reading a newspaper clipping of what happened to some stranger's mother, in some other galaxy. I felt the distance—it was the sort of distance that comes between lovers who have spent a little too much time apart—but I chose to ignore it. I knew he was in excruciating pain, so he was heavily medicated on painkillers for the most part. Something drastic had changed in him. He hardly spoke to me during the day. But at night, he would crawl up next to me and hold me close and make love. So I thought everything would be resolved by love and sex. Afterwards, I'd talk to him about my mother, and how she lived her life, and I'd tell him that he should think about going back to work because the money was dwindling away. He'd mumble something, as most men do in the aftermath of sex, exhausted and weary, and go back to sleep. But as daybreak fell, the distance between us would resume like a half-hearted, limp wave teasing beach lovers.'

She thought that this was just a phase, and he would come around eventually. Everyone does, don't they? But then he became self-destructive. He kept cutting his right hand with razor blades just to feel the blood ooze out. He couldn't feel anything, that hand was lifeless.

'I looked after him during those dark days, even though there was no one looking after me,' she went on.

He never spoke to her much those days but he did tell her to get an abortion.

'My hand can't open toothpaste, how the hell can we have a child right now,' he said to her.

'Why are you talking like this?' my mother asked him.

'I have been thinking about this for a while. The accident . . . the hand . . . I don't know what is going to happen . . . and what I want to happen . . . but I think we should reconsider our relationship,' he said.

'Relationship?' My mother said. 'We are married.'

'That doesn't mean anything,' he said.

'I was too dazed to say anything, Zef. My mother's news, the pregnancy and now this. *This.*'

'But I love you,' my mother told him.

'I know,' he said.

'Is that all you can say?' she asked him.

'See, that's the disconnect . . . I don't,' he told her.

'Don't what?' she prodded. 'I just wanted to hear him say what I didn't want him to say.'

'Don't love you,' he whispered. 'I think there has been a disconnect. I thought I loved you but I am not sure if I do . . . not any more, not like this, and I don't know why,' he told her.

My mother said to me that she may as well have been punched in her stomach with her puking me out.

'Where was your disconnect when you were eating me like a cannibal every night?' she asked him. He remained silent. 'There was no emotion on his face. His beard, that had grown like some sort of a fungus in the past month, hid just about all the emotion I needed to see.'

'I didn't want all this, I didn't want all this . . . my heart is not in it . . . I don't know if it ever was . . .' he told her.

'For how long . . . is it the medication that is making your head feel strange . . . Is it possible?' she asked him.

'I was trying so desperately to salvage the situation,' my mother said to me.

'No . . . I don't know . . . I have been feeling like this for a while . . . I feel we plunged too soon into something I wasn't prepared for, and probably don't even want to prepare myself for, and this accident just made me realize that I can never be sure of anything any more. Not you, not me and not us,' he offered as an explanation.

'Why didn't you tell me? Why didn't you tell me when I was wiping your shit because your hand wouldn't move an inch? Why didn't you tell me before you got me pregnant?' she screamed.

'I should have . . .' he tried to mumble.

He remained silent for a while before saying, 'I didn't . . . I didn't have the courage to bring it up with you,' he said.

'But I am having our child now.'

He was quiet.

'How can you be so cold?'

Silence, again.

'I thought he had a dead squirrel stuffed inside his mouth, Zef, because he just remained silent.'

'Look, you were what I wanted . . . at that time . . . I gave you whatever I could . . . I am definitely not sorry that I met you . . . your smile . . . it can light up the sea . . . but I am . . . also . . . not sorry that it is over . . . the emotion seems to have dried up inside of me . . . and there is nothing I can do to save it, because it is beyond my control,' he said.

'Not. Can't. Won't. The accident not just ruined your hand, it has ruined your heart,' she cried to him.

'I need to leave,' he said.

'But what about your job? The bank will surely find you something easier to do,' she said.

'No. They don't have a place for me any more.'

'We will work something out, the three of us,' my mother tried to assure him.

'I have collected the last bit of settlement they could manage to cough up. It's all gone,' he said.

'Every word that had come out of his mouth was measured, sparse and terrifyingly indifferent. Every word that came out of his mouth seemed as though he was pulling my fingernails out with a spanner while sipping beer with a straw,' my mother said.

'But we can fix this,' she begged him again. 'We are going to have a child together.'

'But that's the definition of insanity—repairing something and expecting it to be different when it cannot,' he said.

That's when she realized that the love he had for her had no weight. It was too skinny.

'But I thought you said you were lucky to have met me,' she said.

'We all use each other as excuses,' he said.

'Running away is the easiest thing. Love takes courage.'

'Then I don't bloody have it,' he said, clenching his teeth.

'It was my turn to stay quiet,' my mother said. 'I wanted to tell him that it wasn't about letting him go, it was about letting me stay. But I stayed silent. I tried everything as a last-ditch effort at remembering how love was in the beginning, just to see if it was worth fighting for, if it was *ever* worth fighting for,' she told me. 'I cried so much but my tears couldn't touch him,' she said. 'I didn't know who he had become.'

They say there comes a time when the person who occupied an important space in your heart, and consumed your soul like a river, becomes someone you instantly recognize in a mist, or in a crowded bus, like a very familiar acquaintance. But there also comes a time when their faces turn a shade that is unrecognizable, somewhere dissolving into rain, that you know that the wall that you broke so many years ago has just gone up. This moment seemed like that. His curiously unfeeling disposition suggested that there was a tone of finality to everything. Lovers make the worst enemies.

'Maybe you give too much,' I told my mother.

'Then get accused of giving a little too much,' my mother smiled. 'But it's hard to give . . . less.'

I liked that. Gravy always used to say 'love you lots' every time he saw me. Lots.

'That night, we had sex one last time,' my mother told me.

It was all they had; the hurriedly whispered lust bites, the tenderness of the quiet heaving breath of their bodies scissoring inside each other, at that hour, in that second. Sex brought them close, but not close enough to stay together. They didn't talk. It was some sort of a final extreme closeness before the goodbye forever.

'But I suppose that silence said all that he couldn't say,' she said. 'At some point, I must have drifted off to sleep.' Because when the morning sun stretched its tired legs, it must have swallowed him whole. 'Just like that he disappeared like he never existed,' she said. 'He disappeared like an imaginary friend, as though he never existed in real life.'

It was my turn to remain quiet.

'It ended just like that, Zef. For no reason, except his own fears and feelings. He didn't want to be bogged down with a family and one hand. He simply didn't want it. He had stopped caring. Some button just went off inside him. There is no explanation for something like this. I kept trying to figure out why it happened, but then the world gave me you. The accident, for him, was just an excuse to convince himself for feeling the way he did, but deep down if there is a lesson to be learned here, it is that loyalties will be forgotten as hastily as lightning. And that there is no certainty about emotions because they can be moulded like clay, they can change just because they can, or if you overstay your welcome-period in your own head. I couldn't understand how people can just fall out of love for no reason in particular, but the reality is that one can. The truth is that the heart is the size of the fist. For some it loves, for others it is merely an organ that mechanically pumps blood, so they can sleep, eat, wake up, go about their chores,' she rambled.

But what doesn't kill can still ruin a heart.

So my mother made her way back to Madras to start a life for herself and for me, doing everything that could keep her from drowning. She was stubbornly vague about what she did but all she told me was that she worked in the same news station, she worked as a secretary, she worked as an extra, she taught needlework classes, she sold her hair, she did everything to survive, for herself and for me.

'It wasn't easy, Zef. But I pulled through because I had a responsibility to be happy for you, to live a decent life for you,' she said.

'Did you look for him after that?' I asked my mother.

'He didn't want to be found,' she said.

'Don't these people have any sense of guilt?' I wondered aloud.

'Men don't think like that, they deal with situations by not dealing with them at all. They deal with something else. Or kill themselves like Gravy,' she said. 'They don't want to acknowledge what they feel because they don't want to deal with what comes with that feeling. For a long time I was so hurt, so sad that I didn't have the energy to be angry. I just didn't understand how people could disappear from your life having lived, loved and been inside you for so long. He didn't even bother checking up on you. *You.*

That's when I realized, I had you, and he didn't. Do you think you will look for your father?' she asked me.

'No,' I said.

Frankly, if you ask me I'd like to go back to the time when I was in my mother's womb, choose XY instead of XX, develop massive nuts, drive a massive tractor, be slightly unhinged, then meet my real father somewhere and drive the tractor over him and beat him up with my bare fists, just because of what he did. And I really hope that he is saddled with a flighty slut who will break his heart in fourteen different places.

But I didn't say all that.

All I said was, 'To me, Gravy will always be my father.'

He was the wall we built our home with, the man who gave me his name, the man who absorbed all our childish (mine) and painful (my mother's) secrets like a sponge. My father loved me with every atom of his being even though I was not a product of his body or an extension of his desire. I owned his love. It wasn't the kind of love that had a measure on it.

My mother told me that when she met Gravy, two or three or four years later, she had no faith in anything and, most of all, in love.

'At that time, Zef, my priority was you. We met at a bus stop, and we chatted like most people do while waiting for their public transport. It became a pattern, he was my 3 p.m. to 3.20 p.m. bus-stop friend. He used to ask me how am I travelling and I'd say the bus, which was why we both were standing here at the same time, right? Then he'd say, "No, I meant how are you?" I thought that was a funny way of asking someone how they were, Zef. Then he started to pursue me gradually, for reasons unknown to me, for more than eight months, maybe more,' she said.

My mother said that he told her something she found terrifyingly endearing, something she can never forget, 'I like you but I think it is more than a little and less than a lot and I can't tell the difference between a little and a lot, and less than a lot and more than a little, but I've usually been guilty of leaving it too late, saying it too late, when there's no time left. I Like You.'

The three little words before the three big words were nice. But she told him that she was incapable of loving anyone after what had happened, and that it would be hard for her to feel loved. But that didn't really dampen his vigour.

'Just because I didn't give in, he didn't give up either,' she said.

Then he asked my mother, 'If there is no struggle . . . does it seem less important? We don't have to complicate it to make it beautiful even though sometimes a little complication makes it more beautiful.'

'I didn't know what to say to that, Zef, so I chose to ignore it. I had now tutored *my* heart to not go astray,' she said to me.

He still didn't give up. Eventually, my mother told him that she will bring nothing to what might be of their relationship other than cynicism and a child. She was a tired woman with a tired life.

'You know what he told me when I said that?'

I remained silent. He told my mother, 'So? That just means more of you to love, then. I am not really sure what you want from me, but I suppose, whatever it is, I could try to supply it.'

'It was some sort of an intuitive love affair,' she said to me. 'There was some sort of a neural harmony around him. I was always in a hurry, running from one job to another, one role to another. But I must have caught the calm from him. We were like close friends that had never met each other before.'

Gravy had the unkempt, slightly concave body of a bachelor who had never been fed right ever since he started living by himself; she looked like an overworked, under-pressure, underfed, newborn mother. He had a nose ring and his breath smelt of anise. She had long, knotted, crimson-titian hair, and she was always on her way somewhere. They just had to collide. It was the perfect after-dream.

Their encounter could be set to music, my mother used to say. Occasionally, our whimsy leads us to the fabric that will be sown deep into our veins, and becomes a part of the skin we reside in, that we wonder what if we didn't have that impulse, would we have been bereft of that important direction that will dictate our lives. But the beauty of this chance encounter was that my mother met the love of her life in the way her personality wanted to meet him: by chance, unknowingly, calmly, patiently, intuitively, accidentally, but certainly.

'I told him that, given whatever had happened, I always got mugged when I trusted too much. And that if we were to be together this cannot be a bittersweet in-between for him and then disappear,' she said. 'He promised me. It was as though we had known each other for years but had to wait until that time to meet,' my mother said. 'There was no sexual intent. He was a man standing firm, collected, strong, and valiantly waiting for me to want him. I thought I would want to hate him but there were too many things we had in common, like laughter, and I ended up loving him. It's funny how our destiny is met in the way we avoid it. I invited him home one day, after almost a year of his persuading me, to meet you, I don't know if you remember that . . . you must have been three or four and we were living in that small flat next to your school in Madras, but you probably do, because you remember everything like an elephant. You just tell yourself to not remember. Anyway, when he came home, he never left.'

She said that she was taken in by his niceness and his honesty. It grew on her. They spoke like siblings. They held hands like lovers. Soon they disappeared inside each other.

It is only now that I tried to dig deeper on remembering how it all had started. All of these things seemed to have happened before memory itself. I had vague visions of a man with warm, caramel hair coming with a long balloon in the shape of a long green snake, a rage at the time, I would imagine. I hadn't remembered it, until right now when I actually told myself to negotiate what I must have made a mental note to forget, and what I chose to remember, and what I must have tried to mould out of my conscious memory for convenience.

My mother had said that he was finishing his doctorate in psychology in Madras, worked in the university library part-time, and shared a one-room flat with an anti-Christ, half-boiled, fully bald, middle-aged (he claimed to be thirty-eight) gent named Vincent, who spoke impeccable, convented English, and spent a lot of his time gazing like an aristocrat and preaching sermons to the ceiling. But it was much later that Gravy realized that he was thoroughly deranged. Vincent, actually aged forty-eight, had killed his wife and two sons and had no recollection of it. In a way, that had made Gravy move in with us on a full-time basis, after that discovery.

But all that didn't faze Gravy. He had loved Vincent either way. It was not as though he was going to love him less just become he was a felon and/or a psychotic beast.

'The love is there,' he had explained to my mother. 'But it must have changed shape,' he said.

That was a good line, I thought, when my mother told me.

'You can't just stop loving someone overnight,' he told her. 'How can you?'

That is true. It's impossible.

He felt bad for Vincent and for his acid brain that had gone for a long walk in the woods and got too lost to find its way back.

But before Gravy moved to Madras to pursue his PhD in psychology, he had just returned from China. See, he had managed to backpack from Madras to London and had made his way back via China. He seemed to have travelled as far into the northern frontier of Heilongjiang, with the full intention of smuggling into Russia for kicks, but he ran out of money, not common sense, and made his way back to India via Nepal and then finally back to where he started, Madras, to nestle into a less nomadic life.

That was when my mother claimed to have met him in that bus stop.

Somehow it seemed that their life together began almost as instantly as they met. ('It was as though he just hopped on to the rollercoaster even if it was moving at full speed, until eventually it stopped and he got off, while I was now left to circumnavigate the rest of the journey alone while throwing up all over the place.')

Even as much as my mother claimed to have resisted her habit of falling in love too quickly, too unrealistically, too fatally, she fell in love with Gravy. I don't blame her. Gravy was a godsend. When she first met him, she had apparently warned him that her skin was merely protecting her broken organs inside. He didn't care about all that. He rearranged her. Eventually when she gave herself to him, she said that she had spent every day of the past years spinning stories, some true, some imagined. He showed her a kind of heaven she did not even know existed.

So it was settled then.

She was his, he was hers, I was theirs.

Sometimes, I suppose, you don't question what was meant to be.

My mother told me that she was scared because there were three entities.

I and love and you.

All three different entities that can be destroyed so easily, but nothing did. Gravy was the thread that bound us tightly together as one.

He made us feel like a composite part of his heart.

And now he was gone.

As hungry as I was to hear the whole story, I was beginning to feel completely drained. But I couldn't tell my mother with all her weary fragility to shut up because that would kill her. Anything could kill her right now. Even a mosquito bite. Because she was just looking for a reason to die. She was that ruined.

The more she spoke, the more I felt physically gutted, as though someone was pulling my kidneys out without my consent, without anaesthesia, without concern, without any need to do so. The more she spoke, the more I realized that the nature of this narrative changes as I discover the atoms that constitute members of my family (the ones who were already dead or slowly dying; the ones who belonged to me by blood; and the one who belonged to me by heart).

I lost my sleep with these dark stories. I was too tired to do anything, and too awake to sleep. I was also a little scared to sleep, to tell you the truth. I didn't want to dream. During the times that I managed to get some sleep, I'd end up waking up to sunset, and sleep at daybreak. Dramaturgy. My brain circled around at lightning speed. Medicine cabinets here had only expired Prozac, and cockroached opium. I'd try to write—to ensure that the truth would refresh my broken mind through these words—by sequestering myself in Don's territorial study.

Don's study was an assemblage of extremes. There were all these eccentric pieces, quite like the emotions or energies that permeated this space. The lime-coloured walls had turned into a shade of fungal green. There were dusty chandeliers above me that seemed as though they were falling from the sky.

But this was the only space where I knew I could be alone in my head and my mother would never enter. 'Too much of Don inside there,' she'd say, standing on tiptoe at the threshold. The neurons must have got mixed up. This room encapsulated a fear for my mother, a fear of finding out something she was better off not knowing, which is a fear she didn't want to confront ever again. What is that they say about once bitten, twice bitter?

Maybe she was reminded of that bastard trumpeter's letters that she found in his desk drawer, who knows?

I still hadn't read those letters. I was only a little too curious. After all, I was an 'inquisitive bob', a name that was given to me by my second-standard teacher, Mrs Russell, a bulldog-faced woman with a braid that consumed almost all of the oil from the Middle East, an absolute cunt who made me stand for three hours in the midday sun and threatened to suspend me because I was making aeroplane noises with my mouth in class just to see what reaction I could evoke. I was six-and-a-half, it was the first time I had been in a classroom of any sort. I was enrolled in my mother's alma mater, a perfidious nunnery called Holy Angels, because it was the only school that pretended to not notice the badly calligraphed 'Fe' next to the 'Male' on my birth certificate. (It was only when I was ready to be enrolled for school that my mother realized that my birth certificate had listed me as a male.)

I looked for the key for the desk's various drawers, which, after much finding, I realized was hidden inside the shell of the taxidermied hamster, named Happy, on his desk. It was a name that fit well, the hamster looked so sickeningly pleased with itself that it made me want to beat it to pulp. But is there any point in killing a corpse? I opened one of the drawers to sniff secrets out of it from forever ago. Everything was there. I knew Don never threw anything away. I found limp, yellow-coloured letters, and read them. It crushed me a bit. A love was lost.

Everything I don't want to see is in these drawers.

Everything that I should untie myself from. All of it was waiting like orphans in a half-way house, waiting to be picked up and nurtured.

Then I found Don's diary, with silverfish bites on it. The calendars were marked for the years that Don must have been in Warsaw. There were a handful of scribbles with words that seemed to be leaning on each other for support. One was this:

The great Roman poet Ovid once said: be patient and tough, one day, this pain will be useful to you.

How can pain ever be useful? Pain is the most nonsense emotion there is.

After I finished reading the diary, I rummaged for more of his life, and love, all lost in these various drawers—it was a huge desk, made of rosewood and brought from Cochin's Jew Town, a treasure trove waiting to be breached.

In one, I found a box brimming with over five hundred different types of corks of wine bottles. On each cork, Don had scribbled the time, place and the name of the person with whom he had drunk that bottle away into melancholia. It was a beautiful idea of preserving a memory, of remembering the ghouls you once laughed with. Knowing Don, he would have kept the conversation going at full speed so that no one could ever notice him surreptitiously writing on the cork and slipping it into his pocket.

I found a set of baby teeth kept in a Ziplock bag inside a plastic box with my mother's name on it. Don had marked each age, month and date the teeth had fallen. Then I found a couple of report cards: one of my mother's states that she was 'a quiet child who stares at the window a little too much, and is very good at watering the plants in the school nursery'.

Beneath these, inside a secret compartment within a drawer, there lay a bundle wrapped up in a muslin cloth. My nose was hit by the familiar smell of citrus. But it was a smell that seemed faint enough to be my imagination. I stared at it for a while, just until the smell subsided into my nose. Then I tore it open. The second I did, I wished I didn't. I wished curiosity never got the better of me.

There were reams and reams and reams of correspondence and money-order receipt slips up to four years ago. The more I read, the more I felt breathless. I was asphyxiated. My right hand began to shake vigorously. My heart was exploding out of my chest. I felt a searing itch in my back, as though I was breaking out in hives. Either way, I thought I was going to die or kill myself. These were memories to curl up and die with.

I couldn't believe what I was reading, and I despised the feeling that it perhaps was my *in utero* destiny to find these pages.

I wished I didn't.

I wished I didn't.

I wished I didn't.

I wished I didn't.

Because the reality was that the relationship that my mother thought was a destined encounter, a chance collision, was anything but. It was, in fact, artfully, cleverly, deceitfully and meticulously planned by Don. The grizzly beast slurring away next door had entered into a monetary liaison with a man to get him to marry my mother, or if not, then at least make an orthodox woman out of her, as a self-serving promise to save her from herself and any further self-destruction, and give her somebody to engage, and love, and someone her child could look up to as a father.

The man with whom Don sealed this deal is now dead. That man was Gravy.

Chapter 9

The smell woke me up. The chilly mix of citrus and Cool Water. It threw my eyes against the rails. It nuked through my veins while I was sleeping.

'Nothing could wake you up,' I heard my mother's voice very feebly in the background. 'I even tried putting a cigarette in your mouth. Nothing could move you,' she said. 'Ultimately, this did the trick,' she said pointing to the bottle of Gravy's perfume and a cotton ball dipped in lime.

The perfume was lying in a satin pouch on the floor. In my head, my immediate reflex action saw me having already reached for the bottle and flinging it against the wall only to see it crack into a million shards. But I remained paralysed, emotionally and physically. Some sort of bile was rising, and receding inside of me.

Just in the same way as the real kept receding, and the unreal kept rising.

I was lying on my mother's lap. My head felt heavy, as though I had woken with a hangover. She smelt like the smoky comfort of the neighbourhood university bar, or the smell of your favourite drug, or dealer. We were underneath the tree inside the house. The branch above my mother's head seemed to be hanging rather tenuously. One small breeze, and it would fall and crash into smithereens. She understood.

'No, it won't fall, the branch,' she said like she was some sort of a coven messiah. 'Its duty is to stay and give us shelter through this wretched winter.'

'There is no winter in Madras,' I murmured.

'Winter of our lives,' she said.

'Oh.'

My brain felt jailed. My body felt like it was some sort of a hollow tin can, empty after I puked my heart out. I was delirious, soaked to the skin, broken between the lungs, trapped in my secrets, covered in rags and heartache. The sheets were breathing over me. I was slowly lumbering my way towards consciousness. I don't know how long I had been out cold.

'I had forgotten that I had brought his perfume in my bag when I came here,' my mother went on. 'I must have brought it with me so that Gravy's smell and its memories would protect us,' she said.

I couldn't find my voice, it was lost somewhere deep inside the folds of my skin, dormant like a seething volcano.

Shreds of beer-gold light filtered in. Maybe it was sunrise, or was it sunset—but whatever it was, it would be a day (or night) the size of hell. My head was everywhere, nowhere but definitely not here. Everything kept melting around me like a Dali painting. My eyelids still felt so incredibly heavy. I saw a hazy version of the beady-eyed, pancake-flat, pixie-faced, cushioned head rest in the distance. Everything around me seemed like it was wilting with trepidation.

She was talking. I wasn't listening. 'He didn't want another child,' I vaguely heard my mother murmur. 'You were the only one for him. Theonlyone. He feared some sort of division . . .'

I stared at her mouth move, like a lip reader. I looked at her big bright eyes shining while I searched for myself in them.

'. . . of love would creep in,' she continued, 'if there was another . . . one of you.'

The words, the worlds, the burnt emotions all seem to be colliding against each other, stretching like the moody, impatient reflection of stars on water.

My mother's crumpled smoke-stained voice splintered in and out of my static.

'. . . you have been asleep since Wednesday, Zef,' she said when my eyes seemed to weakly determine the outline of dark shapes.

'Today is Saturday,' she continued as I stretched my eyeballs with all my weak might. 'No wait, I went to get the drips on Friday. That was the day before, I think. Or yesterday . . . I am not sure but today feels like a Sun . . .'

I stopped hearing her, instead paying attention to a howl of mosquitoes above me. I was going quietly insane. My insides were rioting. Even as I could feel my body waking up, I desperately clung on to the last dregs of my 'industrial strength sleep', hoping to live inside that sleep and be a part of that story, and that what I had discovered would eventually be just a lousy dream that disappears at the arrival of stubborn daylight.

Don had once told me that sometimes the most feral answers to life's problems come to you in your sleep. We wait for patterns to emerge. It draws itself from fractals of thought catalogues lurking in the back of your brain. You hear of musicians humming a platinum-record-selling tune in the middle of their sleep, of your dead grandmother teaching you the right slang of an alien language to help you navigate your way in a foreign country, of authors trying to extricate the titles of their novels in their dreams, of dead fathers appearing inside their children's eyes to remind them to look underneath their bed for a book they forgot to revise for a big exam, only to have the questions from that very book in the test. So you can believe in the power of your dreams, the power of keeping the memory of those who are dead alive.

I thought that my sleep would feed me into a new life with new nostalgias; a new future with no secrets.

But even in that state of despair-filled, toxic drowsiness, I felt my heart being clawed out and being emotionally decapitated. I knew that it was all too true and certain as the arrival of tomorrow morning; that waking up would be a parachuteless sky-dive into discovering the truth behind the financially transacted emotions.

On top of all of this, I am a bastard.

So what does that make Gravy? A star-faced traitor.

'Zef, Zef,' my mother shook me, her voice poking into my membrane.

I opened my eyes wearily and looked at her.

'Oh good, you have your eyes open. Please for God's sake, stay awake. Don't fall off to sleep again,' she cried. 'Do you want a drag? Here, smoke this. I just rolled it for you.'

She put the cigarette in my mouth. I inhaled the smoke like a robot.

'I thought you were going to leave me too,' she said. 'First Gravy, then you.' She broke into a nervous little sheepish laugh.

She put her brittle right hand on my sticky, pimple-bumpy forehead and said, 'I kept talking to you while you were asleep . . . until this fever got out of you. Did you drink Don's opium tea by any chance? You know what I . . .'

I lost her again to the squall in my upstairs' chambers. Ironically enough, I stumbled upon the truth about the man I assumed to be my father in quite the same way my mother realized the truth hidden by hers: by rummaging through items in the study.

Discovering the truth behind Don and Gravy's warped financial agreement was like being electrocuted. All I remember was running to find a way to burn all those shameful papers hidden from us for all these years. I thought that if I set it all on fire then perhaps I could delude myself into thinking that maybe this arrangement between two of my favourite humans was just a figment of an elevated imagination. That the lies will automatically readjust themselves to a more convenient, slightly less grim reality. Silly, I know, and you may chide me into believing that I was a little delusional, but would you really know what to do if you fell into a beehive by accident?

I watched the whole lot burn. In hindsight, I should have jumped into the fire as well but I didn't want my mother to be stranded alone, although eventually she would have ended up killing herself. That would be an orgy of a funeral. If my life had been a movie then this would have been the scene where I was running down a valley or in the rain and the violin and the cello will come on as I burn everything away. But this was real life. The only movement my body could manage was a wobbly walk into the deep end of the rusty garden with all the matchboxes I could find, a bottle of kerosene from the kitchen, the only soundtrack playing in my head was a cheap drum machine against the beautiful piano.

I must have collapsed on inhaling all that smoke. That was it. Then black out. I don't even know how I got to this courtyard, this bench, this day. But just like the deranged Lady Macbeth who shrieked that all the perfumes of Arabia will not sweeten this little hand, I couldn't wash away the stains of all the stale ink—that had marked its territory across my palms—into an estuary of soap bubbles.

I kept staring at my mother. She was made of tobacco, loneliness and beautiful, cracked lips. She was muttering away to fill up the silent spaces. I remained supine, trying to listen to her fatigued voice, while the weariness of waking up to earth-shattering events ate me up.

'. . . found you choking in the garden. What were you burning so furiously?' she asked me.

'Is Don . . .' I started to ask my mother.

Her jaw and neck bone tightened when she heard his name.

'Unfortunately . . .' she said very slowly.

Oh no, I thought. The beast has kicked it. Oh God, no.

'He isn't dead yet,' she semi-sighed. 'He is still alive. I thought he regained some consciousness but he slid back into a coma. He showed signs of waking up but never did. He keeps growling like an old boar. He doesn't show any promise of dying either. Apparently, he had stopped talking or going out after Gravy's death. He just stopped, imagine that. At first, he was just unbearable, now he was . . . is,' she quickly corrected herself, 'unreachable. All he does now is growl in his sleep.'

I was relieved a little bit. This is my reasoning. See, mostly because his being alive was proof enough that my mother didn't know what I had discovered. She would *never* enter that study. It was locked. Unless my father, I mean Gravy, told her during his last days of maniacal blathering, which I was sure he wouldn't have. If my mother had managed to extricate this information out of his skull, she would have killed herself, if not him, and given the ocean of hatred that she had for Don, if she even had a sniff that we were all pawns in his production, she would have slit his throat in his sleep, or poisoned him and watched him die in front of her, and thrown a thundering demolition party to celebrate his passing. Yes, she really would have. She would not have stormed out of the house after discovering something as brutal as this, as she had done the first time her father had betrayed her heart. This time, she would have finished him off till there was no bone left to burn. I was certain of that.

Besides I had burnt all evidence. I was certain of that. I think so. Oh God, did I? I hope I did.

Did Don really think that these papers stammering secrets like lightning . . . did he really think he could keep it lying around like this, without my finding out? Unless he *wanted* me to find out?

Or did he not get the time to throw them away, or decide what to do with them himself? He controlled everything. Surely he was far too sly to let *this* secret slip.

And now that I've found out what am I supposed to do with this filthy seminal information? It was a secret as absurd as a father who checks into a brothel only to find his daughter as the whore on call. Exactly how would you break it to the mother?

I couldn't tell my mother, not just yet.

This bloody imbroglio, it spread like a slithering noxious sea inside me.

This pretty little lie wrapped in a muslin cloth was just too much to bear.

Even the truth about my grandfather's preferences for consuming continents of gin and *garcons* didn't seem half as disturbing as realizing that the man whom I had accepted and grown to love as my father, whose blood I had tattooed under my own skin, was actually paid to play the part.

Now what? On top of all this, the man was dead.

If he had to die, he shouldn't have died *in media res*.

He left a can of poisonous worms that were crawling unattended. How do you row yourself back to shore when you have no arms?

Discovering this secret just made me want to love my mother a little more, if I could. For all her nuttiness, she turned out to be the one sincere half of what made me. We were bound by blood, not any financial bond. Her womb had been my sky at one point.

The more I seemed to learn about my life, the more I died. Silently, all the forms in the smoke started to make sense, before they disappeared. The reason why Gravy brought me to meet Don against my mother's wishes, the underlying tension between the two men, the role that the two played—Don as the truant, Gravy as the rescuer; that horrible fight between them years ago, how Gravy still never stopped me from coming here, and, most tragically, why Gravy killed himself—the guilt—it must have hung like a millstone around his heart, like a 100-ton weight tied to his hair. It must have pecked on him like some sort of a razor-toothed rat nibbling away at a building of cheese till it died of gluttony.

'Zef . . . are you even listening to me?' My mother shook me.

I stared at her languidly, a little preoccupied with connecting the invisible dots in my head. She was growing bald. I could see some patches of her scalp amidst strands of the Technicolor rusty-red hair.

'Is Don . . .' I asked her . . . or did I already ask her . . . I couldn't remember . . .

'Yes yes yes the old bandicoot is still alive,' her voice bellowed with an exasperation that comes from repeating the same answer. 'Don't worry he won't die until he speaks with you, until his time is up.'

'How do you know that?' I shot her a quick question. Did she know?

'I just do. He hasn't spoken to anyone after Gravy died. Chances are that he might speak to you. He won't die so easily, I wish he would, but he just won't . . . go that easy. That's Don for you,' she intoned. 'He's too clever for heaven. He's too deranged for hell.'

I suppose. Wonder what Gravy is doing now, I must have mumbled.

My mother mumbled back, 'God knows whose soul he might be haunting now after leaving us.'

I remember an incident that Gravy had once told me about his childhood. One day when he was thirteen or fourteen, he ran away from the house. He told me that at the time he claimed to have felt lonely in his heart. But in reality, he had failed a year in school and had decided not to inform his parents. But his siblings had found out about it, which led to a terrible fight between them. Gravy had decided that he just didn't want to live with them around him so he wanted to leave home. His parents just assumed that he was late from school. Finally, when the slumber of twilight sneaked in, so did the worry. Fear always seems to peak when the heart of darkness breathes. After searching for him incessantly, his parents lodged a complaint. The policeman took them to the local quack who specialized in bringing back runaway children. After travelling for over five hours into the night, they finally reached the home of the patron saint of runaways at around five in the morning.

'He didn't seem to be the slightest bit miffed that a search party had descended on his doorstep hoping for him to work a miracle in the next five minutes,' Gravy said what his mother had told him. The quack's room was sparse except for one cot without a mattress. Everyone expected him to look like a saint with benign eyes but he was wearing nothing but a pair of striped Bermudas and his dry eyes seemed frozen in thought. His ruffian's beard was turmeric coloured and his bald head seemed to morph into this mosquito bite, red, like a wound that you wanted to keep scratching. Eventually, he helped them find Gravy by asking his twin sister to gaze into a water bowl and explain what she saw. When she said she saw nothing, he asked her to stare harder. Finally, within the next hour, the twin was able to spell out the name of the café and the beach that my father had gone off to in Goa. It was spot on. When they got to that spot in Goa, they found Gravy sitting in a corner and sipping on a straw from an empty bottle by himself. When they finally held him, he pretended to be someone else, feigned ignorance and pretended to not understand the language. But who was he fooling? His parents hugged him and wept blood. Apparently, he came home and continued to not understand anything for another week. Then one day he woke up and started behaving like he always did. He never spoke about how he escaped, why he escaped and when he escaped. He must have just hung on to the wind, trampled ahead and understood the signs as though he was reading some sort of Braille. When Gravy told me this as a bedtime fable, I listened in amazement, wondering how he could do what he had done. It seemed too unreal. But then if he could have been paid to play his role as my father, anything was possible.

Wasn't it Hamlet who said to Ophelia that God has given you one face, and you make yourself another? That's exactly what Gravy did. He betrayed our destiny. He was not who we imagined him to be. He was messy in life, as he was in death. And death is a more unifying force than life. It is a great determiner.

Was he worried that we wouldn't love him if we came to know the truth—which was probable but not really possible? Because the truth was that we didn't know how to not love Gravy. Hating him would have been an alien emotion. How do you replace the taste of uncompromising love—like Gravy showed us, was paid to show us—with impossible hate? My body of emotions did not have an on-and-off button. Like Gravy said about Vincent, you can't stop loving someone overnight. How do people do it? How do you tell your heart to stop loving immediately? And more importantly, how does it even respond to that command? I've never understood how lovers become friends when one of them changes their mind on the kind of love they want from the other. Lovers till lunch, friends from dinner. How do you rearrange all those emotions? How do you tell them that after you make love with the fury of animals this morning on a bed that has been your temple for weeks, that it will be a different kind of love from this afternoon? I still love Gravy, I think. No, I know that I do. That sort of love doesn't just go away. And now he is dead. What's the point hating someone who is dead anyway, when he can't experience all the venomous missives. But I think that maybe that love I had for the man who took on the role to be my father has now changed in size and structure to some loose, ill-fitting shape, somewhat in the same way he changed. It seemed to be hiding somewhere inside the baggy folds of a bigger love. Like a skeleton hiding inside a XXXL T-shirt.

Maybe it wasn't guilt that killed him. Maybe it was love.

Chapter 10

Don was still alive.

My mother and I were also alive. Somewhat.

It had been two and half weeks since I came to Madras, learning every secret, and unlearning my life.

It had rained last night. Some sort of a biblical summer rain. The room seemed faded for my eyes, as though the rain had flushed the colour out of it. Don had still not woken up. He showed signs of life as I kept pacing up and down his room, watching him slur and sleep, sleep and slur, and grunt. His breathing was getting sluggish by the day. His slow decline was like the path of a dying comet. The wrinkles on his face would collect like a bunch of broken lines connecting tapestries of what I assumed to be scattered thoughts, and merge with the thick forest of his eyebrows, while his nostrils remained in a state of permanent flummox. His eyes were moving inside and seemed to be busy chasing some unicorn in his own north pole, inside his dreams, in his darkness.

After I came here to Madras, my mother made herself scarce around Don, allowing me to take over her nursing duties. In a way she was just waiting to dump it all on me, like some type of avenging angel, so she didn't have to deal with the old man. She walked around Don like a champion eye-roller, equipped with the indifference of a night-watchman in a morgue, blocking her ears to his incessant drawls.

Today, she had left the house to get us something to eat, or to sort some matters out, or to clear her head. One or all of the above, I don't remember. Me, I was tired of taking long walks in my head. But today smelt different. There was something about the air, the thick visibility of it. I didn't know what it was, but you know that strange feeling deep inside your bones, when you know that if something was changing, it will make itself known? It felt like that.

So I sat in Don's room, and read a bit but I couldn't put my mind to the sentences. There were just words, blurring in front of my eyes. I gave up. I saw the scar on Don's belly moving up and down in an uneven, slow pace. My eyes kept darting, spinning around every corner crowded with Don's elegiac world. The room and everything inside was silently sweating from its fears. The benevolence of these days allowed me to see Don for not just how he was, but how he was once upon a time, the various lives that he lived, its layers, its skin.

I had questions reeling in my brain as if we were locked in some subterranean prison camp. I was preparing myself to talk to Don. The thought of shaking him up so he could sit up, pour himself a drink and tell me what really happened occupied me. But I could do nothing but wait for him to wake up. He *had* to wake up. I prayed for it desperately. Perhaps he was waiting for my mother to fill me in, like those jigsaw pieces. Who knows? I kept checking if he was still breathing, hoping that it hadn't stopped. Each time I thought he let out what seemed like a closing sigh, a penultimate breath, it was followed by another—as though his weak breathing carried him forward.

'Good God, child, that is a prodigious stare,' he said so calmly while I was busy staring at him.

I felt as though I was electrocuted. I had gotten so used to staring at him and his not responding that when he did, I didn't know what to say.

I don't know if I dreaded this moment or longed for it.

His sleep-waxed eyes crinkled open slowly.

'You are alive, yes,' I blurted out. I didn't know whether to laugh or cry.

'I woke up five minutes ago or . . . maybe yesterday. I am alive for you, my love.'

'Oh.'

'Did you think that I died?' he asked me.

'I didn't for a moment doubt you were dead,' I lied.

'I'm too young to die,' he said. 'Fifty-seven is no age to die, is it? I lived my age by choosing it at a younger age.'

'I agree,' I tried to smile but it was a bit difficult. Don was a real *rara avis*. He was eighty-one. He lived as though he was eighteen, and had told people that he was fifty-seven for as long as I could remember.

'You know, they couldn't find my vein when they were trying to bring me back from the dead. I heard someone mumble that it was too thick, too toxic, too tight. Bloodless bastards,' Don whispered. 'Oh wait, that's me,' he smiled. Tried to smile.

I remained quiet, trying to adjust my eyes and ears to the sound of his feeble drone.

'What is the emotional temperature out there?' Don asked me in a barely audible sigh. He had a voice that was built for rage but he sounded like a cat that was tied up to its whiskers.

I didn't say anything; I didn't understand what he meant.

'How are things?' he persisted.

'Things are strange,' I said slowly, trying not to tear up. 'How . . . how are you feeling . . . ?' I asked.

'Alive from the knees down, dead from the neck up and quite numb in between. Near the temple, but far from God,' he said as his mouth ran dry. 'I feel handcuffed to a machine gun at the back of a truck,' he pushed the words out of his mouth.

I have to remember that line, I thought to myself at the time. I looked at him. When the body breaks down, it does not all go at once; it goes piece by piece. Don was too weak to go but still not strong enough to surrender. His cheeks sagged so low to his chin that all I could see of his lips was a dry little slit. His nails, once so beautifully clean, now curved like a crow's claws. It all looked grey. Still, even in this state, his huge, wet, haunted grey-violet eyes had an abstract tenderness and his face dazzled with some absurd, crazy nobility. It seemed to be the only living thing in this war-torn area.

Don whispered to me that he lay in some state of suspension, somewhere between heaven and hell, not fully alive, but not fully dead either. He said that even in his sleep, in his coma, he was fully conscious. Sometimes the voices and the noises from our past (and present) life never really disappear. They come at us in our sleep, they ridicule us, and hover over our forgotten conscience like a blood-drunk mosquito that keeps coming back for another round, and another round, and another round, till we wake up and crush it. And then ruin our peace and sleep forever.

'She's here? I know she is. I can smell her,' he asked me, referring to my mother.

I nodded my head.

'She's stepped out,' I said. 'I'll get her for you when she is back,' I said.

'I don't think she wants to see me alive,' he said.

Don looked hard at me. He knew that I knew. I didn't know how he knew that I knew what was not meant to be known but he knew. He was Don, he knew everything. He controlled us as puppets. He remained quiet for a while, trying to reassemble his mind to speak. I suspect nothing concentrates the mind more than the prospect of death, and Don was getting ready to exfoliate his brain before calling it a life. He was struggling to talk, and tried to joke saying that his voice was on loan, but when he started talking feebly he was somehow guided by this eerie intuition that this was his last chance to wash himself clean.

'It . . . Gravy . . . was the only way I could be in touch with you,' he started. 'When she . . . your mother was pregnant with you, I wanted to be there for you, to get to know you. I had lost everyone that mattered to me,' he said. 'Your mother . . . she wanted nothing to do with me.'

Don whispered to me that he tried various ways of seeing me but nothing seemed to work. At around the same time, he met a poor research student, Gravy, at the Theosophical Society Park. Gravy was reading a book with lunch. Don had smuggled in drinks for some of his friends. The two of them crossed paths and straight away became best friends. With Don everything was immediate: friendship, marriage, romance, lust and love. Nothing was delayed, everything was hurried.

Don spoke about the people who used to crowd his home, this home, and how he drove them all away, and how he wanted to establish contact with me. Gravy then suggested the plan of his befriending my mother and then bringing me to Don. And my grandfather was instantly convinced by the prophetic power of that idea and embellished it out in his brain like a business transaction.

'Why?'

'It was the least that I could . . . that I thought I could do for your mother, providing her with someone to love her . . . for breaking her heart because after she left this house . . . my home . . . our home . . . strange men were tearing her apart and passing through her like cruel spirits . . . I wanted to end all of that. She lost her virginity, and her brain . . . I wanted to give her someone to love and someone who would love her . . . because she was waiting to be loved. And you needed a father, and you *needed* to know me.'

Ha.

'Gravy became greedy,' Don went on speaking. 'He'd keep asking for money, and I'd scrape it together somehow and send it because he did a good job of looking after the both of you. Sometimes he'd ask for more . . . but I didn't mind that . . . because I didn't want to risk not having you in my life. Your mother . . . she hates me . . . and if she knows . . . about this . . . she will hate me even more if she could,' Don cried. 'It . . . it was . . . I had to do this for her.'

'You gave her Gravy like you gave her a new pet.'

'Only if you put it like that,' he winced.

When Don speaks, he grips you even in his fragile state, and his words all make perfect sense. It's only when he stops talking that it stops making sense. It's only when Don left destruction in his wake that you realized that you were merely the dramatic vehicle for his sordid plan.

Frankly, I didn't know what to make of all this. One passing comment from a stranger to satiate an old man's quixotic whim and it changed the course of my life, my memory of a life that chose me. It seems like my part was ghost-written by two drunks.

'I feel the error of my ways,' Don sighed. 'But you . . . you are young enough to believe in redemption,' he said.

What was that even supposed to mean? I stayed quiet. What redemption was I going to get when the man was dead? It was like plastic surgery gone wrong, and rectifying it would only make you look even more terrifying to little children and dogs.

'He really began to love you both,' Don said, almost in consolation.

'How do you know?' I shot back.

'Because he never left you,' Don said instantly. 'He could have walked out of the arrangement but he didn't. His love was so evident in the way he raised you, and your mother. Your mother held him, Gravy, like a crutch against life, against me . . . he was her rock; she was a sponge. He stopped taking the money I sent after the last time he came here . . . after we had that . . . little tumble,' Don said.

'That fight . . . three years ago . . . it was . . .' I said, trying to find all these invisible links to make sense.

'Because,' Don interrupted, 'because . . . he must have got disgusted with himself, with me and the way I treated him . . . who wouldn't, if you come to think of it. He . . . Gravy started worrying that you and your mother would find out, he was ashamed of himself for living a lie. I don't know. But he was convinced that he might get caught out . . . so he . . . he wanted to stop . . . and I didn't.'

'Stop what?'

'The payments. Only the payments. He wanted to continue being your father. Don't get him wrong. He wanted to clear his conscience.'

'Where did you get the money from?'

'That doesn't matter. Money is money. It comes and goes. Somewhat like people.'

I kept quiet, waiting for more explanations.

'He had agreed for money, after all. And . . . and I was worried that he might poison you against me. He didn't, but what if he did? He wanted me to trust him and believe that he genuinely began to love you both but I . . . I wanted to keep all the evidence . . . because just . . . in case he turned . . . then I too had proof . . . I didn't want to be the permanent villain for your mother, as I had always been, and to you. I wanted you to never stop loving me. Gravy wanted me to destroy all the papers, all the receipts, everything. But . . . I . . . I kept them . . . because . . . I shouldn't have. I did it out of love too. I didn't want him to leave you or your mother. It was my way of controlling this situation . . . the desire to see you, and . . . and . . . to make sure he never left you. But then he became the better bloody person and went and killed himself.' Don was pleading but he also managed to sound a little miffed.

My grandfather was noble in thought, but weak in action. He was buried in remorse, love and loathing.

'I wanted to throw it all but then . . .'

'You fell sick,' I completed his sentence.

I wish my mother was here. Where the hell was she? I didn't know what to believe. A part of me wanted to, a part of me needed to.

'Do you still love him?' he asked me.

'I tried to hate him. But it's hard. I want to but I am still not able to,' I told him. 'Maybe in a few years I will be able to . . .'

'Able to . . . what?' Don asked.

'Hate him,' I said, 'but for now I think there is still some love left for him.'

'Do you still love me?'

'I don't want to but it's hard not to.'

But then it's not always love but other things attached to that emotion that makes it a trifle dangerous. Things and emotions seemed to get stuck inside my heart.

'Holding a grudge was a waste of time,' Don sermonized. 'Why invite someone to stay inside your head, and allow them to drive you insane?'

I managed a laugh.

'Don't condemn him. It's not worth the extra burden. Hate me instead,' Don explained. 'I loved you from the beginning, remember that. Gravy . . . he was a few years late in loving you but he did. I promise you that he did. That's why he killed himself. Because he loved you more than anything in the world, and your mother,' he said.

Then after a while, he asked, 'Your mother . . . she doesn't know . . . does she?'

I shook my head.

'If she knows, she will hate me even more if that is even possible. Promise me you won't tell her,' he pleaded.

There was very little left of my mother, so why ruin that, I wondered. I decided not to tell her, for now. Don probably didn't envision the whole thing blowing up like this. In his impossibly twisted and optimistic brain, he must have imagined all of this would continue forever. That all these lies will somehow change into a bitter truth. In the middle of our lives, it just added up into a colossal mess. Eventually everything does catch up with you, whether you choose or not. There is no escaping the fatality of fate. Hearing all these stories, each nesting like a Matryoshka doll, was like being on a constant heroin trip because of the weird connections that eventually led me to understand the construct of Gravy, Don and my mother, and what bothered them, the secrets that they hid and the ones that eventually destroyed them.

'I am so sorry for your loss, darling, I really am,' his voice quivered. The tears turned his eyes bloodshot.

I should have been angry with him but I was too tired to be furious.

I just started to cry.

'Why didn't you come for the funeral?' I asked him.

'If you aren't informed about someone's death, chances are that they don't want you to come,' he said.

'Who told you?' I asked.

'I saw it in the obituaries in the paper,' he said. 'In the same way I saw Sancho's death in the paper.'

'I know what I have done to hurt your mother but I also know what I have done to protect her, and you,' Don said.

Perhaps, in his own perverse way, Don was trying to be the protector of his child.

He was trying to be a parent in the only way he knew he could be, struggling to pick up the pieces even when it was too late, by slyly controlling things that shouldn't be controlled.

It probably stemmed from his unhappy childhood. Don's real

mother carried him to term in her belly. One day she was shot on the street, in stray gunfire. While she died on the spot, Don was taken out of her belly and he survived. His father married a much younger woman, a distant cousin of sorts, and she left him as she had some sort of a nihilistic incestuous connection brewing with some gent who persuaded her to leave her family to start one of their own. Upon trying to explain to a teenage Don where his stepmother was, his father very matter-of-factly advised him that she had gone on a long holiday to the village, and that he had to make his own meals, wake up and get dressed for school on his own, and then his father headed off to work or wherever. Her affair sunk like a fused rocket and Don's father took his scarlet wife back into the fold and things went back to pseudo-normalness. Only semi. The lady nearly tried to kill the young Don by bathing him in boiling hot water and once spilled hot coffee on his belly—which explains the scar that I was staring at earlier. But she pulled another one out of her immoral bouquet and disappeared with her husband's brother or friend, or both. She was a midnight nympho, I was convinced. Don's father became chronically depressed and constructed a tree house to seek solace for himself, leaving his son to grow up on his own. The sad truth under it all was that Don grew up unloved and without any dominant parental force around him.

'I know what it is like to be unwanted as a child for no fault of mine, but then I was not wanted as a parent, and it was all my doing. Imagine living in a world when you know no one loves you. I was tired of waking up to that. That's why I tried to control a little bit so I could have your love.' Don sounded like a convict on death row. (Which, to tell you the truth, he was.) 'Once I had your love that was enough for me, Zef. It gave me a reason to wake up and now it will give me a reason to die,' Don said. He spat out the words in one breath.

'Don't say that,' I mumbled.

'I am, after all, waking up to die.' He let out a laugh.

'If you knew then . . . about yourself, then why did you marry Sancho?' I asked him.

'It was the right thing to do for me, but it was wrong for me to do it to her. But then that's the thing—sex is desire. It is pure savagery. It led me to a sub-arctic cold, dark place that was devoid of any compassionate emotion, and was so frightfully, overwhelmingly consuming. I lost my daughter because of that, and I nearly lost you,' he said.

I suppose lust can be blinding.

'I loved . . . loved her too much, Sancho . . . too . . . maybe . . . definitely not in the way I should have, not the way she wanted me to.' Don puffed the words out heavily. 'I didn't deserve Sancho's love . . . yet she loved me, a little more than necessary,' Don wept. 'I died when she died. I was the one who placed her obit in the paper . . . in the hope that it would reach your mother's eyes. I saw the obit in the papers here . . . Sancho had told that church to release it in Madras so I could chance upon it, and she knew I would, and . . . when I saw it . . . I put it in the paper . . . everyday for a month all across the Konkan coast so that it would reach your mother somehow. I was hoping she would see it. She . . . she needed to know . . . that there was no one . . . no love like Sancho's.'

'How did you know where my mother was?' I asked.

'I was never as uncaring as she made me out to be,' he said.

'You say you loved Sancho but . . . but you ran behind men,' I blurted out when I shouldn't have.

'There were some women too . . . but yes, mostly men,' he tried to joke but he started coughing, and with every cough, he sank even more towards his end.

'Sancho was Sancho,' he said. 'She was *sui generis*.'

'Like you,' I smiled.

'You know Sancho, she ate flowers, mostly dried roses, she drank rain water, and was obsessed with picking out dandruff and ear wax, like some tropical monkey. She loved me with all her heart and continued to love me till she could even when I made a mess of her life, our lives.'

'Then why didn't you take her back?'

'I don't know. I was too . . . too greedy . . . too vain . . . too rich . . . but mostly I don't know,' he sighed. 'I miss the sound of a family . . . you know that sound that you take back with you when you leave me. It's somewhat . . . like the sound of dampened silence after rain.' His words came out slowly, painfully. He went on, 'Zef, you know that saying "some people should be around your whole life and others should never make an appearance." I should never have been there.'

'You gave me a father,' I said.

Don had never been this open with me. He spoke to me as an adult in the past but I always knew he held something back. But now, the more he talked, the more I asked.

Every traumatic recollection that he confessed, he discarded a part of his past, slowly understanding that it could no longer hurt him. There was no time for regrets, no time for the future. He was rushing to reach some kind of a sordid nirvana, to a point where he could be brave about facing the quiet murmurs that will gnaw at him in those last-minute-moments before the big sleep.

We remained silent. I wondered where my mother was and when she was going to return and if she would be keen to make her peace quickly so we can all start moving in some sort of a line towards the life that is awaiting us. In that silence, I tried to imagine her sound, her clothes swishing across the marble floors. But I didn't hear her. She mustn't have come back. We remained in that moment, Don and I, digesting each other's words. A silent army was road-rolling inside me, occupying the insides of my body and pressing me down.

'Why don't you get some rest . . .' He didn't let me finish.

'Rest is for the wretched. Wrecking is for the brave,' he said, smiling as much as his weak face would allow him.

I started to tuck him in to sleep.

'There will be no one at my funeral,' he said.

'We will be there.'

'Remember to dress me up well when I die. Get me out of these horrid clothes. Make me wear a hat and socks. Add a bow tie while you are at it. A nice shirt, something linen, it's going to be hot down there,' he said as though he was giving out last-minute instructions.

'You aren't going to die,' I said.

His eyes spun around the room, visually cataloguing everything. Then he said, 'All these things make one think that I lived a glorious large life when I rotted here all alone in terrifying hospital silence. What's the point of all these possessions, all these things . . . everything seems hollow . . . when your daughter hates you, Zef. And that no matter what I do, I seem to disappoint her all the time. Now I seemed to have snatched away Gravy too.'

'Don't say that, Donna.'

'But I do know that I have a heart because it is breaking right now,' he cried. The tears were falling at a rate that was too fast for my hand to wipe away.

'When I die you can say here lie the bones of a broken heart.'

'Stop being so dramatic.'

He laughed. 'Can you feed me some cognac in a spoon?'

'All the drinks are dead,' I told him.

'Did you finish them off?' he smiled.

'It doesn't matter who finished them. You shouldn't have it, that's all.'

'Don't be evil to a dying man,' he said.

'You are not dying.'

'Blood may be thicker but cognac is better than blood. It is liquid gold.'

'Say what you will but I am not feeding you any alcohol.'

'Don't think of me as dead when I am dead. Perhaps you can think that I have gone to a bar for a lifelong happy hour,' he said.

He appeared to be thin as paper but still kept deliriously asking for his pipe and his cognac. I suppose he wanted to die in a state of dizziness, the same way he lived, instead of being dragged down lethargically sober by the wretched weight of time pressing his heart more and more towards his grave.

'I am dying, let me have a good taste before I die,' Don pleaded.

I fixed him a drink and fed it to him with a tablespoon. We sat in silence, he slurped noisily. With each gulp, a moor got unfastened from his body. He felt lighter, I could tell. He felt like he was floating away into the golden ceiling of another world.

We never spoke about tomorrow. I wondered where the hell my mother was and if she would make it before death left, taking Don away from us.

I bent forward to hug him. My cheeks felt wet with his tears.

'A mind has many seasons,' he mumbled between the tears. 'It's not working . . . the cognac, the medicines.'

He fidgeted a bit, signalling me to take out the book from underneath the pillow.

I took out the velvet bag by gently shifting his sweaty head.

'Open it,' his voice was straining.

It was that precious, dog-eared, much-loved copy of *War and Peace*. It was the same copy that Sancho had bought for him. His name was scribbled on it along with these words from *Anna Karenina*:

> . . . but I always loved you, and if one loves anyone, one loves the whole person, just as they are and not as one would like them to be . . .

Don wouldn't have given me this book, in which he kept his heart, if he didn't know he was on his last legs. Those words were a reminder that his world was ending in those sentences. The breaths were numbered. Isn't that the most tragic goodbye—the one that we can never speak of, but deep inside we know it is all over?

I heard the gates open. I heard the sun struggling up ahead. I heard my mother's clothes twirl.

Don heard it all, relishing the sound of his daughter.

'Do you think she will forgive me? Maybe even love me when I die?' he asked me, sounding like a child.

It's true, isn't it that in our lives, no matter how far we go, and what trophies we bring home, what wars we fight and emerge undefeated, no matter the applause, no matter the medals, there are only a few people whose approval we seek, whose attention we crave, whose passion we want to stir, whose love we want more of, whose face we wish to see before we die. It's our parents, children, lovers, ex-lovers, siblings, best friends, best pets.

I wished I could have been some kind of a Santa Claus to make Don's dreams come true. But I was dealing with my mother's hatred. And if there is one thing that I have learnt it is that you can't reason with emotion. You can change people's minds but you can't change their hearts.

'Bring her to me, please,' he whispered. His heart must have quickened for his own good.

I ran out to find my mother. She was organizing our lunch. But she was mostly drinking the lunch. I told her Don had woken up. She dropped the bottle. I watched the 'liquid gold' (as Don would call it) slither like half-hearted blue-balled piss on the marble.

'He wants to see you.'

'I am a bit busy now,' she mumbled. Now was not the time to be stingy with movement.

'He'll be dead in five minutes if you don't rush,' I pressed.

'I am scared,' she said letting out a fart in her nervousness.

'Come on,' I said. I took her in.

But I was too late. Don had switched off by then.

Isn't it annoying that people who are dying often wait for the few seconds when you leave the room to die. It was a moment over-filled with what ifs and if onlys. He spoke his truth, his version of reality, and made his peace, and died.

His bony face was deathly hollow, the brown molten skin just about serving as the coating for the skeleton underneath it. His toes turned blue. He hadn't worn socks.

My mother stared at him and I stared at her staring at him in the same way I stared at my father, a year ago, memorizing his face to not miss a scar, a mole, a hair, an eyelash. There were stains of tears that had crawled onto the sides of his eyes. They seemed to have dried as we stared at his face. He had by then adopted his dead face to have an air of elsewhere, that he was looking through you to somewhere else that he'd rather be. Ideally, I was sure he would have liked to have had a bath in his bronze bathtub underneath the stars and welcomed death, fresh, scrubbed up and sufficiently intoxicated.

Just a few seconds later, the perilously hanging branch of that tree inside the house fell on the floor with a thud, and smashed into smithereens.

Somebody once said that there is a time for departure even when there is no certain place to go.

That's what happened to Don.

My mother left Don's funeral halfway. I suppose she walked away, hoping to run into a better tomorrow.

I was standing there alone, watching the last dim flicker of fire crackle away. I tried to think of nothing, trying to be safe in the absence of a thought. I thought of Don, whose life was destroyed by the ravages of love and lust. He was mad when he was alive, I hope he becomes sane when he dies. Both Gravy and him were made in love, and had now vanished deep inside it. Most definitely probably. And love is a madness most mottled.

There was no one else here. Most of Don's friends were dead, or had disappeared quite like the goodtime drinks he gulped with them. Except for a tired, thin priest with his ribs pressing against his tender, underfed, sun-tarred skin, some odd cleaners scavenging the grounds for some bones, some money, some jewellery, some elements from a dead life. It was all quite godless, really. But there was nothing about Don worth taking, except for his life and his mad sense of it, and his wholesome, twisted goodness. I took his Byzantine ring, and hung it around a string found in his jamboree of collectibles. It beat close to the thump of my heart. I wore his glasses, as he wished. I was a vision of a midget with pickled eyes.

As I walked home, I felt the sky sinking inside my ears. Thoughts of Don's hungry face frozen in discomfort and his eyes, which contained my world inside them, invaded my head. There was a summer storm that stirred in the middle of this thick, visible heat. I imagined flying monuments everywhere; tombstones somewhere soaring high like soccer balls. There was a dirty shadow against the sun. By the time I reached home at 2.00 p.m., the day, which never belonged to me, had quickly lost itself to darkness as the Rothko red clouds rumbled as though they acknowledged my pain. It was all Dickens; the day shifted from yellow to red to grey to gory. Dark and windy quite like our bleak life ahead.

I looked around the house; it had reached this level of terroristic shabbiness fuelled by sorrow and shame. I looked for my mother. I looked for her in the empty pool outside. I looked for her in the study. I looked for her on the terrace. I looked for her in the kitchen. I looked for her in her room. I looked for her inside the guestroom. I looked for her in Sancho's room. I looked for her in the bench underneath the tree inside the house. I kept colliding against furniture that splayed itself in front of me like left-over guests from a party in a previous lifetime. All these rooms reminded me of an abandoned amusement park at sunset while my mother and me were suspended from the highest rim of a Ferris wheel. Finally, I stayed put, in that dusty corridor with the footprints of the past, tired in the continual calm under the furious sepia sky, welcoming the arrival of an invulnerable silence to smother the bells tolling in my head. Then I heard whispers of tears coming from Don's room. I found my mother sandwiched between Don's mattress and his bed.

I helped pull her out. She sat on his bed and petted it. She looked like a raccoon. I wanted to put my arms around her face. I don't know when we had finally fallen asleep but when I did open my eyes, I saw that I had woken up to a chillingly unfamiliar sound.

I walked out and saw my mother sitting on the stool in front of the piano. It was greased with salty dust. There was yellowed sheet music unopened and stacked with disdain. She had opened the music that was hidden inside the piano, locked away for all these years.

She played from memory, reading the notes from inside her eyelids.

It was beautiful. It was balletic, this lightness of the sound, the space in the noise, the tremor of wood.

Don was right. This sort of music sways inside your veins, it goes right inside you, snipping away the chords of burden, floating on a plateau bereft of anxiety. She blew out the day, the dawn, the dark. She threw out the stars. She didn't miss a beat. She could stop a war. She brought the rains with her fingertips. It wasn't any ordinary rain. It was cinematic in its pour, this movie rain. When she stopped, a few hours later, the anxieties of the room had shifted. She realized that her fingers had bled. I found her a band-aid and while I was fixing her up, she started to cry.

I started to tear up seeing her cry. She repeatedly kept saying that it was her fingertips that were burning. But we all know that that sort of a physical pain is worth a pithy little stubbed-toe cry, a slight scream here, a shoddy squeal and you are done. But her sobs seemed to be echoing through these illusive, insincere walls. I was also trying to tranquillize my own head, trying to process what Don had confessed to me.

In between dialogues with my upstairs chamber, I heard snatches of my mother's ramblings.

'There were so many times . . . that I wondered how Don lived with himself . . . after what he had done to Sancho . . . and me. I tried very hard to allow all those memories to lose their way back to me . . . and Gravy . . . he was there, he was always there . . . I don't know what it is like to feel anything any more.'

I didn't either. Gravy's suicide had destroyed my mother's emotional index. Don's final confession had rattled mine. Exactly what does one do after a cyclone passes by, besides dealing with its legacy?

'What are you thinking?' my mother asked me.

'About Don,' I said.

'He was such a bloody Madame Bovary, wasn't he?'

I remained silent. My mother continued to speak but she may as well have been speaking in other tongues. I tried to listen, but I couldn't get myself to do so. Her voice seemed to stretch and bend, roll and drop, intonate and belch like an android losing its battery, like the sound from an old, corroded magnetic tape.

'Zef,' she shook me finally. 'Zzzzzeff.'

'Sorry, what were you saying?' I managed.

'I just said that we should go back.'

'Where?'

'To our home . . . our home that Gravy built. I've had enough of this house, its lies, its betrayal, its bad memories. It never provided any sort of solace to anybody except for Don. Even the air here is so claustrophobic.'

She was right.

'I should never have come back here,' she said. 'I should have never let you come here now or before with Gravy. It was always a bad idea. You didn't need to meet Don. But Gravy . . . he would never listen. I tried to tell him . . . so many times but he just didn't hear me out. He didn't care. He was adamant; he wanted you to know Don. And what was the point in that? Sometimes I used to think that Don only came into my life to create nothing but chaos. Remember how he threw Gravy and you out? But your father . . . he was patient, he didn't care, he was never the kind to hold any grudges. He still let you go to Don. Gravy wanted you to know this beast because he only saw the good in people. He didn't allow my hatred for Don to influence you or him. That was the kind of person Gravy was . . . he was such a nice human, maybe that's why he didn't belong to this world . . . this world that the likes of Don had inhabited.'

This was the moment when I thought about telling her what Don had told me—that her father was a different kind of monster from the one she suspected, and Gravy a different kind of saint. It would be fair to Don.

But I couldn't.

Telling her would be like gently pushing someone—who was already teetering on the edge of life—in front of a speeding train at just the right time. Then it'd be my turn to wait in the middle of the tracks, waiting for a train to put me out of my misery and the guilt of killing my mother.

Gravy was the only beautiful force in my mother's life. He didn't care for her history; he only cared for her as his present. His was the only real love that didn't disfigure her. Why let that love kill her? It would be heartless of me to ruin that memory with a dose of unjust, imbalanced truth. My mother had become far too frail to handle reality, its many unedited levels, its averse versions. The two people who created the mess were gone. The fragility of a normal life loomed in my mother's horizon. Why disrupt her chance at it? She was already so far gone from the kerb.

Should the realm of the dead continue to exert power over those of us who still had to get through life?

'Let's go back home,' I said.

I could already feel the burden of that many-voiced secret grow inside me like a restless tapeworm. It was terrible—the quiet horror of knowing but not having the strength to reveal. Ironic isn't it, my hurricane family had almost made it a tradition to live and love with secrets, and here I was just following suit until my blood ran stale. It made me realize that the only constant in my family was inconstancy in flesh and soul. There was nothing but a permanent paralysis of the hope gene.

I didn't know how I was going to continue living after the intensity of these weeks, with all their confessions. Byron may have said that the great art of life is sensation, to feel that we exist, even in pain. But I was terrified of my own grief.

At some level, I thought that writing on paper in ink and blood would help me atone for what is left, peel off dead sins, and reorganize my past. I thought it would be so liberating, writing it all out and getting it out of my body, and all this would help me walk into bigger, clearer skies, and give birth to a new centred skin where everything was less strangled, and more worthy of living. None of that happened. But we write what we know and sometimes, as I have discovered, it is best to not know anything at all. All these words turned out to be wretched custodians of memory. They cut me to the core and taught me that absences have a presence too.

Everything I wanted to forget on purpose ended up resurfacing like placards for future remembrance. Now I just wanted to return all this memory, sealed into a brown envelope. Thanks, but no thanks. Remembering all of this made me want to disown my mind.

It's true, isn't it, that memory is a beautiful, generous thing.

But it is also such a bastard.

Gravy was right. It is the contamination of the mind.

Ibid.

A Note on the Author

Supriya Dravid has worked as a journalist in both print and broadcasting. This is her first novel.

A Note on the Type

Garamond is the name given to a group of old-style serif typefaces named after the punch-cutter Claude Garamont (latinized as garamondus). It is considered to be among the most legible and readable serif typefaces for use in print applications and one of the most eco-friendly major fonts when it comes to ink usage. A direct relationship between Garamond's letterforms and contemporary type can be found in the Roman version of the typeface Adobe Garamond.